MW01608918

# My Life
# &
# Other Short Stories

# Table of Contents

*****

# A Week in the Life

When a blank page stares me in the face, it's a daunting task to fill it with words that actually mean something. I love to write. But it helps, doesn't it, to write something interesting and meaningful to somebody?

Not meaning to be presumptuous, I'm grateful that I have that gift. I put a lot of years into the practice of effective writing. My jobs included newspaper editor and high-school teacher, and when I get an urge, either sitting by a lake or seeing a sunset, poetic words pop into my head unbidden. I've always been that way.

I volunteer as a visitor in various seniors' Homes around the Niagara Region, spending maybe 30 minutes with the shut-ins to make their day more interesting. Some of these people are senile, and victims of Alzheimer's and Dementia, so it requires some skill to visit with them. I dropped in to see Vic recently. He was a member of our church and always sat in the same pew. I would not have known Vic had any problem. All of a sudden, I hear he's in the United Mennonite Home.

He did not recognize me when I visited. I brought a Louis Lamour cowboy book to read to him. He did not respond, just looked blankly at me. He was busy fingering a belt on his wheelchair over and over again. When his wife dropped in though, his face lit up and I could see the spark of recognition there for her. Alzheimer's can make memory of certain people so selective. Who knows if that spark of recognition for his wife will eventually fade out.

Being mad at God may be a waste of energy. However, prayer must be some sort of comfort to the family.

I don't know. I'm just rambling. I don't know where my writing is going. It's just forging ahead with no purpose in mind. This is an experiment to see if my meandering thoughts have any connection with people at all, and if these sentences hold any jewels of meaning for somebody, anybody. This writing is just a mish-mash of things, and if you find relevance, I'm happy for it. If you don't find anything meaningful, then read Lee Child or David Baldacci. This willy-nilly writing is grasping at any haphazard topic to see if it can mean anything to anybody and still be a well-written flow of consciousness. Besides, I'm learning technical things about the appearance of paragraphs.

I needed a paragraph at the beginning just so I could learn how to create a "Drop Cap". I've just recently learned to justify my paragraphs and also to create headers and footers. But to learn those things, you need to have written a paragraph in the first place. I wanted to see if my purposeless writing would help me to learn technical skills: a drop cap, justification and also a header and a footer, and at the same time, relate something meaningful to the reader. As you can see, I was successful in my drop cap. It's the first W above. The paragraph is also justified, and it has a header. I don't need a footer. I think my writing as I go, also has meaning.

So, how do you make a Drop Cap? First, highlight the first letter in your paragraph > Click on Insert > look for Drop Cap to the right and click it > Pick Dropped. And there you are; your highlighted letter will become a drop cap! This gives a lovely stylistic touch to the start of your paragraph. Along with justifying paragraphs and adding a header and a footer, I should be able to produce books that are nice looking now and ready for publication.

# 1. My Second Language

English is my second language. I read Dick and Jane stories in grade 1 when I was learning English at the foot of a Catholic nun at Sacred Heart School in Kitchener, Ontario. Ah, grade 1! That's where I got beaten up by 5 Polish kids after school for wearing my Lederhosen [German leather shorts] to school. My introduction to Canada was not kind. The principal who was a Nun lined the offending parties up in front of the class and strapped each one of them. After that I was inspired to learn English...very fast! By the time I reached high-school I was writing poetry in English. My first language is German, of course, and thanks to mom and dad, I can swear in about 3 different languages.

Short stories and novels came much later, after a varied career as a newspaper reporter, an editor of a small-town paper, and then as a high-school teacher. I only taught high-school because the money was far better than a reporter's and I could finally pay the bills.

I wasn't good at disciplining teenagers teaching high-school. Hated that part of the job, so eventually I quit. Became a wedding photographer, a web designer, and a novelist. I was a rolling stone as far as jobs were concerned! I even took two years of Bible College at CMBC in Winnipeg to find God, and decided I did not have the makings of a pastor. My wife and I went to France instead. We lived in Perpignan where I attended the university to get a B.A. in French. You have to do these sort of things when you are still young and foolish, I suppose. Your health cannot afford to move all over the place when you are old.

Albert was a former pastor in our church years ago. Pastor Albert got early dementia at the age of 46. I remember his determined personality as a pastor, that he had to have control of everything. I don't know if God would approve of such a personality. Pastor Albert needed to dictate everything in the service and the music. Pastor Albert argued with my brother-in-law, Kenny, about the songs that were picked, even though Kenny was a gifted young singer. Pastor Albert himself was gifted with a 4 octave range but Kenny had a nicer voice. Well, that's all gone now for both of them. Pastor Albert got dementia, and Kenny, died of lung cancer at the age of 37. We don't see Kenny's kids anymore.

I'm an insomniac, so I will often close the door to the bedroom and boot up the computer at midnight. I stare at the blank screen for a bit, and it's amazing how it fills up in no time, like this page is doing right now. Hmm, must be a gift, or maybe a curse.

At least, I don't have the gift of gab. I don't like to listen to myself talk which could be a curse to a lot of people. I'm sure I'm not like that, though my wife says, that sometimes I tend to demand attention like a little kid, "look at me, look at me!" Sometimes I can't resist talking about my latest novel, or about my websites.

Oh, didn't I mention my web design? I picked up that skill so I could show off my scenery photography and my writing. I went to night-school to learn HTML and web design. Worth every dollar of the tuition. My Webmasters Certificate from 2007 hangs on the wall to the side of my computer.

I should have run out things to say by now, but Karen Carpenter sang, "It's only just begun." I have a knack for tying in lyrics from songs to whatever I'm saying. It's fun. I promise I won't sing the lyrics.

Actually, sometimes I stoop to the temptation to do just that, and friends either smirk or smile at me because I do not have the most melodious voice. I joined the choir at church to help out with the basses. I'm not a great singer, but I participate and that's what's important, to give me something positive to do on

Wednesday nights at rehearsal, and on Sunday mornings at the service. When I used to take pictures of scenery, I'd often say, having a camera beats having a gun. How could we, in general, do away with destructive behaviour with all people who are supposed to live in a civilized society? Using the power of the written word is better than flying a plane into the Twin Towers.

I guess, if anything, the purpose of this writing is to make you think about values. Where do you place your moral compass? I must admit though words don't always have an effect and are not as explosive as dynamite strapped to one's chest. But then with so many innocent deaths from terrorists, one wonders if their message gets lost after they push the button or after they die from a sniper's bullet? Do you remember any of the manifesto from a fanatical bomber?

Years ago I took a writing class, and one of the lessons made us think about the value of each word. Some words had a 0 value, some a 1 or 2, and other words a 5. The placement of the words within the sentence was important too, how you strung your words together. Some words can be put together in a very ugly way. Other words can hang together like little jewels. That's when you get beautiful prose or poetry. I'm still learning how to do that. It's a craft, and a gift.

I write poems now and again during retirement. Sometimes I spin a yarn or short story, and if I've got the fortitude, I even write a 300 page novel. It takes me about half a year to write a novel. I love fabricating things and if I need to stretch the story out a bit, I concoct a sideline for one of the characters which gives me another 50 pages or so. The ladies at prayer meetings on Tuesday mornings ask how I can have such an imagination. I think in a former life I kissed the Blarney Stone, so that when I write books, words just flow out of my fingertips in a never ending stream of enjoyable exaggeration. I have to watch I don't sell myself short though, because sometimes I have a tendency to do that. Being able to spin stories is a gift for which I am grateful.

I once heard of a story about a grad student who was accused of gushing too much with his prose. But he defended himself. "It's not how much you gush, but how well you gush!" I prefer to take Ernest Hemingway's viewpoint. He says that prose should not have elaborate descriptions. It should not be decor, but architecture. I agree with him. Get to the point with streamlined writing and get on with the plot. But, of course, you can't do that if you are sick, drunk, cursed by Alzheimer's...or dead!

My knee is aching now of arthritis. It's time to stop my typing, and head to the couch to read a bit of the Louis Lamour cowboy novel. I'm taking lessons from him about writing one of my own cowboy novels someday. Louis Lamour died in 1988. He wrote over 100 novels in his lifetime...and what's more important, he made a living at it. He was a national treasure for the United States. I don't know if I will ever become a national treasure for Canada, but I hope some people will appreciate what I write about and what thoughts I have. I'm intending to use the same mantra which Jacques Pepin used at the end of each of his cooking shows, but instead of "Happy Cooking", I will end the Preface or Synopsis of my stories with "Happy Reading."
This mish-mash is turning out to be more of a Blog. I don't like Blogs. They remind me of Facebook. Too personal and gossipy. Oh well, it's sharing that counts!

We went to lunch at the church today, as a sort of farewell to Adelaide, who is about 85, and in really good health. Her grown up kids have arranged for her to pack up her belongings here in Vineland and move out West to Winnipeg. The movers have packed the heavy stuff. Adelaide and her son will drive in the car all the way around Thunder Bay, along the lake and along the Canadian route. It's amazing that she, at that age, still has the stamina to start a new life in a new place. Some people are so blessed.

I was swimming at the Kiwanis pool and puddled around with Jack who was also 85. I complained about all the arthritis in my body, and Jack blithely said, "Oh, I got no problems like that." This kind of unequal dispersion of health, and gifts leads to resentments, just in case there is a spiritual Being  out there somewhere listening.

People pray anyway. I just finished the nightly prayer with my wife. I closed the bedroom door, bidding her sleep tight. I can't go to bed as early as she can because I am a night owl. Also she still has to go to work in the morning as a teacher, and won't retire for another 3 months. I've retired 15 years ago, and so I habitually close the bedroom door early, and wander off to the computer to write or to the kitchen for a snack. This time, I sauntered into the kitchen, took down the KAVI bottle of whiskey, and took a swallow, which a friend of mine told me would help me to sleep.  Instead of taking a shot glass, I take a swig straight out of the bottle and measure what I think is a shot worth inside my mouth before I swallow. Drinking whiskey is not an exact science, anyway. I prefer the KAVI over the Courvoisier Brandy. The brandy burns like hell. Real burning stuff. I'm taking the Brandy to my brother-in-law's with the hope that he can use it with his coffee. Brrrr.

I never did get to my cowboy story about how far Milo Talon got in tracking that kidnapped girl. So far, he's riding around the open plains more than he is squaring' off with any bad guy with his six shooter.

My INR, which is my blood thinner, has to be checked at Lifelabs tomorrow, on Monday morning after swimming. I'm taking two books along, one the Milo Talon, cowboy story, and the other, "My Dad Got Sick" by Jay Perry, whose father died of lung cancer a couple of years back. Jay and his mom were the caregivers. Jay is a superb photographer of fashions and people. I guess that's where the money is.    I specialize in scenery photography, so I don't have to be superb.

The reason I have to get my INR checked is twofold. First, I've got a 32 year old artificial Teflon aortic heart valve clicking away inside me. That's why I have to take 2 mg. of a blood thinner each night, called coumadin. If the pill makes my blood too thin, then I could bleed to death. But hey, the choice is get the level right, or get a stroke! I need to check my INR on Monday, because I am having a tooth pulled later in the week, on Thursday. Let's not have me bleeding all over the food as I heal.

I haven't decided yet if I will get the implant done at a cost of $4,500, which, by the way, is the cost of getting a book published and marketed. Unfortunately, there are no more agents and no more publishing houses that pay you money to publish your book for you. Unless you are Lee Child or David Baldacci.

Well, the whiskey has not kicked in. I might just open up the Milo Talon novel and see if he tracked down this kidnapped girl. EeeeHaaa! Ride em cowboy. In fact, he found her and after a shoot-out, rescued her. That's a happy ending. Well, maybe another shot of whiskey might do the trick for me tonight.

# 2. Beautiful Music for a Crazy World

I did have a relaxing Sunday. I love to lie down for an afternoon nap, and listen to radio 96.3FM "Beautiful Music for a Crazy World". Kerry Stratton is still on at 3 p.m. on his program called "Conductor's Choice". Kerry was diagnosed with ALS, Lou Gehrig's Disease. The disease has a 3 to 5 year's of life expectancy once diagnosed. Kerry is a marvelously gifted conductor and had a great bass radio voice. Now-a-days, his voice sounds cracked and feeble. You can tell he is losing his ability. What a wonderful man. I enjoyed him sharing his little jewels of musical knowledge in between the various classical pieces he chose for his program.

I knew Kerry personally back in 1980 when I lived in Grande Prairie, Alberta. He was just a young conductor then starting out. I was a newspaper editor there for *Grande Prairie This Week*. I got promoted as editor after the former guy fell off the wagon and had to dry out in the emergency ward of the hospital. The publisher asked if I was up to taking the job. I said, "Yes, I can do it." The pay increased by $3,000 per annum.

I remember Kerry conducting the *Grande Prairie Symphony Orchestra*. We rehearsed in the college auditorium on Monday evenings. He had such a dry sense of humour and was very patient with all of us amateur musicians. I played first violin, behind the concert mistress. Kerry inspired the best in all of us.

Years later, when my wife and I moved back to the Niagara area, I listened to the Toronto classical music station, and whose voice should I hear over the radio but Kerry Stratton's? He went on to record music with one of the best orchestras in the world, the *Prague Symphony*. His specialty was Dvorak. I went on to continue playing in amateur orchestras, specifically the *Peninsula*

*Orchestra*, when we moved to Vineland. We played concerts at seniors' homes around the Niagara Region.

So Kerry moved to Toronto and became world famous. I moved to Vineland and remained an amateur musician. I tore the tendons in my shoulders several years ago, so I can no longer play violin. But despite my aches and pains, I'm still mobile enough to go swimming to the Kiwanis Pool twice a week, and I've got my mental faculties, sharp enough to write books.

As far as the mobility issue goes, I hire teenagers to do my yard work. Kerry on the other hand has contracted Lou Gehrig's Disease, otherwise known as ALS. He can no longer conduct. Even his voice on the radio, which used to be such a rich, expressive baritone, is faltering now and sounding like an old man's voice.

Kerry Stratton says on his radio show now, "I will continue to do this until I am no longer able to." I hope it won't be soon.

ALS is such an insidious disease, so unfair, but then what disease isn't? At the end, It's a battle that is finally reduced to a private matter between him and his family, and then finally just with him alone in his final moments. Each one of us has to face that final curtain in our own way, no matter how much support we have. We all pray for a miracle at the very end. Some of us for a quick finish, not wanting to drag out the pain. But sometimes we have no choice. Not a happy thought to end this stint of writing on. It's time for me to sneak back into bed.

*****

Monday, Monday, and rainy days always get me down. It was sprinkling a bit when I fired up the car to drive along the QEW to get to the Kiwanis Pool this morning from Vineland. It was only the second week of spring. My headache usually grows on a damp day when the temperature bounces up and down like a yo-yo and when the air pressure gets heavy. I took a Tylenol before I left, swallowed it with an instant coffee, in which I pour some

International Delight Hazelnut for flavor. I didn't take time for breakfast and just snagged a nut power bar out of the box to eat on the way over to the pool.

I was lucky to get the handicapped shower because it is so much more convenient to use than those push button cubicles. Dousing yourself with water before you go in is just a policy the lifeguards enforce but I doubt it does anything.

There is a group of 4 or 5 of us, a quartet or quintet of walruses that bop up and down in the warm pool, chatting about hockey or politics. I do that for a bit, and then I puddle away to do my own exercising, like water walking, so my achy muscles get stretched.

Dave is nicknamed Bernie, because he looks like Bernie in the movie, *Weekend at Bernie's*. He takes over the hockey talk. Jim is the statistics and numbers guy because he is a chartered accountant. Lu lets you know all about history, politics and Trump. He used to teach geography and history in high-school. Phil, like his namesake, is the philosopher of the group. He always has a smile on his face, maybe because his wife lets him drive the Cadillac. John, who wears black horn-rimmed glasses, is the quiet one, the listener who keeps his own private counsel about things. Me, I'm the occasional smart alecky remark guy. When Klaas is here, he takes over the conversation and knows everything about everything. His focus is mostly health, medicine and doctors. He's not here. He is luxuriating on a sunny beach somewhere by his condo in Florida. Even in his absence, he gets the biggest portion of what I've written.

It's clear when I've had enough gossip about Trump or whether the Leaves will take the Cup or not. I puddle away from the group to do my strokes in the deep water so I get my muscles moving. My knee is killing me. I could hardly stand up this morning when I got up.
I kept an eye out for 8:45 a.m. when I know Angelo will limp over from the exercise end of the pool and head for the handicapped

shower. It's a race between him and me. I lost this round though, heading for the steps. He was already closing the door to the men's shower room. Boo! Angelo walks with a real stooped handicap, like a waddling chimpanzee. Poor guy. Oh well, he needs the handicapped shower more than I do. He has a rough gravelly voice with a heavy Italian accent. And he swears a lot. Must be a European thing. Sanovabeech!

I was fortunate that the rain stopped by the time I had coffee with the gang in the foyer of the Kiwanis Pool. Coffee is $1.00 now. Used to be .50 cents last year. Like the gas prices, prices to up. Somebody up there is pulling the strings. Profit is the bottom line. After the swim, I headed to Lifelabs to check my INR. Lu gave me a book to read before I left. "I think you will like this one." One of the ladies, manning the counter, her daughter is also a writer. Lesia Annastasia Chytra. She's a young teacher living in Toronto. Maybe there are better connections there than Vineland for authors.

# 3. "My Daughter is an Author Too!"

Lesia Annastasia Chytra wrote *Tarnished*, a novel about the way life was for Tasya in 1942, a girl living with her mother in a Ukrainian village on the Polish border. Tasya is forced to work in Germany as a labourer. Yes, the author is a pretty young woman, and obviously talented. Her mother, Mary, works as a receptionist at the Kiwanis Pool. She  must be awfully proud of her daughter. I was surprised two years ago when I bragged to Mary that I was an author and had two books out, Mary said, "My daughter is an author too". That kind of took the wind out of my sails. I felt like everybody was an author, like everybody was a wedding photographer too now-a-days with a digital camera.

Anyway, once I finish reading Louis Lamour's cowboy novel, Milo Talon, I will read this book *Tarnished* about wartime 1942. It will mean switching mental gears drastically to a serious topic away from my popcorn cowboy reading material. Different genre.

Sitting at Lifelabs took a good hour because I never register online, so I just brought a book along to keep me busy until eventually I get called. I finished the Louis Lamour book. Milo shoots the bad guy. He gets his $1,000 for finding the lost girl, Ann, and at the end, he rides his horse out of town, heading to the West where he can live under the stars and build a campfire rather than go after the million dollars in cash stashed away somewhere, according to the girl's secret ambition in the book. As a scenery photographer, I could appreciate Milo's riding off into the sunset, though I must admit finding a million dollars could buy me a lot of new camera equipment.

My blood was finally taken by a technician who looked like she had recent Botox injections in her lips. I don't know why women

do that to themselves. It looked weird, like she had unnatural lips that stuck out like swollen flaps above her perfect teeth. Yuck.
I wonder how much Lesia Annastasia Chytra had to pay for the publication of her novel, *Tarnished*? Or did the publisher sponsor her as a prospective best selling author? The book looks very professionally done, better than I can design through Kindle Direct. Maybe it's a matter of technical experience with Microsoft Word. I prefer the the creative process of writing over the technical expertise knowing how to do layout,  justifying margins and how to create a drop letter at the beginning of a chapter.

Chytra, Lu tells me, means very Clever, in Ukrainian. I wonder how clever and well-written this novel by this young teacher is? It's bound to be pretty smart, since she is young and looks perky.  I'm 73 years old and often tired. I must be on the way down the incline in my mental capacity. Oh well, we each have had our own chance and our own time and  our own era.  In the meantime, I've got a continual headache, and I need another Tylenol. Perhaps a little lie-down, and some classical music? I prefer the Pavanes of either Faure or Ravel.
But before my planned lie-down, I had other things on my mind other than reading a book about World War II. Chores have to be done, before my wife comes home from work. So, I headed to the sink and washed pots and pans, and dishes.

Then finally, I was free to read, *Tarnished*. The author used a word like "incessant" in the first paragraph. That's got to be a good sign. She does build the personalities quite credibly with apt descriptions and dialogue getting the tension across between the granddaughter, Sofiya, and the grandmother, Anastasia. Sofiya's husband, "the Canadian Jeff", strikes me as a bit of a jerk because he wears a T-shirt with a hammer and sickle on it, not appreciating the historical significance of terror and abuse to Baba's ancestors in Ukraine. He thought wearing the T-shirt was "cool". The introduction to the book is an economical short 3 chapters where Anastasia has her daughter persuade the mother to sell the house and move into a seniors' apartment. No sooner is that done when the dumpster shows up at the house in front of her driveway. "She found herself arguing with both her daughter and her granddaughter about what should be kept and what should be thrown in the trash." [p. 13]

The younger generation did not realize the symbolism of all those things in the grandmother's house and how they attached to her memories. The introduction is short and sweet giving the reader an anchor from which to navigate into 1942 and the grandmother's past. She was known as Tasya then, and lived a different life than what she now lived in Toronto. Yes, a well written and researched book after all. I was glad to read something of different personalities than cowboys and something of credible wartime history from 1942 in Europe.

The whiskey did not work well last night as far as a "night cap" goes. My friend, Google, says that alcohol can enhance blood thinning if you are on coumadin. Actually my INR was 2.2 today, Tuesday, and that's pretty good for a guy with an artificial aortic heart valve. The Teflon valve keeps on ticking! I think I will phone the periodontist anyway on Wednesday to see if the tooth could be pulled next week instead, not because of cowardice, but because our family is having a family get-together on Saturday, and want to be able to eat, talk and enjoy the company. I know that specialists make their own schedules and the patient is lucky to get in, but with all the money he's making, I should hope he can nudge his time around a little bit. Let me see, where was I going at the beginning of this paragraph. Oh yes, I will lay off the whiskey.

Besides, if I can't sleep, I may be awake enough to write the great Canadian novel. I wonder how many great works of art and literature have been produced throughout history by insomniacs? Or maybe it wasn't that they couldn't sleep; it was because they were hyperactive  geniuses to begin with.

When I came to Canada in 1954, the nuns at Sacred Heart Elementary School in Kitchener, Ontario, put me in grade 1. I was already 8, but a small 8, so I fit right in with the grade 1's. I suppose the principal thought  this would be just a temporary measure until I learned the language and then they'd move me up to where he should be. Well, that never happened. Mentally, this adjustment was traumatic for me, especially when other kids found out I was 2 years older than they. I remember the IQ test in grade 7. They were big on IQ tests in those days, back in 1961. They gave me the test twice. I thought, since I was older than the other kids, maybe they were making sure to see just how dumb I was. Kids are so impressionable. Now that I'm 73, this doesn't matter anymore, and probably in another decade it will matter even less, if I'm dead. Anyway, I did learn English without an accent by the time I was in grade 3, and by the time I was in grade 7, I was reading James Fenimore Cooper and Mark Twain. What a lovely language, English!

I spent most of the day, today, revamping my http://johnhartig.ca website. I use Dreamweaver to redo the scripting in HTML, and then I upload to my server, godaddy, with the Ipswitch WS_FTP program. I think my new banner looks cleaner on my site, and I like the fact that I slipped in thumbnail images of my novels and short stories into the Home page. I have links there to Kindle and Amazon for purchasing the eBooks and Paperbacks. Maybe I can get some money out of this strategy to pay back for what it costs me annually to have websites.

I'm still using the Macromedia Fireworks program which I inherited from my dead brother-in-law so I can produce "png" images, which are "dynamic" images, so I can change text and sizes within the layers anytime. Wonderful stuff.

I design my own book covers with  this program which I prefer doing over the templates that Kindle and Amazon provide, though it is a courteous and free gesture on their part, once you get an account with them.

I confess though I did glance at David Baldacci's website for a bit and noticed that he has changed his colour scheme and also his header, but he still likes his name up there in huge letters. So I went big too, -JOHN HARTIG-, right up there, centered in the banner. Hey, you need to blow your own horn, at least a little bit.

We talked about the difference today at prayer meeting, between Pride and being a Doormat. It's necessary to be proud of things you do or have, certainly not arrogant. I do envy David Baldacci somewhat. He is so successful with his writing that he doesn't have to concern himself about marketing anymore. At least, I don't think so, and he certainly doesn't have to take hours designing his own website. I'm spending lots of time resizing images and HTML pages when I'd rather be writing another short story.

At least, I had a little break at about 3 p.m. today where I packed up the book, *Tarnished*, and sat at the local library for about half an hour reading about Tasya, the 15 year old Ukrainian girl, whom the family wants to send off to Germany as a *Zivilarbeiter*. Germany was demanding that outlying countries send them workers for the war effort. The older girl, Kateryna had already had her turn, and now she was pregnant. Not so easy a life in 1942, compared to Canada in 2019, with universal healthcare, easy student loans and cell phones. Oh, and by the way, colour flat screen TVs.

I've read another couple of chapters in the *Tarnished* book. The girls, Tasya and Hanya are now on a cattle car headed from Poland towards the German border and eventually Dusseldorf. They have a bucket in the train for peeing and pooping. They ask why, if Germany is so great ,why do they have to live like this. Hanya asks if her friend ever feels like just jumping off the train? Tasya just hates her mother and sister for getting her into this mess, as the sacrifice to be sent to Germany. Otherwise the whole family would have had to be conscripted.

I wish I could remember the two books I read about World War II a few years ago. One about a little girl in Hungary, about 11, who was blind and her papa helped her survive. She eventually became an oceanographer when she grew up. The other war book was about another girl, a German one, Manci, who survived the war in a little village. I've forgotten most of the book despite the fact that this was autobiographical and was reproduced through the precious memory of the author. And here, I can hardly remember where I left my toothbrush.

It's 9:45 p.m. and I've taken my third sleeping pill, my Oxycocet and Tylenol. I feel sleepy and tired and I might just try a small shot of whiskey, and slip under the covers. Thank goodness for electric blankets.

The Bursitis on my right hip is aching.

If I ask, will God make it ache less?

# 4. Sprinkles & Hockey Buddies

Wyatt Earp, Wyatt Earp,
Brave courageous and bold.
Long live his fame and long live his glory
and long may his story be told.

*The Life and Times of Wyatt Earp*
*starring Hugh O'Brian 1955*

I make a ritual of watching the Wyatt Earp TV series with my breakfast every morning after my wife goes to work. It's in black and white. I'm glad I get "gritTV" with my outdoor TV antenna, no cable, no satellite. I'm happy with my 23 channels. It's amazing how my TV watching has gone full circle because these are the exact episodes I used to watch on a Friday or Saturday evening when I was a kid in the 1950s. I asked my historian friend, Lu Cekota, if cowboys wore guns in the old West like they show on TV. Apparently, they did to protect themselves from wild beasts on the plains or in the mountains, to fend off cattle rustlers and also to shoot a horse if it broke a leg.

Farming was back breaking work in those good ol' days. People died young.  I guess certain types of men preferred robbing trains and banks to honest farming. Either way, making a living wasn't easy in the 1800s. There were no cars, no TV and no student loans in those days! I ate my Cheerios as I watched an episode of Wyatt Earp where Ringo wanted to reform as a gunslinger, get married and move to California. He was fed up working for the Clantons.

I phoned the periodontist to see if I could postpone tooth pulling until next week. I wanted to be able to chew my food during Saturday's family Easter supper. However, Deidre, the receptionist at Dr. Fritz's office told me in a nice voice, that cancellation required a heads up of 2 business days, so no-go. The receptionist was encouraging, telling me to cut my meat into smaller pieces at the family function and chew on the opposite side. As long as it wasn't steak!

My next chores later this morning included getting a bag of sprinkles at Bulk Barn, so the kids at our family get-together could put something colourful on their French Vanilla ice-cream. I've got to drop in to the Amica senior home this morning too, to visit Lynne Kositsky and drop off her drawing of the two little doggies, Doritos and Nachos, about which she and her husband are writing a children's story. Lynne is a published author whose health really declined over the last couple of years. They used to live a few houses down from me on Menno Street in Vineland. In fact, getting to know them and having tea time together at 3 in the afternoons prompted me to become a published author myself.

Since self-publishing houses sprang up all over the world like weeds, it seems everybody's become an author. As long as you pay money, I guess you can get anything published. I assume my stuff is good. In fact, I know it's good. Are these famous last words of arrogance or megalomania? I suppose Hitler must have said, I'm right I have all the answers for Germany in 1939, as he bombed his way through Holland and France. But let's not make ridiculous leaps from simple pride in a writing skill to supreme arrogance in taking over the world!

I still have to buy the sprinkles this morning. Then there's a swim at 11 a.m. and later at noon, lunch with my old hockey buddies. I used to play Old-timers' hockey until my knee gave out 4 years ago. Woody and Peter are still playing, gliding along the ice, occasionally making contact with the puck. Woody is 85 and Peter is 81. I'm home typing away in my sunset years wanting to become a respectable author. Jim Croce used to sing a song, "I've got a name, I've got a name."

In front of me, on my desk, rests the 18th edition of *The Canadian Writer's Market*, the 2010 version. Useless, especially since self-publishing is "in" and since you can get things published on the internet through Kindle Direct Publishing.

I paid $3,000 to Tellwell Publishing t back in 2015 since I thought I might die with my next heart operation. I wanted to leave something behind that I'd written. I hated getting a box full of 20 books delivered by UPS from the company. I had to approach the local library to get my book catalogued, and I felt like I had to peddle my books at cost to friends.

Kindle Direct Publishing has made publishing books for authors much cheaper and easier and to get only the copies you want. So now I can die peacefully!

I can enter the Pearly Gates with only one copy of my book to give to Saint Peter, instead of stooping and shoving a whole box full of my books through the Pearly Gates because of a package deal for $3,000 from some publisher.

It's time to pack up Lesia Annastasia Chytra's novel, *Tarnished*, my glasses, and my list of chores, and head for the door. I better not forget my swim trunks. I will touch base with this short story about my week when I get back.

I left Tasya on the border of Germany, as I recall. Poor girl, 15 years old and a stranger in a strange land, 1942. I will stop at a Timmy's as I do my string of chores and see how the girl is doing.

Some time later: I never had time at Timmy's. I parked the car and dozed in the parking lot at Timmy's and then it was 12:45 all of a sudden, time to meet the guys for a beer at the West Hill Bar and Grille. I ordered a beer and fries. That cost me $9.00, a buck more than what the guys pay when they share for a beer and a pizza. I can't have pizza any longer because I'm gluten free now. I explain it to them, "That doesn't mean glutton free!" No laughs.

Anyway I gave Peter the book back on Old-timers' Hockey, *Overtime.* It gave the whole history of the growth of old-timers' hockey in Canada since 1952, the resurgence in 1977 and the health of the game for old-timers in 2018. There was quite a bit of emphasis on competition, competition, competition throughout the book, except at the end where Eric Nesterenko said, old-timers hockey should be fun, not competition. Good for him.

I did get my half hour swim in before noon, good for me. And before that I had a lovely visit with Michael and Lynne Kositsky at the Amica seniors' home. They were glad to get that drawing of the two little doggies back. Apparently their children's illustrated book is done and they are expecting a proof within the week.

I told them about the 1942 book I'm reading. Michael mentioned the book he's reading: "Mama's Last Hug." He told me that he was fascinated by it, a book which explores the world of animal and human emotions. Primatologist Frans de Waal spent four decades at the forefront of animal research and explains how similar primate emotions are to human feelings. Apparently apes even smile. Michael sees safari hunters of the 1950s, in fact in any decade where it was allowed, doing a disservice to nature and morality by killing animals for sport. Michael launched on a premise that morality for humans evolved as a result of their being a society because of the concept of co-operation and of "do not do to others what you don't wish done onto yourself." I could also see religion coming out of a group co-operative behaviour, where individuals ask each other, where does this come from and how does this work? But more so, there is the need of primitive mankind to ask each other, where does the universe come from, how did we come into existence. To explain everything that primitive man did not understand resulted in what historians called, "the God of the Gaps". I did not feed Michael many comments on these ideas because I did not want to get trapped in a lengthy philosophical discussion. I wanted to go swimming.

Now, that I'm back home, I don't know what's happening to Tasya and her new life in Germany, so after a teeny nap, I will open up the next chapter of *Tarnished.* Maybe I will force myself to do the dishes before I lie down. Then a nap, then the library.

Okay, Tasya and the rest of the girls have been processed by German soldiers some of whom speak Polish or Ukrainian. Name? Village? Age? Tasya lied about her age, and said she was 16. They were ordered to undress and parade around the table of the officers. The officers laughed and enjoyed the show. The girls were put in barracks which had barbed wire around the compound. They were fed soup twice a day. The girls stopped menstruating after a week. They did not get any pay to send back home like they were promised.

I had my little nap, my little read at the library, and now back home again, I took out a slice of cheese from the package to nibble. I noticed that the slices are no longer square. The company took about half an inch off one side to make the cheese more rectangular, i.e. smaller, and yet, used the same old package size. Cost cutting for them, same price for me, profit making for them. We get less for more!

The same goes for the price of gas now-a-days which rose by 10 cents per liter since last week, from $1.12.9 to $1.22.9 this week. They can do whatever they want. Yet, Premier Ford figures that "a buck a beer" and "tailgating" at sports events is okay! I didn't know what tailgating was until my wife explained it to me. Funny that she should know. It was being able to bring your own beer to sports events so you could party outside in the parking lot cheaply with your own beer putting your truck's tailgate down for comfort before the game. Now, passing a law to allow that is a real governmental priority!

I had better get ready to go to choir practice at the church. It starts at 7:30 p.m. We are picking songs, lovely songs, which pertain to the Easter Advent service. Pastor Louise asked me to join the choir a couple of months ago. I don't know if they were hard up, or if she thought I could sing nicely during one of the songs at the Tuesday morning prayer meeting. Anyway, I am pleased to participate. It's something positive in the big scheme of things. Before bedtime I intend to read a bit more of *Tarnished*, to see how Tasya is coping in the German brick factory in Dusseldorf. She and the other girls are overworked.

I also made it a point, before bedtime, to google Hugh O'Brian, the actor who played Wyatt Earp in the TV series. When he got married, he and his wife spent their honeymoon studying philosophy at Oxford University in England. I suppose the royalties from his TV series helped to pay for that unexpected way to spend a honeymoon. Hugh O'Brian was a humanitarian and developed a charity for young people, the Hugh O'Brian Youth Leadership, HOBY, program. The gun-totin' marshal in the TV western, is quoted as saying this: "I believe every person is created as the steward of his or her own destiny with great power for a specific purpose, to share with others." That belief really figures with him and his wife spending their honeymoon studying philosophy at Oxford. I hope they, at least, toasted to their honeymoon with champagne.

Now, to *Tarnished*, and then to bed!

Whoops, I just thought of an image for a new business card. I designed it in Fireworks. Not glitzy, rather chunky and utilitarian. 3 things noted: Canadian Author | Web Design & Hosting | Niagara Scenery.

I threw Google John Hartig in there, as well as Search Amazon and Kindle Store. Included my Contact Information: website address, my phone number, and my e-mail address. And what the heck, I threw a Happy Face in some white space that I had left over on the card. I used Photoshop Paint to give my card a zigzag border.

Now it's time for a Tylenol, a few chapters in *Tarnished* and then to bed.

# 5. Dry Socket & Web Design

Dr. Peter Fritz pulled my tooth today at noon, a premolar on the lower left side. That sounds like the lower left side of town. Is that the poor side of town? Anyway, the tooth has been bothering me for 2 years. Apparently the root canal didn't take 2 years ago, and then when a huge filling was put on top of it, the filling acted like a wedge which when grinding on it,  eventually split the tooth like a piece of wood. Out with the offensive thing! It cost me $351 to have Dr. Fritz pull the tooth over the lunch hour. Nice lunch money!

I will have to think twice about the cost of the implant though, if I really need it at 73 years of age. Wow! $4,500, plus another $1200 for my regular dentist to put a crown on it. Everybody wants a piece of the action. Not that a specialist shouldn't get paid big bucks for specialty work; it's just that it costs so much! People cringe when I ask for a $300 in website!

At least, I had the comfort of listening to Tom Petty singing "Don't Do Me Like That" on the way home. I might have preferred Doug and the Slugs singing "Day by Day".

Dr. Fritz is doing a nice thing though, a fund raiser, Paint A Paddle, for ALS disease. I promised to put him in contact with the 96.3 Classical Radio station in Toronto because a man who used to be my conductor way back in 1980, Kerry Stratton, now a world famous conductor and a radio host on Conductor's Choice, Sunday at 3 p.m., has contracted the disease. It's public knowledge, and Kerry said he will keep doing his radio show until he cannot do it any longer. It's a rough road ahead for him and his family!

I will have to keep on putting gauze onto that dry socket every 2 hours, and no eating. At least, I'm allowed to eat supper if I nibble little bits delicately on the right side.

I will have a lie-down, I think, until supper time. Change my gauze bandage. Maybe listen to 96.3 FM radio, "Beautiful Music for a Crazy World."

My wife came home at 5:00 p.m. She is having scrambled eggs. I am having soup. She told me that the principal has her slated for .75 Learning Resource Teacher next year, with a part-time teaching load. She is already doing full-time LRT work. She won't be there next year because she is retiring at the end of June. She has not told the principal yet.

Aunt Martha worked for Bethesda years ago. Bethesda is an institution which takes care of mentally handicapped adults. Anyway, Aunt Martha did everything from accounting to the dishes. She asked for help repeatedly and the administration said, "You are doing fine. You don't need any help." When she finally quit to move to Winnipeg, Bethesda had to hire 3 people to replace the work she did.

I've been thinking about what Hugh O'Brian said: "I believe every person is created as the steward of his or her own destiny with great power for a specific purpose, to share with others." Sure, if you are healthy and gifted, you can make your own destiny. Easy for you to say! I just don't agree with him on everything. He was quoted though as saying that not all people are created equal. There I agree. Not only are we born into different societies, but we also have different DNA and different levels of gifts.

Therefore, we have our hands tied from the beginning when it comes to making our own destiny. There's heredity from our parents, our social station and also our country of origin and economic opportunities. So many boundaries fence you into your destiny.

Mind you, some of us rise above circumstances, but it is difficult. I suppose a belief in a purpose and in a God is like a life preserver which keeps you afloat above the chaos of this world. But some people's destiny is not equal to other people's destiny. That sounds a bit morbid and fatalistic. People still need hope don't they?

It's time to change the gauze on my tooth. What a bloody mess! It does not help to be on coumadin. But then I need that for my artificial heart valve. Sort of caught between a hard place and rock. A "mithing" tooth and a dry socket.

Perhaps, I missed shaping my destiny when I wrongly chose my subjects for my M.A. year in English Literature. I chose Milton and Chaucer which should have been Modern American Lit instead and maybe Literature of the Victorian Era.

I chose Milton and Chaucer haphazardly, well because they sounded cool, and I thought I would educate myself in something I did not know. I did not enjoy them, and I found the profs stuffy. Within the first month, I should have read the signs and switched my courses. The prof for Chaucer did not recommend me for a Ph.D. "Hartig's work is poor. He is not recommended for a Ph.D." And that put the nail in my post-grad coffin. I gave a half deflated defense of my thesis, as well, "John Milton and the Art of Logic". The argument was supposed to be that John Milton applied his treatise on Logic, the methods and devices in it, to his epic poem, Paradise Lost. How did I ever latch on to that as an argument for my thesis? I felt saying so was obvious and did not need a defense. Anyway, Paradise Lost was a lost cause on me. I just did not have the mentality or the appreciation for this 17th century classic.

Yes, I had a chance to make my own destiny here but not with those authors. No Ph.D. for me. I suppose at the age of 73, I don't need to pine about this anymore. Should my gravestone read? "Here lies John Hartig, no Ph.D."

Instead of a path to higher grad school, I chose a path to Teacher's College, and then, not being good at disciplining teenagers, I took a job as a newspaper reporter, at a minimum salary. My first newspaper job was a miserable experience. Office politics opened my eyes, and in fact, opened deep wounds in me. I could not play arrogant games. When I switched jobs to Grande Prairie, Alberta, I blossomed. Just loved being a newspaper reporter there, but I still hated the low pay. "Well, that's what everybody gets paid," said the publisher. "Yes, but for 60 hours a week?"

So, Hugh O'Brian is right, you are the steward of your own destiny, provided you can break out of the box you're in. There's your DNA, your culture, your hang-ups and your gifts or lack of them. Actually, it's your gifts which may be your ticket out! It was nice that Hugh O'Brian was able to take his wife to Oxford University on their honeymoon to study philosophy. Not bad for a rootin' tootin' shootin Marshal Earp of the West! Not every cowboy can do that.

I know, I know. I shouldn't complain. An old girlfriend called me a complainer once. "Well," I answered, "that's because I have something to complain about."

But the fact is I'm alive, and for that, I am grateful. When I got my poor paying job as a newspaper reporter and then a little increase in pay by becoming an editor, I said, the heck with the money. I celebrated my promotion by going to the restaurant one morning and ordering steak and eggs for breakfast. In all those years of low salaries, I haven't starved. All I suffered from was a lack of status, the absence of a big pay-cheque and no Ph.D. I can still afford to go to Timmy's though, once in a while, and read a good book there.

I just changed the layout and wording in my new website. I must say, it looks fine! Very fine!

After another little lie-down during which time I hope my dry socket will stop throbbing [I took another half Oxycocet], I have a choir concert to look forward to tonight at the church. The Mennonite High-school from Kitchener is singing.

Well, I'm back. The Rockway Mennonite Collegiate was not as good as previous years. I would have stayed the whole concert, but my dry socket was really throbbing again. I came home and took another half an Oxycocet with a sip of water. I removed the gauze bandage and the bleeding seems to have stopped. That is a hopeful sign for enjoying the food at my sister-in-law's on Saturday. There will be ham and mashed potatoes. And of course, a mountain of desserts. I'm glad I got the sprinkles from Bulk Barn for the kids. I bought more than my wife said I should.

My bedtime reading will be the 1942 story, *Tarnished*. The girls sneak out of the barrack after supper and go into Dusseldorf to beg for food. They are thin and starving, and in fact, Elzbeta died of a bloated stomach. Tasya has hidden a gold ring which she hopes she can barter for something later on when needed. Terrible times!

I barely escaped from those terrible times, born in 1946 in Austria. One generation away from World War II. In fact, the first 8 years of my life were spent in a refugee camp, in barracks, in Lager Wegscheid, just outside of Linz. The Luftwaffe had been using those barracks during the war, and when the Allies took over, the Allies put displaced persons into them because DPs had no place else to stay. My father, Michael Hartig, was a Siebenburgen Saxon coming from Romania. He was fleeing the Russians. My mother, Rosa Guenter, was a Donau Schwabian coming from Serbia. She also was fleeing the Russians. To think that only half a year before I was born, the Nazis were still incinerating people at the Mauthausen concentration camp.

Mauthausen is a small market town in the Austrian state of Upper Austria. It is located at about 20 kilometres east of the city of Linz. And to think how close I was to those terrible times.

I had an aortic artificial valve replacement when I was 41 years old in Winnipeg, Canada. That all came from the rheumatic fever I had as a baby in Austria. I was also sequestered in a sanatorium for 2 years in Linz so I could recover from tuberculosis. My mother tells me that I got lice from the little Saxon girl in the crib next to me. Now, that I am aging, I attribute my current health problems to life in the barracks in Lager Wegscheid and the hard times after World War II. Hence, the necessity for my aortic valve replacement, and also for the diagnosis of another recent disease called, "aortitis" which is inflammation of the arteries. Canada's been good to me, I confess, because I have had a good education, good medical care and a good life here. I am grateful.

The nurse at the periodontist's office told me to cover my pillow with an old pillow case in case I drool blood during my sleep. She told me not to keep the gauze on the dry socket at night, in case I swallow it. I don't feel like I should need that gauze now, and I'm ready, I think, to go to bed, maybe not for sleep, but at least for a rest. I can't have the radio on though. Marjorie is asleep, thank goodness. She gets herself ready for school at 5:30 a.m.

# 6. One Week From Good Friday

Last prayer meeting, I asked the pastor what was so good about Good Friday when the Romans crucified Jesus? She didn't know why people called it Good Friday, when there was nothing really good about it.

Well, at least, this Friday, today, is good. It's just one day away from our family Easter supper at Marilyn's, my sister-in-law's place. The nieces and nephews, the kids, the father-in-law, in fact the whole family will be there. Marilyn's table will be laden with victuals, meat and potatoes, veggies and juices. Later desserts [plural] and coffee. I can almost taste it now, despite my "mithing" tooth. The dry socket is shaping up to be in good shape for the feast. I am no longer stuffing gauze into that space of my non-existent tooth. As long as I chew on the right side, I will be fine and my tummy will be happy.

There is nothing on the agenda this Friday for me except to read *Tarnished*, write more of *My Life and Other Short Stories*, and go to the bank to pay off my credit card. It's after midnight now. My wife just opened the bedroom door and went to the bathroom. On the way back, she asked, "Are you coming to bed soon?" I'd better go.

*****

It's true what they say, "Tomorrow is another day." So I've started mine. My wife is off to work. I might just be healed enough to eat waffles gently, and sip a cup of warm coffee. There's Wyatt Earp on TV to go with Friday morning breakfast.

Whoops, change of plans. My wife left me oatmeal for breakfast. There's brown sugar and mango to mix with it. Heat the bowl of oatmeal for 1.5 minutes.

Wyatt Earp doesn't sound interesting this morning. Doc Holiday had a notion to buy the American Hotel and rename it something fancy with a new purple sign with golden letters. We will leave him to his ill advised investment, and let me get back to the golden nuggets here in my writing. I better throw some cold water in my face. I'm still  groggy. The sun is breaking out this Friday morning, and it's forecasted to be a milder day today.

I haven't seen old Doug this morning walking his dog. He is about 85 years old and single. His little dog's name is P.J., a friendly little thing, loves sniffing your leg. Doug is a white haired gentleman who moved into a cheap rental unit down the street about half a year ago. He's a tall guy, and walks stooped with his head leaning down to his chest, the reason being that he broke his neck some years ago on a construction site in Florida. When he lay in bed propped up on pillows, a young surgeon asked him how his line of sight was. Doug said, fine, he could see okay. The doctor set his neck that way, and Doug has had a crooked neck every since, with chin pointed down to his chest as he walks. He might be okay lying down.

I picked up my recycling bins on a Thursday morning a few months ago. As Doug walked by with little P.J., I introduced myself. We went out for coffee a few days later. He told me all about the places in which he was project manager as a pile-driver engineer. Bangkok, the Middle East, Africa, South America, anyway a bunch of places all around the globe. He told me about Viet Nam and friends who got shot up there. I found out that a "guppy" was a type of helicopter. If I would have had a recorder, I would have loved to record his monologues. One could write a book with his stories, but like his memories, his words come out too fast and are too fleeting. His wife died some 15 years ago, and I never found out what she thought about them moving all over the world. Doug has a 4 day a week job now as a security guard, at nights, I think. When he's not making his rounds, he's reading Clive Cussler. He got me to read a couple of Clive Cussler novels. I think I'll call it quits on him. I find his style a bit too "erudite". Give me Lee Child or David Baldacci any day! Slam, bang, kill the bad guys and move out of town.

I've made some headway in *Tarnished* by Lesia Annastasia Chytra. She's a good writer. I'm halfway through. Tasya survived the bombing by the river in Dusseldorf, and was taken underwing by a rich lady, Frau Bamm, to be the new chambermaid in the house. Hanya will work outdoors on the farm. This is a godsend for the two girls. The first thing that Tasya, now called Tasi, was treated to in the kitchen was a slice of bread, a bit of ham and some real soup. No more work at the brick factory and being starved!

When I was a child in Austria, we fared comparatively well in the barrack. We had our own little garden in front of our window where Mutti grew tomatoes, carrots and potatoes.

I remember being sick an awful lot when I was a kid. Mumps at the age of 7. And then high fevers where I became delirious. I went through a bout of pinworms, teeny white worms in my rectum, and mom would pick them out of my butt. Maybe that's too much information. Somehow I got cured of them.

There was an American army chaplain, Dale Ackerman, who drove his jeep into the refugee camp. I was on his list because I had TB. He brought a Care package with food and clothing in it. I remember getting Clementines at Christmas. I wrote to him faithfully until I was 18 after we moved to Canada. He was from Pennsylvania, I think.

I was a stinker when I was a kid. Probably would have become a criminal in Austria if we would not have moved to Canada, the land of milk and honey. Mom told me I was expelled in grade 1, for misbehaving in the back of the room. My teacher, I can still see his face in my mind, his big pick-marked nose, glasses, and one of those green German hats with a feather, he would walk up and down the aisle, stop where a kid wasn't doing any work, and pop him one on the forehead with his fist. I was one of those kids. I was no scholar. I remember mom and dad having a meeting with him. I believe that might have been where they discussed my ultimate dismissal from grade 1. It didn't matter anyway. The following year, we moved to Canada, and I started grade 1 all over again in a new language.

There was a cripple, an older handicapped guy, in the wheelchair in the camp. He sold chocolates. We used to make fun of him, and I was one of the more crude offenders. He enticed me closer to his wheelchair with a chocolate bar. "Come here I want to show you something." I approached, and should have seen it coming. When I was within reach, he slapped me one, fast as lightning. I deserved it. Who knows how this guy ended up after we moved to Canada. Whereas I, in my ignorance, had a second chance with a new life and an education in Canada. How lucky I was, not deserving it.

For fun, we used to pull pranks at the common toilet in Austria, a barrack used by the whole camp. The barrack was divided in half, half for females, and half for males. There was a row of sit-down holes all the length of the barrack. The men also had a funnel, or runnel, all along the barrack for peeing. No dividers for privacy. Are you kidding!

As a seven year old, my buddies and I would bring in a long stick, wait until nobody was on the men's side, and then look down a toilet hole to see if any woman was sitting on the other side. If there was, we'd go opposite the hole, put the stick under, and whap the lady on the bare butt. She yelped, and we'd laugh and high-tail it out of there before she cleaned up. We'd drop the stick after using it and see all the rats scurrying around down below in the poop.

That was considered fun and a big joke among the boys in the camp. Now, it seems pretty stupid, cruel and a low kind of humour. Something to be ashamed of. As I say, if it wasn't for the move to Canada, I probably would be serving a prison term in Austria somewhere.

Europe was pretty much destroyed after World War II. It's funny that foreign countries often say, if you want free money, just get into a war with the United States. The Marshall Plan was an American initiative passed in 1948 to aid Western Europe, in which the United States gave over $12 billion in economic assistance to help rebuild Western European economies after the end of World War II. Maybe that plan had not kicked in yet around Linz in 1954, but Canada was accepting immigrants to help build up its own economy in the late 40s and early 50s. Construction was booming around Kitchener, and that's where the family headed for work.

We landed at Pier 21 in Halifax on November 22, 1954. It was foggy and cold. Mom and dad were sick as dogs during the 11 day voyage across the Atlantic Ocean. I was the only one not sick, being a rambunctious 8 year old boy, and eager to discover the nooks and crannies of this huge vessel, the S.S. Neptunia. My little sister was 5, and my half-sister Nevenka, or Nellie, was 16. Dad got work mixing cement and mortar on construction and eventually became a forklift operator. During my high-school years, I always had a summer job waiting for me with G&A Construction.

I remember Pier 21, and the customs officer lifting the towel in dad's suitcase. Dad had stashed away two bottles of his best homemade wine. The officer just put the towel back and waved dad through. That would not happen now-a-days.

Well now, this little tangent has gone far astray from Tasya and her story after the Dusseldorf bombing in 1942. I'd better get back to see what is happening in her life. The sun is shining quite brightly now through the windows of the Great Room. I'm halfway through the book. Tasya tried writing Hanya asking how she was doing on the farm. No reply. Two German officers have just knocked rudely at Frau Bamm's residence. Tasya is told that she has to be reassigned for work to a truck making factory in Cologne because she is an "Auslander", a foreigner. I left off where Frau Bamm slipped Tasi some money and the girl packed a bunch of clothes in a pillow case, then was driven by the officers to Cologne in the back of a truck.

I put the book down. Took the car to the Grand Oak Barn to buy the gluten free carrot cake. Half of a cake costs $8.00. I mentioned the pot holes to the proprietor, Jane, and she said they are looking into fixing them with asphalt. To do the whole parking lot would cost them $30,000. I thought, hmmm, just like the gluten free carrot cake.

I paid the $651.23 Visa bill at the bank. I asked for the balance in my special account which I created just for the money I'm making in my eBook and paperback sales. So far, $63. I've written 10 books, a combination of novels and short stories. It's a good think my wife and I are not relying on that income for a living.

We will be glad when the end of June and her official retirement comes. The principal has been hinting that the board wants to cut her LRT time back to .75 and add a couple of subjects for her to teach next year. I don't know if that's a manner of seeding paranoia into teachers employed in teaching special needs. Cut backs all over the place by the government with the objective of balancing the budget in 5 years time. Slavery is still alive and well in the teaching profession in Ontario. My wife might break the news about her retirement to the principal at the next staff meeting. By the time the government balances the budget, she'll be retired by 5 years.

When I drove home from the bank, I noticed that the price of gas is now $1.22.9 cents per liter. It sort of leveled off at that price this week. How nice for the oil companies! Well, a bowl of soup is waiting for me. I might have a piece of bread with it and also a pepperoni stick. The gluten free carrot cake is safely tucked into the fridge. The icing really looks good. I say, look but don't touch!

# 7. Finding Connections

This Friday afternoon, I thought I'd nip over to Costco Pharmacy to pick up my Peridex mouth rinse, and then scooting back to the Rittenhouse Library to read some more *Tarnished,* while sitting by the big bay window. Maybe I can finish the book by the this weekend, which is also the intended finish for this short story on My Life. I hope you will stick around to peck away at the 8 other short stories which follow. I promise you each one of them is entertaining, and make good reading with a coffee and muffin, even without!

It looks like Tasya is not doing so well in Cologne in 1944. She is 18 years old now and working at the Ford-Werke factory. Because she insisted, during processing, that she was Ukrainian, not Russian, she was labeled as Ostarbeiter, i.e. Russian anyway, which was not a good thing. She pulled the night shift and her job was to install the front windshield in the Maultier trucks on the assembly line. Herr Bamm pulled strings and got her to come to the old household once every two weeks to spend time with the family there on excuse that she was going to do housework there and therefore work a double shift with her factory work, thereby disguising the visit as a sort of punishment.

When the Allies liberated the Displaced Persons, the DPs, Tasya and her friend, Alyona, were left to fend for themselves sheltering in the cold basement of a church. The German army and factory workers had fled. Tasya and Alyona found the Bamm household  empty and abandoned. Many people were starving in the street.

A Russian administrator tried to get the girls to sign up for a train going East, promising them that this would get them back to their home villages. Two young Ukrainian soldiers warned them not to go because the Russians were taking people to Siberia to work in labour camps. Both girls signed up because they were eager to get home. At the last moment, Tasya took her suitcase and held it out the train window. She told the Ukrainian boys to grab it; she was getting off the train. That was a moment of decision which determined a different direction in her destiny.

She said to herself that no one was ever going to make decisions for her again about where she could go and what she could do. "...she would no longer allow anyone to dictate the shape of her life, ever again." She tried to persuade Alyona to come with her. "Come with me, and later we can figure out how to get home..." Alyona ignored her friend.

From the dock, Tasya saw Alyona's face become smaller and smaller as the train picked up speed. The two young men took Tasya to a British camp, called Muenster-Lager. There were other Ukrainians there. Tasya heard that Soviet agents roamed the streets in jeeps looking for young Ukrainians to kidnap and force them back to Russia. Tasya got friendly with Stephan, a young Ukrainian soldier, who said he wanted to be his own man and have Ukraine be its own country. "We stand for self-determination. We fight against the Russians. I am Ukrainian, not a Soviet." They become an item. Tasya learned English and excelled. She also taught embroidery in the camp. Stephan was dealing in the black market, got caught and was put in solitary confinement for two weeks. He was released in August, 1946.

I would like to note here that I was 7 months old when Tasya's Stephan was released from prison. She was angry with him and told him, "I told you so", about dealing in the black market. It was also the time when Tasya was 3 months pregnant and Stephan and Tasya talked marriage.

They were in Muenster-Lager; I was born in Lager Asten, and moved to Lager Wegscheid just outside of Linz. The word Lager means "camp". Stephan signed a contract to work in a mine in Sudbury in order to come to Canada. He would send for Tasya and the baby, Alya, later. Tasya and the baby finally arrived in Halifax in June 1948, sailing from Hamburg. That was 6 years before my family arrived at Pier 21. We left Bremerhaven and arrived in Halifax in November 1954. June sounded like a more hospitable month than November to cross the Atlantic. I recall it was cold, snowy and windy. The train ride across Quebec to Kitchener was a wintery experience. We got off at the Kitchener Train Station with heavy winter coats waiting for a car to pick us up and take us to Oma and Opa's. They'd been in Canada for two years already.

I find it personally interesting that, years later, Alya, [or Tasya's daughter] studied History. I took a double honours B.A. in History and English at the University of Waterloo from 1967-1971. The generation that Alya lived through is the very generation in which Janis Joplin died of an overdose of heroine in 1970. This was the same generation which affected me. Rock music and experimental drugs! I find it so ironic that Justin Trudeau got marijuana legalized in Canada in 2018, a thing that would have gotten me arrested back in the day. Hypocritical, if you ask me. But then, the 1920's had alcohol prohibition, and now it's all reversed again, made legal, under the limit, of course.

I thought the end of the book, *Tarnished*, came appropriately back full circle into the 1970s after Tasya's terrible life during World War II. The last few chapters of the book get nostalgic, and remind me of a lot about my life in Austria. Apparently dad, Michael, had to marry my mother Rosa when she got pregnant. Not sure, but that's Aunt Sophie's opinion. She doesn't even know if I'm part of the legitimate Hartig family. My brother and I look so alike that it's no mistake that I am a Hartig. Dad Michael came from Romania; Mom Rosa came from Serbia and met in the refugee camps of Lager Asten and Lager Wegscheid. That is sort of like Ihor and Kateryna in the *Tarnished* novel. Except Ihor and Kateryna stayed in Poland; my parents moved to Canada like Tasya and Stephan. Tasya's village, Horayetz, no longer exists. My birth place, Lager Asten, still exists but has remained a small village, known now only as Asten, having dropped the "Lager". My wife and I drove through Asten in 20 minutes when we visited in 1989. "Yep, I've seen it. Done it. Let's get out of here."

The questions that Anya often asked is what I've often asked myself. What would have become of me, had the family not moved to Canada? I certainly was not a good student when I was in grade school. Dad was a steel worker, and we did not have money for higher education. Canada offered bursaries and student loans when I graduated high-school, and that is how I got to university. But those were the Pierre Elliott Trudeau years when money flowed to get every young person into university as a "right".

The perspective on destiny is interesting. Hugh O'Brian, the cowboy actor, says you are the steward of your own destiny. Tasya, in fact, took her future in her own hands when she decided, on the spur of the moment, to get off the train, instead of being driven to Siberia. Yet, years later, at the Ukrainian festival in Toronto where she gets up to announce the names of the relatives she has lost, including her brother, Mychaylo, she says to her daughter that it was worth everything that she and Stephan had sacrificed: "Worth everything that I've been through, everything that your tato went through. It wasn't of our choosing, or our doing, and yet we managed to survive and make our way here, to Canada, to Toronto. It was all worth it."

This admission about destiny recognizes that we are often victims of forces, not of our own choosing, which shape our destiny. We are not necessarily self-determining people, with "the will to power", like the philosophy of Friedrich Nietzsche, that the superman creates his own destiny. It may be okay for the supremely gifted or strong, but not for the average man or woman who is buffeted about through circumstances like a Second World War. Maybe Hugh O'Brian with his royalties from his cowboy movies could afford to shape his own destiny and take a philosophy course with his new wife on their honeymoon at

Oxford University. By contrast, Stephan had to come to Sudbury, get a job in a mine and save up money for two years to bring Tasya and little Alya to join him in Canada. There are different destinies for different people. Not all of them can make their own destiny. Some, in fact, are victims of fate. There are 6 million Jews who attest to that fact.

As I read the last few chapters of this book, and how Stephan is described, very opinionated about politics, and religion, and very argumentative, I cannot help but think of my half-sister Nellie's husband, Paul. He loved to drink with his buddies, and argue politics and religion. He hated the Pope, just like Stephan hated the Ukrainian Church. Paul was fiercely critical of corrupt government, and was proud that his 3 girls were getting a good education in Canada. Stephan was proud of Alya.

Ukrainian nicknames, in the book, are associated with my own family history too. I can't help but see the similarities. We used to call my grandmother, "die alte Baba", i.e. "the old grandmother". Baba was the same in Serbian , same in Ukrainian. Languages are funny. I'm so glad that Anastasia [Tasya] and her brother, Mychaylo, got together at the airport after 30 years.
Well, I've finished reading the book, *Tarnished*. It is a well written book by Lesia Annastasia Chytra. Nicely done! I can now give it back to my friend, Lubomir Cekota, whose first name means "lover of peace". He is always introducing me to new reading material, which I deliberately squeeze in between my efforts to write my own books.

Because of the many similarities I found between my family's life during the Second World War and Tasya's life, I have named this mini-biography, *A Week in the Life*.

I intend to finish this little bio/ blog/ fiction/ fact with a recounting about the Easter get-together at Marilyn's. The food should   be   good   and   the   kids   should   be   fun.

# 8. Easter Before Easter

I slept a bit late this Saturday morning. The sun was shining and I listened to classical radio. When I got up, I had oatmeal, watched The Life and Times of Grizzly Adams, and then got the vacuum cleaner out. My wife does not expect me to do the dusting, so I have programmed her into the futility of getting me to do so. I am going to ask the other church [we share the building with another denomination] to see if they can get 2 teenagers to come and do yard work for me for $15 per hour. Our own church, the United Mennonite Church, is made up of seniors. Members who had teenagers have basically left. I'm hoping I'll get a response from the Adoration Church to help me out. My knees and shoulders are just aching and I use a cane now-a-days to walk, or rather hobble.

Today, Saturday, is grocery shopping morning, maybe an afternoon of proofreading, and then going to Marilyn's for supper by 5:00 p.m. We are bringing the dessert: carrot cake, the "tall cake", ice-cream and sprinkles.

*****

When we got Marilyn's, the kids were playing some board game like monopoly. Tara was already in the hole, having to buy a mansion for $120,000 when she did not have the money in the bank to cover such an expense. That was ironic because her husband, Andrew, and she have bought property in Nicaragua so they can open an Air B n' B down there. They want to build within the next two years. They are young and are full of dreams.

44

Andrew is a chef at Christian Ministries outside of Beaverton, a Christian outdoor camp, called Fair Havens.

When we finally sat down for supper, the food was delicious: ham, mashed potatoes, fried veggies, salads, juice and white wine. I had a cup of coffee with my dessert. Talk around the table took in anything from the latest movies to the latest Lee Child novels.

Dad talked about his days as a principal and the types of teachers he had. There was an older overweight lady who couldn't teach, utterly incompetent. Dad recounted how she tried to keep her grade 7s in line. "If you don't behave, I'll take my hearing aids out!" The kids thought that was laughable and just continued to do what they were doing.

The superintendent and principal drafted a letter which asked her to resign. Within two weeks she had a massive heart attack. At the next principals' meeting, the administration felt very badly about this, feeling that they had practically killed the poor lady because of the letter. Her principal got up at the meeting and reached into his pocket. "Guess what? I forgot to mail the letter." So guilt-wise, the administration was off the hook. The board thought they were also off the hook, because they thought the heart attack was so bad that she would not be coming back to teach in September. "Well guess what?" asked my father-in-law. "In September she showed up. But she only lasted 2 days. The stress was so bad. The board hired a teacher more capable of controlling grade 7s."

In my own teaching experience, I have seen both teachers and principals who should not have been in those jobs. Maybe that includes me. I was never good on discipline and never had the quick come-back to put a kid in his or her place. I looked for office support when I had continual problems, and of course, office support was never forthcoming.

Principals hated to have things sent to the office. Teachers had to sink or swim on their own. I admit some teachers shouldn't be in the classroom, but by the same token, some administration people should not be in a position to govern. One wonders how some people in power get to those positions. I think they call it the Peter principle. The Peter principle is a concept in management developed by Laurence J. Peter, which observes that people in a hierarchy tend to rise to their "level of incompetence".

One of my principals, when I started teaching, believed that all kids were naturally good and that if a kid misbehaved, it was the teacher's fault. I had a particularly bad couple of years while that principal ran the school. When I asked for help, there was none there. It was always the same one or two kids who caused the trouble. Talk to them, the behaviour did not change. Send them to the office, they got sent back. Separate them and put one in the hallway, the principal would sent the kid right back into the classroom, because he's got a right to learn. What about the right of the other kids to learn?

I'm sure that I'm not the only one who has had such complaints about the lack of support from "the office". Oh well, that's all water under the bridge, something I'd prefer to forget.

I was glad to see that Dad had an appetite as the ham was passed around. He put a liberal spread of mustard on his ham. Dad sipped a glass of white wine as he ate supper. He will celebrate his 90th birthday in June. The family has already planned a big birthday party at St. Ann's Community Church.

My wife confided in Dad that she has not told her principal about her retirement yet. The board is already planning on giving her .75 LRT time next year, and .25 for teaching several extra subjects. Actually, the .75 LRT work will end up taking a full LRT load because there are more identified kids coming into the school, and the whole load of work just has to get done somehow. We wonder what will happen in the school once my wife doesn't show up next year.

It's a good thing that Marilyn has a little Shih Pooh doggie, named Bria, who scoots around and plays with the kids. The kids

My Life and Other Short Stories                    John Hartig

just adore her. Mason is Marylin's 8 year-old grand-son who has a lively mind connected to some very creative thinking. For instance, he decided to create a dog sitting business recently for which he would charge $2. He already planned out his business cards and he wanted to thank people publicly for supporting his business.

I asked Mason if he heard about the black hole that scientists had discovered in outer space. I said, they took a picture of it, and the picture was black. "Of course, it was black," he said, "that's obvious". He concocted a story of his own about Queen Bria. "Once upon a time, there was a Queen Bria and she was attacked by hair balls." The story was already getting pretty hairy. I left Mason to his imagination, and looked at the TV screen. The Masters Golf Tournament in Augusta, Georgia was on.

We had a relaxing drive back home in our Subaru Forester. It's easy for me to get in and out of that vehicle with the high frame. We brought home the rest of the ice-cream, cake and sprinkles, which I can use for coffee breaks during the week as I put my new series of short stories on the internet. I still have to design a book cover. Probably the silhouette of me holding a book as I stare poetically out over the sunset on the Niagara River. The camera was put on a self-timer.

*****

Well, tomorrow, Sunday, is another day, and the final one for "A Week in the Life". I'm glad I finished the book *Tarnished* as planned, and that Marilyn's early Easter get-together went off nicely. You know what they say about the plans of mice and men and how they go awry? Unlike Robbie Burns' tragic incident with ploughing over field mice, our supper plans went splendidly. The whole family enjoyed the food, the kids and the company. Even the doggie was happy.

47

This weekend is turning out great, sunny on Saturday and a bit cool and rainy today on Sunday, Palm Sunday. The theme of today's sermon was "Paradoxes". I appreciated Pastor Louise' sermon. It underscored the human condition of hypocrisy, and how people can be nice in one situation and turn their backs in another.

Apparently, there were two leaders who rode into Jerusalem on Palm Sunday. Pontius Pilate made his triumphant entry riding in on his chariot from the West. Jesus rode in on a humble colt from the East, with people praising him and throwing their coats under the colt's feet in honor of the Messiah. These same people turned their backs on Jesus the next Friday as they shouted, "Crucify him." Then on Easter Sunday, Jesus rose from the dead, which is the whole basis of the Christian Faith. The moderator gave the blessing at the end of today's service, telling the congregation to go in peace and love.

I was pleased to sing in the choir today. It is a positive participation within a group that makes a positive contribution to the community. This afternoon at 2:30 p.m., we meet at the UM Home to sing a few songs to the old folks. That breaks up the day for them in a nice way.

When we got to the auditorium at the seniors' home, I noticed 99 year old Wycliffe Godjer in the front row. He was an engineer who worked on the team that developed the jet engine after World War II. He had a bandage on top of his head, which covered a cancerous area. People are like old tree trunks which are prone to fungi of all sorts. Pastor Louise does a wonderful service by bringing the choir to the UM Home to sing.

April 7 to April 13 is National Volunteer Week. That's a great idea. I volunteer my voice, whatever quality it is, to bolster the bass section of our choir. I also visit seniors occasionally as part of my duty to church and to society. In Hebrew the phrase good deed is "mitzvah". In the Old Testament, a mitzvah refers to a moral deed performed as a religious duty. The term mitzvah has also come to express an individual act of human kindness.

So, the end of *National Volunteer Week*, is appropriately the end of this short story, *A Week in the Life* of John Hartig. I started out with a paragraph wanting to learn how to make a drop cap, and then I just kept on writing, hoping I could find things to say which would resonate with somebody, anybody. I think I did just that. I hope you stick around for the rest of the stories within this collection, "My Life and Other Short Stories".

"Happy Reading,"
John Hartig

*****

# Saint Peter Needs Help

## Crowd Control

- Jean-Baptiste Lully [1632-1687]
- François Couperin [1668-1733]
- Jean-Philippe Rameau [1683-1764]
- Jean-Marie Leclair [1697 – 1764]
- Pope Clement XII [1652-1740]
- Jean-Pierre Guignon [1702-1774]

## Synopsis

**Jean-Baptiste Lully**

One would think that the Pearly Gates to Heaven would have a big welcoming sign. Not so! Not if you have to face a grouchy Saint

Peter who guards the Gates with the calloused hands of a fisherman, who is flustered with this new job of "roll" keeping and getting the names right on his list. One can't really blame him. New job, more bureaucracy. Fishing was simpler. So, in a rather unsaintly voice, Saint Peter had to tell people to take a ticket, and get in line!

Since the Earth made it a busy business to go out and multiply over the past millennium [maybe more], Saint Peter meant to ask the head guy, or at least the second head guy, for an administrative assistant, but the top guys always seemed so busy themselves. All Saint Peter seemed to be doing lately was "just coping". He longed for his old job back.

There were days [if there were "days", as such, in front of the Pearly Gates] when he thought he'd just pack it in, buy a boat, and go and row out on the Sea of Galilee to see if any fish would bite.

However, he had been given this job by Jesus who considered him a rock, and had confidence in him that he could handle any problems that came up to the Pearly Gates. At least, he had a job, and he did promise to be the Keeper of the Keys to the Gates of Heaven. Did the contract say, "Forever"? He still couldn't understand why the Gates had to be Pearly, being a simple fisherman and all.

Not too long ago, he couldn't remember when exactly, he had to deal with a couple of argumentative painters, Michelangelo and Leonardo something or other. Anyway, there were two of them, and a couple of Popes, he recalled. Not a happy experience. He really needed that administrative assistant!

Jean-Baptiste Lully [1632-1687] was the first one of the new crew to pop into existence in front of the Gates. "Here we go again," he thought. He got his clipboard out and licked the tip of his pencil. Shortly, 5 other persons would pop up like popcorn, and he would get flustered. Who were the other fellows on the list anyway? At least, he got the memo. Oh, yes:

- François Couperin [1668-1733]

- Jean-Philippe Rameau [1683-1764]

- Jean-Marie Leclair [1697 – 1764]

- Pope Clement XII [1652-1740]

- Jean-Pierre Guignon [1702-1774]

\*\*\*\*\*

# Preface

"Again I tell you, it is easier for a camel to go through the eye of a needle than for a rich man to enter the kingdom of God." [Matthew 19:24]

Sometimes I feel that way about writing. In the old days, if you were good enough, you got a contract. They wanted you and you got royalties. It seems lately, mainly with the internet, you have to pay them, the publishers, to get published and printed. Royalties yes, but you have to do the marketing yourself, unless you pay extra big bucks. I know nothing about marketing, and would much rather just write.

Well, whether you write a novel or a novella, or anything, you have to do "research". You don't get an hourly wage for that, unless you work for an already established author who is already making big bucks. But complaints aside, research in itself does have its own rewards. The wonderful thing about research is that you uncover all these historical gems, some shiny, some just stone, but really neat stuff about people and events. Writing is a way to share these treasures with others.

Yes, the Pearly Gates should have a warm welcoming sign. Maybe a Timmy's coffee shop there would help, with free coffee and Timbits.

I'm sure that when Saint Peter's six new candidates came up to the Pearly Gates, five violinists and one Pope, they felt like they were at the other place. Especially with a grouchy and strung-out Saint Peter in front of them. When the Keeper of the Keys told them to take a ticket and get in line, they might have thought they were really at the gates of Dante's Inferno, "Abandon all hope, ye who enter here."

Again, I can't help but picture myself there in front of the gate of a publishing house with a manuscript in hand, wondering if I should just trash the thing in the closest Timmy's garbage can. Except there is no garbage can, because there is no Timmy's at the Pearly Gates and no Welcoming sign. Hmmm. Would the Golden Arches of McDonald's be a good substitute for the Pearly Gates? Something to think about. How did I get on to this topic? Maybe it was something I ate or maybe it's a mid-life crisis? If you see this in print though, there is hope!

Saint Peter is just a figment of my imagination. I hope you get a chuckle or two out of his dealing with Violinists waiting at the Pearly Gates, ticket in hand.

*****

# Knock, Knock, Knockin'
## On Heaven's Door

"Halt, who goes there?" challenged Saint Peter. It was not a friendly greeting from the Keeper of the Keys to the Gates of Heaven.

Jean-Baptiste Lully [1632-1687] was the first one to arrive. "Am I early?" he asked.

"No, no one is ever early," responded St. Peter. "They always come late," he said. "Maybe that's why they call all the arrivals here, 'the late...so and so'." St. Peter chuckled at his own little joke. You have to have a sense of humor to work here because new people were coming up to the Pearly Gates all the time, not early, but always "late" arrivals.

Some of them shouldn't even have come here; they should have gone straight-away to the other place. "That would make the names less messy in my book keeping," complained St. Peter, "sometimes I have to erase things, or redirect people, which is always an unpleasant chore."

"Like the song says," he said, almost singing it, "when the Roll is called up yonder!" He continued his train of thought, "It would be great to have the names stay the same, but sometimes they change, and sometimes I have the unpleasant job of telling my new arrivals, they came to the wrong Gates; they have to go to the other place instead. I can't stand arguments. Maybe if I had an administrative assistant?"

"Well," said Lully, "do I have clearance or not?"

St. Peter said, "Yes you do, all in God's good time."

St. Peter explained that there was a bit of a delay in Lully's case. It was a matter of the profanity he let loose when he stomped his big toe accidentally as he was conducting his orchestra with his big staff. Lully challenged, "And what would you have done if you'd have pricked yourself with a fish hook being a fisherman? Or even Jesus, being a carpenter, and banged his thumb accidentally with a hammer?"

Lully mulled this over, massaging his sore toe. He imagined it still hurt. He was looking at St. Peter for for some sort of understanding. "Well, you are a Saint, after all. And Jesus, he is the Son of God. I'd say those were unfair advantages compared to us poor mortals."

St. Peter said to Lully, "Well, maybe that's why you're standing in front of the Pearly Gates, because God understands, instead of sending you straight to the Fires of Hell. We do take extenuating circumstances into consideration up here."

Lully kept rubbing the imaginary pain in his big toe. "That's phantom pain," said St. Peter. "We've run across it before in the Big Battle between the Angels of Dark and the Angels of Light. That was even before Mankind got booted out of Paradise. We won, of course, in our big skirmish, but some of our Seraphim and

Archangels came away with various scrapes, scratches and broken wings in the fray, and well, they've had phantom pain too."

St. Peter explained that there was a Canadian former preacher, from Saskatchewan, who turned politician, who was a feisty little guy who spoke passionately about a unique concept of healthcare. "He passed through the Gates some 250 years in the future, after this group you're in, Lully," said St. Peter, "and he was so convincing about his idea of universal healthcare that God adopted the idea retroactively, stretching the benefits back in time to the very Battle of the Angels."

St. Peter explained that the plan paid for all personal damage, including broken wings. That took care of the injuries to two-thirds of the Angels of God, and that meant a lot of broken wings among hundreds of thousands of them.

Lully asked, "What about the healthcare and broken wings on Lucifer's side?" St. Peter said firmly, "Let them get their own healthcare."

God pinned a set of golden wings on the lapel of that Canadian, Tommy Douglas, in a special ceremony of recognition. Tommy said before one and all, "What's a Heaven for, if it can't take care of its own citizens!" St. Peter admitted that he'd never been prouder to let a politician pass through the Gates of Heaven, than Tommy Douglas. Tommy Douglas got his wings in 1986.

"If there would not have been an Angel rebellion, and if Mankind would not have fallen," said St. Peter as an afterthought, "there would not have been the Pearly Gates, and I would not have a job."

Then with a more kindly voice, St. Peter asked Lully to take a ticket, step aside and wait in line because there were more arrivals expected. The Pearly Gates loomed high above Lully. They looked formidable, like a Wall to keep the riff-raff out. He had clearance though; he was not one of the riff-raff.

François Couperin [1668-1733] shimmered into existence next, if you could call it an existence, in front of the Pearly Gates.

"So," asked Couperin, "what are we all doing standing around?"

St. Peter stood in front of him officiously. He was tired now of explaining, if not justifying things to his newcomers. "Just take a ticket and get in line," he said. Couperin wasn't used to being shuffled about this way. After all, he was "Couperin le Grand", Couperin the Great, to distinguish him from other members of his overly talented musical family.

"Reminds me of another family, the Bachs," said St. Peter, "although they haven't arrived yet, thank goodness! I'm still keeping up with the new names here on my Heavenly roster. Oh, I surely could use that administrative assistant!"

Couperin tugged on St. Peter's sleeve. "I have one question, Peter." He dispensed with the title of "Saint". He only asked what was most pertinent to himself, "Do you have a 'clavecin' beyond the Pearly Gates?"

"A 'clavecin', what's that?" asked the big fisherman.

"Why, it's a harpsichord. Since I died, I missed my usual six hours of practice. Got to keep those fingers nimble you know. Who knows I may have to perform in front of God, or Jesus, at the least."

"I'm sure that can be arranged," admitted St. Peter. "We have advanced classes in the harp, and as you say, the 'clavecin' or harpsichord, also the violin and this new instrument we just ordered in, the 'piano-forte'. We prefer the shorter term, than the Italians use.  Bartolomeo di Francesco Cristofori , the inventor, called it, 'gravicembalo col piano e forte'. Since God himself likes piano music, not just the harp, in fact all kinds of music, except maybe rap, Cristofori was waved through to Heaven immediately without ceremony."

"How much for lessons on the piano or the harp?" asked Couperin. "I don't know if I brought enough change with me."

"Oh, lessons are free of charge," said St. Peter. "As long as you put your heart and soul into practising."

Couperin seemed content with that. He grasped his ticket firmly in his hand and stepped to the side of the Pearly Gates to make room for any new arrivals who might just "pop in".

Jean-Philippe Rameau [1683-1764] shimmered into existence next at the foot of the Pearly Gates. Then came Jean-Marie Leclair [1697-1764], right behind Rameau.

"Well," said St. Peter, "you two did die only a month apart. So it is expected you'd show up here one after the other, at about the same time, even though we don't have time up here as such."

St. Peter observed that this double appearance was putting stress on his nerves. "I do need that administrative assistant," he asserted, "I will have to talk to Jesus about it. I don't even know if God is listening."

Rameau, in the meantime, was admiring the sight of the Pearly Gates."It beats the sight of the other place!" he said to himself. As an ironic afterthought, he muttered, "At least, they have a sign there, but I don't like what it says."

Rameau. by the way, was born in Dijon, France. Dijon was the city that the famous Dijon mustard was named after. But Rameau had established his name for more important things than mustard.

Jean-Philippe Rameau had replaced Lully as the lead composer for opera in France. He also composed for the harpsichord, and like Couperin was eager to see what this new 'piano-forte' could do. He didn't mind paying extra money for his lessons, although he was most happy to get them for free.

Having been a miser during his old age, he could quite well afford to pay for lessons. After all, he died with a big bag full of gold coins, specifically, 1,691 "gold Louis d'or" which were found in his room after death. When he was alive, he lived in apparent poverty, wearing old clothes, a single pair of shoes and playing on a battered old harpsichord. Had Charles Dickens been around and written "A Christmas Carol" one hundred years earlier, Rameau would surely have been called "Scrooge" by his neighbours.

"It will be nice playing on something new," said Rameau to himself, "and hopefully in tune." As he eyed the formidable height of the Pearly Gates, he muttered cynically to himself, "Surely, Heaven can afford free lessons and a good instrument, with all the talk about Pearly Gates and streets of gold and all." He took his precious ticket, and stood behind Couperin.

Jean-Marie Leclair had been standing quietly by, saying nothing. "There we go," thought Leclair to himself, "I'm standing on the side-lines again." He felt like he always missed the limelight, even in death. Leclair had been stabbed three times, just one month after Rameau died of natural causes. "Ouch," commented St. Peter, "that must have hurt."

"Oh, not so bad," said Leclair, "what really hurt was that the killer wasn't considerate enough to kill me later, putting some respectable space between Rameau's death and mine, so I would, at least get a few more headlines when I was dispatched." As an afterthought, Leclair commented, "I'd like to be known for more than just the way I was killed!"

Whereas Rameau took to opera writing like a duck to water, Leclair wrote only one opera, "Scylla et Glaucus", and gave up on making that the new direction in his career. He stuck to what he knew best, which was composing concertos and sonatas for the violin. Leclair is known as the founder of the French school of violin, and rightly earned the titles of "the French Corelli" or "the French Bach".

Ironically, Leclair was killed by his own nephew, a fellow musician and violinist, who was envious and wanted his uncle to put in a good word for him to King Louis XV of France about his amazing playing talent. Of course, the nephew had no talent, and nothing was ever said to the King about it. Perhaps Leopold Mozart was right when he advised his young son, Mozart, some years later, not to trust musicians.

It seemed like 1764 was a bad year for composers. Pietro Antonio Locatelli died first, an Italian who made good his career in Holland, passing away in March 1764. Then Rameau died with a bag full of coinage in Paris in September 1764, and finally Leclair passed away, murdered in October 1764, stabbed in the back by his own nephew, and dragged into the vestibule of his own home. Leclair was more irritated about the date which his nephew picked to kill him, than about the fact that he was murdered by stabbing.

"It was too close to Rameau's death," he complained to Saint Peter, "that I would have to share the announcement of my death with another composer. Couldn't my nephew have at least waited just one year?"

Leclair, the latest to arrive, asked one more question of St. Peter, "But what about the different dates in all of our deaths? Here is Lully who died in 1687, and then myself, way later, in 1764!"

"And may I add," lamented Leclair, "I wasn't even ready to die!"

"Well, no one is ever ready to die," said St. Peter, "except maybe some Christians who don't see that the transition may be painful."

St. Peter explained that there was no "time", as such, at the Pearly Gates. In fact there was no space or place either. "No space-time continuum as Einstein understood it," he said, "or didn't understand it." In fact, St. Peter confessed that he didn't understand it himself, which was excusable for a simple fisherman.

"We might just have anybody popping in at anytime, from anywhere," said St. Peter, "that's why I find my job so frustrating. I really do need an administrative assistant."

Before it took the time to say, "Pope Clement XII", Pope Clement XII himself popped in at the Pearly Gates. Pope Clement was Pope from 1730 to 1740.

Born Lorenzo Corsini, the Pope belonged to the Florentine nobility. His uncle promoted him in the practice of law. Years later, when he became Pope, he was blind and confined to bed. He surrounded himself with capable officials, many of whom just happened to be his Corsini relatives. Pope Clement also picked his own nephew for the Cardinalate. He knew the meaning of "nepotism".

"That," admonished Clement, looking accusingly at Jean-Marie Leclair, "is more than you ever did for your nephew, Guillaume-François Vial!"

"Well, maybe your nephew actually had talent," countered Leclair.

"Boys," said St. Peter, "before we get into a heated discussion here, remember where you are!" St. Peter did not want to go through a repeat of what he had gone through with that other group, those painters, Michelangelo and Leonardo whatshisname, and those Popes who got into heated words in front of the very Gates of Heaven. How inappropriate!

"Besides," said St. Peter, "the only reason you qualify, Pope Clement, is that you restored the papal finances and fired that corrupt Cardinal Niccolo Coscia. You also promoted art and architecture when you were Pontiff in Rome, creating lots of employment for artisans, artists and tradesmen."

"All for the glory of God," said Pope Clement.

St. Peter responded, "God doesn't need your praise or glory. I'm sure that erecting an eye-catching chapel dedicated to your 14$^{th}$ century kinsman had a lot to do with promoting the Arts in Rome. Anyway, go get your ticket and stand in line with the others."

Even though he died a decade after Jean-Marie Leclair, and a good 34 years after the Pontiff, Jean-Pierre Guignon [1702-1774] popped in to get his name registered with Saint Peter. "Better late than never," he smiled. Saint Peter raised one eyebrow. "Here's a ticket, get in line," he said.

Guignon saw Leclair ahead of the Pope. He reached out with his violin bow [always ready], and poked Leclair with it. "What say, to a violin joust while were waiting?" "No thanks," said Leclair, "I had enough of that in my lifetime, and especially with you." Guignon smirked and stared up at the Pearly Gates, with obvious impatient body language. He moved his head up and down in time to some music only he could hear between his own ears. He raised his chin and nose to Leclair, as if to snub him.

Guignon was not exactly a friend of Leclair's. They used to play in the same orchestra together for King Louis XV, and in fact, they had violin jousts on several occasions for the public in Paris, in the public music series called "the Concert Spirituel". Those competitions or jousts seemed to go over quite well with Parisians, but Leclair couldn't stand Guignon and vice-versa.

So, before it was Guignon's turn to take the first violin chair in the orchestra, Leclair simply packed up his fiddle and quit. In 1737, Leclair moved to the Netherlands "where he was warmly received". Well, that's all history and water under the bridge now.

Saint Peter was eyeing the Gates with unease, as if expecting something. All of a sudden, the Pearly Gates shimmered and melted away into another dimension. Lully, Couperin, Rameau, Leclair, Pope Clement XII, and the late arrival, Guignon, all took on new bodies of light. Lully thought he not only heard but saw music, the Music of the Spheres. Strangely, he no longer thought about his sore toe.

Couperin imagined himself playing a pretty tune on his "clavicin". Rameau and Leclair saw themselves playing their fiddles, as did Guignon. Pope Clement was just content to be there, a rarity for a Pope to be in front of the Pearly Gates. One and all shimmered into the other side of Eternity, and into the light,

"You know," said St. Peter in a final word to the Pope, "you are lucky. There is a saying, that it is easier for a camel to thread through the eye of a needle, than for a Pope to sneak through the Gates of Heaven...or something to that effect. I never could get it quite right. I really do need that administrative assistant!"

\*\*\*\*\*

# Leonardo and Michelangelo
## At the Pearly Gates

**A Short Story**
**By John Hartig**
February 2018
12  pages 5,000 words

"Hey Michelangelo, what are you doing here?" asked Leonardo, as Michelangelo himself, shimmered into existence. Well, you could call it a sort of existence, as it happened to be in front of the Pearly Gates.

Leonardo arched his eyebrows upwards, eyebrows which were distinctly bushy in this spiritual realm. Always polite, Leonardo answered, "I'm waiting for a ticket to get in."

"So, why are we waiting? What's keeping us outside the Gates?" asked Michelangelo, obviously impatient.

"Maybe we've been bad boys!" commented Leonardo.

"Maybe it was the fact that you were gay and liked boys!" accused Michelangelo. "Everyone in Florence talked about the red tunics you wore."

"I was proud of what I was and am!" rebuffed Leonardo. "And speaking of secrets in the closet, I heard a few things about you!"

Michelangelo took a long time to answer but finally admitted, "Well, since we're in front of the Pearly Gates, yes, I was gay too, but at least, I tried my best to follow the church's teachings. I should be rewarded for my hidden suffering."

"It could be that all that doesn't matter to God," said Leonardo, "maybe it's other things we did which are holding us outside the Gates. When I knew you, you were such, what shall I say, a bastard about people."

Michelangelo pursed his lips in disdain. His anger rose and he was about to swear.

"Tut, tut," broke in Saint Peter. "We'll have none of that here." He wanted to hear what the two men were arguing about, especially since they were at the very threshold of the Pearly Gates. "Look," said Saint Peter. "Neither of you is getting a ticket in until we settle this thing. Bickering is just not allowed in the Kingdom of Light. So let's settle it, right here and right now."

Of course, 'right here' and 'right now' meant nothing there in front of the Pearly Gates. This argument could potentially stretch out forever like a tedious ping-pong match until one or both of them put down their paddles. Saint Peter eyed the two men and sighed philosophically. "Forgiveness is a long and winding road. Sometimes, it never ends."

He pointed to the Pearly Gates. "As you can see, this is a gated community," he said, "and we just don't allow any old riffraff in."

Michelangelo was somewhat miffed. "Riffraff?" he asked.

Meanwhile, Leonardo smiled quietly at Michelangelo, and nodded, as if to say, 'if the shoe fits...'

Saint Peter jumped in before things heated up again. He explained, "in the old days, we categorically kept Unbelievers out. But recently, there's been a change in policy. Belief is not used as a measure any more; it's Kindness."

No, Michelangelo didn't like Saint Peter's remarks, at all, or the look in Leonardo's eyes. Michelangelo came to the Pearly Gates with a bad reputation to begin with for being unkind, a real grouch, during his lifetime. He was a contentious even with his patrons, especially in Florence and Rome. According to him, you shouldn't base Heaven on just being "kind and nice." Michealangelo had his own idea of standards in mind. How does God justify endowing Leonardo with divine genius when after all, he didn't even believe in the same

God that the Church believed in? Besides, as everyone knew, Leonardo was gay and never felt guilty about it. If suffering alone was a criterion, as it should be, then Michelangelo should have had a free ticket into Heaven.

Michelangelo was testy, especially since his osteoarthritis was acting up. They weren't in Heaven yet, where all the pain and suffering for those heavy of heart would one day end. While on earth, Michelangelo had pounded away at marble all day long, day after day, liberating figures like David who were frozen in the marble. That obsessive chore came at a high price. His long gnarled fingers ached. He did lighter work in painting only as a welcome relief because the paintbrush was easier to lift than a hammer and chisel. Besides all that pounding on marble gave him a headache.

He felt that Leonardo had it easy. Everything was easy for him. Leonardo was always a pretty boy with a straight nose and a handsome face framed by tight curls, and he had a muscular physique! Leonardo paraded his homosexuality openly in the streets of Florence. He was a well-dressed dandy and enjoyed life. On the other hand, Michelangelo was tortured by his sexual proclivity through no fault of his own. He kept "the big secret", wearing dark clothes and swearing to a life of abstinence and penance.

Leonardo acted younger than Michelangelo, even though he was 23 years older. He enjoyed designing costumes and the theatrical machinery for parades and pageants in Florence and Milan, so he could regale the royalty and princes there. He would prance around in his red and rose coloured tunics telling his underlings when to bring in the next float or to pull which wire to make a cherubic angel fly. Admittedly the glitter and glitz of such showy pageantry won him the admiration of the art world of the High Renaissance. And because he was good at everything he did, his rival, Michelangelo, cast eyes of Envy upon Leonardo, who eventually became the true definition of a Renaissance Man, excelling in painting, anatomy, engineering, mathematics and even in Michelangelo's own specialty, sculpture. Oh and before we forget, Leonardo was also an excellent musician, inventing new instruments like the key-board operated bell. His biographer at the time, Giorgio Vasari, wrote, "he sang divinely, improvising his own accompaniment on the lyre."

The two men pursued their argument, ignoring Saint Peter, taking up their verbal fisticuffs again.

"I don't like you calling me a bastard about people," countered Michelangelo. "If anyone, you're the real bastard!"

Leonardo deftly swiped the remark away, politely observing, "I prefer the word 'illegitimate'!"

Leonardo's own father, Piero Fruosino di Antonio da Vinci, made a peasant girl pregnant, a tradition which was a common practice in those days, but Piero never legitimized his son. Maybe that was for the best because Leonardo was apprenticed to Verrochio to become a master painter, and thereby escaped his father's boring profession as a notary public. Leonardo was a laid-back kind of guy. He accepted being illegitimate and being gay. What's the big deal? You are who you are, you make do, and you got on with life. In this respect, Leonardo was the better man. He had never expressed envy over Michelangelo who was born legitimately within a family of minor nobility.

Saint Peter stepped in because Michelangelo was still in a belligerent mood. "Now boys, we don't have name-calling beyond this point." He drew a line across the doorway of the Pearly Gates. They sparkled and the air beyond them shone and shimmered with a soothing warmth. The two artists shut up and kept their own counsel. They wondered how long they'd have to stand outside the gates, or if they'd ever get through.

Saint Peter said, "You know guys, it doesn't matter whether you're gay or not, what matters is your heart and soul, and in the depth of things, your kindness towards all living things." The two men seemed somewhat chastened. But there still was something hard in Michelangelo's eyes which was unyielding.

Maybe this friction, this unspecified tension between the two men, came from birthrights, from genetics, from temperament and from the difference in gifts? Maybe all this made them each a puppet in a cosmological play, even more than masters of their own destinies? Who knows? The fact was they didn't like each other. Physically, personally, nor how they approached their art.

Michelangelo with his long bony face and receding hair line. Leonardo with his straight nose, pretty face, long curly hair and muscular body. Temperament-wise, Leonardo, was an easy going sort of person, who often did not finish his commissions. He put his curiosity first in studying the flight of birds and how water currents swirled, before he considered the size of his income as a painter.

Michelangelo painted like he sculpted with strong striking lines. Leonardo, on the other hand, used the 'sfumato' style to create less distinct lines, softening them, sometimes even smudging them with his fingers tips to create an ephemeral look in the features of faces, like the smile of the Mona Lisa. Sometimes he left a fingerprint on his work. He imagined God doing the same thing when He smeared the cosmological gases of space into existence and into the shapes of stars, planets and even galaxies.

All this being said, Leonardo was quite happy with his place in the universe and his sexuality. He flaunted this with flashy clothes, and had a young man, Salai, 28 years younger, as his companion. Michelangelo was a devout Christian and was tortured by his secret sexuality. He often wore dark clothes and apparently imposed celibacy upon himself. He was grumpy and grouchy all the time.

Michelangelo's nose was out of joint in more ways than one. In fact, it was permanently disfigured because he got into a fist fight, actually more on the other guy's part. That other guy was Pietro Torrigiano, a young artist who was drawing alongside Michelangelo in a Florentine chapel. Michelangelo made a remark and boom! Torrigiano popped him in the nose with such force that he gave Michelangelo an unattractive bump there which he had to live with for the rest of his life. Michelangelo also earned an unsavoury reputation for bad body odour, going unwashed for days. He had stooped shoulders, as a stark contrast to Leonardo's straight muscular physique.

But Saint Peter did not take stock in such comparisons as the three of them stood there in front of the Pearly

Gates. He wanted to weigh each man on the scales of Faith, and more importantly on their soul and inner fibre. Leonardo had no personal religious practice, didn't think about God much or Religion. He liked to think about big questions, what were stars made of and why was the sky blue? He wanted to describe the tongue of the woodpecker. Who would think of such things? Such questions to Michelangelo were of no use, and well, just not practical. And yet for such questions, Michelangelo was secretly envious of Leonardo who was blessed with the curiosity to ask such questions.

"It's you who are envious of anybody finding out your secrets," accused Michelangelo. "Why else do you write in mirror image in your notebooks?"

Leonardo explained, "That's easy. I'm left-handed and by writing from the right to the left, I avoid smearing the ink on my page. Besides, I enjoy doing things that nobody else can do. I love riddles and brain-teasers." Michelangelo could only come up with a silent look of disdain.

Saint Peter, by the grace of God, knew all of this about the two men. "I've got a difficult job," he said, "being Saint Peter. You may think it's an easy job, but you just try filling my shoes!"

It seemed like no time at all had passed by when the two men started throwing disparaging remarks at each other again. Michelangelo looked like he wanted to take a swing at Leonardo's nose so that they'd both have, at least, a level [or rather unlevel] playing field in the ugly probosci department. However, Saint Peter, ever vigilant, and also a stout fisherman, intervened. He spread his arms out in the form of a cross, and by sheer force, kept the two men apart.

"What you need, Michelangelo," said Saint Peter, "is some anger management." In the twinkling of an eye, the archangel, Raphael, appeared. "This is fitting," explained the keeper of the keys, "Raphael is the angel of healing, and what you need, Michelangelo, is healing of your soul. You have been battered and twisted by the church's teachings, so that your soul is sick and unhappy with itself."

Saint Peter continued, "I know Raphael here is also the name-sake of your bitter rival in Rome. Raphael, the painter."

"Therefore you need to learn forgiveness and humility," said the keeper of the keys, "or you will never get into Heaven. Even here your Envy and your Anger will grease the slippery slope to the Eternal Abyss."

Michelangelo put a rein on his feelings, and nodded his head in submission. Deep down, he did want healing. Leonardo meanwhile had not said a word the whole time. He was ever the observer of details and facial expressions. He itched to sketch Michelangelo's face, but found that in this spiritual realm, which was devoid of time and space and matter, he had no pen and paper at hand.

*****

In another twinkling of an eye, Pope Julius II appeared. "Long time no see," he said to Michelangelo. "It's been years, since I commissioned you to do the Sistine Chapel!" The whole sequence of events seemed out of synch to Michelangelo because the pontiff had died in 1513, whereas Michelangelo himself had died in 1564.

"Well, what's time anyway?" asked Saint Peter, "except an illusion."

"Sometimes God makes people appear here or there in an instant. He must have His own reasons for doing that...even though I can see Leonardo asking, why? In the long run of things, what does it matter?"

"Hey," said Saint Peter as an afterthought, turning philosophical for a moment, "That reminds me of a joke. Did you ever ask yourself what is Mind?" After a brief moment, he said dismissively, "...uh, no Matter." With perfect comedic timing, he next asked, "What is Matter?...uh, never Mind." The Saint chuckled at this stand-up routine which was so out of place in front of the Pearly Gates and in front of such a poor audience. All the faces stared blankly at Saint Peter.

"Gee," he affirmed, "I'm working in front of a tough crowd!"

At least, At least, Michelangelo was coming around and showed an amused smirk on his face. Leonardo was merely amused, showing a tiny hint of a Mona Lisa smile. Julius II looked like he was ready to kill somebody. He, in fact, had earned nicknames like "The Fearsome Pope" and "The Warrior Pope" during his lifetime. He had ridden into battle and slain people to protect his power. He had a daughter out of wedlock, and was reputed to have had homosexual lovers. No sense of humour there, only serious plotting and killing to maintain his hegemony over other city states. No time for jokes or laughter.

"Let's get on with it," he cajoled, "the Pearly Gates are right in front of us, within our very grasp!"

Julius II thought he could simply march on through the Pearly Gates, no obstacle there, because he deserved to seize the Heavenly Prize and Eternal Bliss. After all, look at what he had done for God and Man, and the historical heritage of the Roman Catholic Church. It was, after all, on record!

Julius II had commissioned Michelangelo to paint the ceiling of the Sistine Chapel back in 1508. The ceiling was originally dotted with golden stars set in the background of a blue sky. How unoriginal was that! Michelangelo was hard at work on the ceiling for four agonizing years, redoing the fresco which inspired ecstasy in its admiring onlookers. It was painful work for his back and joints. Raphael meanwhile imitated Michelangelo's style but painted far below in secret and in safety decorating the papal rooms, while Michelangelo stretched and strained on the scaffolding high above. Michelangelo disdainfully dubbed Raphael a plagiarist.

Somehow Leo X next appeared at the Pearly Gates. Poof! He stood there beside Julius eyeing his predecessor up and down. "I thought you were dead!" he said. "I got news for you," said Julius, "we're both dead."

"Well, this is a fine how-do-you-do!" exclaimed Michelangelo when he saw the new pope pop up out of nowhere.

Leo X caught Julius up on the latest papel news, remarking that his investment in Raphael, the painter, was paying off. "The kid's got talent and is doing a marvelous job which everybody is admiring," he said.

Michelangelo only harrumphed at that with obvious disdain.

Raphael, the archangel, tut-tutted at Michelangelo, who immediately simmered down. Leo X, as every history buff knows, depleted the papal treasury in his huge expenditures on art for the papacy. He was also the pope who excommunicated Martin Luther in 1521, not taking the Reformation seriously. "That's just a phase," he said.

Leonardo remained quiet, observing all the details about what was going on and making his own quiet judgments about things. He wished he had his invaluable notebook in his hands. When Leo X popped in, Leonardo thought that the Pearly Gates were already overly crowded, when poof, yet another historical figure popped onto the scene, completely out of synch with both time and space.

*****

Einstein blinked into existence, and said, "Hello."

Michelangelo raised his eyebrows and snidely asked Einstein, "What? You forgot to comb your hair?"

"You need to talk!" countered Einstein, "you stink!"

Saint Peter stepped in, backed by Raphael, his formidable archangel. Archangels don't come in small sizes, you know.

"Either I'm at the end of the universe, or I'm in a place where time and space don't exist," surmised Einstein. "Hey, this place could use a restaurant here at the end of the universe where a fellow could get a cup of coffee and a bagel."

The two popes having had little to say up to this point interjected. First Julius, "I'll have you know, we are at the very foot of the Pearly Gates!" Not to be left out, his successor, Pope Leo, added, "Can you believe it, we are only a stone's throw away from Heaven?"

"But I don't see any stones," said Einstein. Leonardo, tired of being quiet, finally remarked, using the familiar form of address, "Look Albert, it's just a figure of speech."

"I know," said Albert, "I'm not stupid."

Somehow through supernatural intuition, Albert knew who all these people were. "This is quite an august assemblage," he said. "Is this really the end of the universe? And are we really in front of the Pearly Gates? Why are we all just standing around? Why not crash the gates?"

What a remark! You'd almost think Pope Julius had said it. Generally Einstein had a reputation for being a reasonable soul. But then again he came up with the idea for the nuclear reaction which would make an Atomic Bomb possible, which in fact, was the case when the Americans levelled Hiroshima and Nagasaki in 1945. So, there was, at least, some kind of gate crashing capacity within the brain of this allegedly peaceful man.

He said again, "Why are we all just standing around? Why don't we crash the gates?"

This got Saint Peter upset, and he finally spoke out, obviously irate. "Gate crashing? We'll have none of that here!"

Thunder and lighting reverberated across the sky at that very instant, or what purported to be a sky and an instant. The Pearly Gates shook and shimmered but only momentarily.

"Fascinating," said Einstein. "It would appear that there is an Intelligent Design after all. God does not play dice with the universe."

Einstein, like Leonardo, was an observer. They observed each other. Finally, Einstein said, addressing Michelangelo, "Now, don't get me wrong, Michelangelo, I've always liked your work. David was simply divine. But some of your paintings? Well, I hate to kvetch, but they look stilted to me, like that Doni Tondo, for example. The lines are too chiselled, like they're sculpted in stone and not painted."

Einstein was treating Michelangelo like an apprentice art student. He lectured, " Lines, like the universe, should be fluid and not solid."

Einstein pointed at Leonardo. "Now there is a man who knows what I'm talking about. He knows a thing or two about soft lines and how to make a woman's face both beautiful and ethereal."

The archangel put his hand on Michelangelo's shoulder soothing the storm rising up in Michelangelo. The great artist took a deep breath. He counted to 10. Anger left him like the sweet breath of spring.

"Still," conceded Einstein, "you did good work, Michelangelo." With that concession, he turned his back on Michelangelo and again addressed Leonardo, heaping more praise upon him. Michelangelo counted to 10 again, with the archangel's supportive hand on his shoulder.

"I just love how you used the technique of *sfumato*," observed Einstein, "I guess God did something like that in creating galaxies. He smudged quirks and quarks into the Big Bang and then let them play, popping in and out of existence in all the shimmer and shine after the first millisecond of creation. Nothing is really real and there are no definite lines anywhere on the quantum level."

Einstein finally proclaimed, "$E=mc^2$," with conviction.

"What's he talking about?" asked Leo X, looking at Julius puzzled.

Raphael happened to have taken a special course on that very subject some eons ago. He said, "Einstein is correct. It has to do with the theory of relativity, quantum physics and sub-atomic particles."

Raphael harrumphed to get everybody's attention, since the popes weren't listening anyway. Raphael drew himself up and assumed the mien of a guest lecturer. "After all," he said, "I was there some 13.82 billion years ago when God held a full-day seminar on this very topic for all of us angels, even the fallen ones. If I recall, the agenda for the day was 'Understanding the Inexplicable Universe' and 'Why Everything Was the Way it Was'."

Raphael faced Einstein and qualified, "Though God had a knack for making everything clear, much clearer than you, Albert!" He reminisced, "Ah, I remember it like it was only yesterday." Einstein felt somewhat slighted...but then God was God, and Einstein was only a mere genius.

The popes, meanwhile, raised their eyebrows. *What are these guys talking about? Was it just crazy talk or plain heresy?* Pope Leo and Julius came to an agreement, "Wait until we confront God about this matter, once we get passed the Pearly Gates, of course!"


\* \* \* \* \*


At the mention of the Pearly Gates, two more figures popped up out of nowhere. Salai and Melzi. Leonardo felt like he was at a family reunion.

"Boys!" he exclaimed, "I'm so glad to see you!" He went over and hugged both of them.

Sadly, he felt a certain tension between the two young men. Salai was his long-time lover, younger by 28 years, and Melzi was, best described as his adopted son, the son he never had, younger by 39 years. When Melzi came into the fold, Salai was obviously jealous.

Of course, it was a miracle that both young men were still that, young, exactly how Leonardo remembered them. Salai died in 1524 at the age of 44, unfortunately from a cross-bow duel, and Franscesco Melzi died in 1570 at the age of 79, some 21 years after Leonardo's death. But years and dates did not matter here in front of the Pearly Gates, because it was devoid of time and space. Einstein, himself, used to say, "What is time anyway, but a number that doesn't count." Jack Benny, the deadpan comedian, was 39 years old until he finally died at the age of 80, the day after Christmas in 1974.

Saint Peter internally quipped, So what is time? It doesn't matter...oh well, never mind! However, he figured his comedic timing still needed work, so he kept quiet.

Anyway, there they all stood at this point in time and place with however they looked whenever they were young or younger. Well, maybe that rule did not quite apply to Einstein. It seemed like he was always old. Photographs of him always showed him with a mustache and crazy hair. The hair defined the man, like he had just put his finger in an electric socket and instantly discovered electricity.

"Boys!" Leonardo addressed Salai and Melzi again, "I'm so glad to see you!"

Leonardo was not surprised to see his former secretary and scribe, Francesco Melzi there, in front of the Pearly Gates. Leonardo had taken the young boy under his wing when he was a mere youth of 14. It was never clear if there was anything sexual between the two. However, there was trust and affection there. Melzi had a steady temperament and became a good artist, as was expected if you were a protégé of the great master.

Salai, on the other hand, was another story. Leonardo took him into his household when Leonardo was 38 and the boy was only 10. Salai became a life-long servant and again an artist, though of mediocre quality. Things might not have become sexual between the two until Salai himself turned 15. Salai was described as a pretty boy with curly hair and "a devilish little smile." His nick-name, in fact, means "Little Devil" or "Little Unclean One." Leonardo had written about the boy as a thief, liar, obstinate and greedy, and yet kept him on in his employ for some 20 years.

On this point alone Leonardo might have been accused of pedophelia. Who knows? The mores of the Italian High Renaissance was more open about sexual misdemeanors than most people know about or would tolerate today. Leonardo raised many young protégés. Was this a good thing? Or was he linking his homosexuality to humanitarian acts of kindness in that class-conscious society of the High Renaissance? God only knows.

When he was 24, Leonardo was arrested along with three other young men and charged with sodomy. It came from an anonymous allegation and involved a 17 year old boy named Jacopo Saltarelli. No witnesses appeared and the charges were dropped. The case was probably dismissed since one of the young men was married into the rich Medici family. It is also interesting to note that the young men received a strong warning, "with the condition that no further accusations are made."

A modern student of history can appreciate how acceptive Florentine society was in the matters of sex. The Germans, for example, being less tolerant, used the slang word "Florenzer" as an insulting term for homosexual.

Machiavelli, who wrote The Prince about political opportunism had a son, Ludovico, who had a boyfriend. Machiavelli asked his friend, Florence's ambassador to the Papal Court, at the time, what to do about his wayfaring son. The ambassador's reply unveils a lot about the broad attitude about sexuality in those days:

> "Since we are verging on old age,
> we might be severe and overly
> scrupulous, and we do not
> remember what we did as
> adolescents. So Ludovico has a
> boy with him, with whom he
> amuses himself, jests, takes
> walks, growls in his ear, goes to
> bed together. What then? Even
> in these things perhaps there is
> nothing bad."

According to his contemporaries, Leonardo was pleasing in conversation and showed generosity in his blessings. Leonardo's biographer, Vasari, wrote, "He was so generous that he sheltered and fed all his friends, rich or poor."

So in terms of sin and pedophelia, only God knows. There are not enough written accounts to convince the church that Leonardo was destined for Hell. To later historians and theologians, Leonardo made a better candidate for Heaven than a lot of popes.

When Leonardo died in 1519 on French soil, he bequeathed half of his Milanese vineyard to Salai and the other half to Melzi. Leonardo was 67 years old, and as legend would have it, he died in the arms of Francis I, King of France. When Salai himself finally died, 5 years later in a crossbow duel, somehow the Mona Lisa turned up in the inventory of the man's estate, a sign that Salai's sticky fingers had never really reformed.

That's why Leonardo was somewhat taken aback when Salai popped in at the Pearly Gates.

"I thought you'd gone to the other place?" asked Leonardo.

"Well," said Salai, "you can never tell who ends up in Heaven. What are these popes doing here?"

The popes snubbed the remark, ignoring the implication.

"Oh," said Saint Peter, "don't any of you take anything for granted. Things could still swing one way or the other as long as we are standing outside the Pearly Gates."

Leonardo thought, *As long as the Pearly Gates are the dividing line, maybe I can go back to earth for a second chance, maybe I could still come back with an earthly breath, take back my vitality and finish that horse, "Il Cavallo."*

He looked beseechingly at Saint Peter and the archangel. But they both knew what he was thinking and they both shook their heads, to indicate a clear, No!

"It doesn't work that way," said Saint Peter finally. "You had your 67 years, and you used them up. Unlike the centenarian you dissected, that was all the time in the world that God gave you."

"It was worth a shot," commented Leonardo. "At least I learned one thing through my 67 years, and you can quote me on this, "As a well-spent day brings a happy sleep, so a well-employed life brings a happy death." Actually Leonardo had written that down some 30 years earlier when he was only 37 years old.

"Unoriginal," said Saint Peter, "but well worth remembering."

"I think I used my time well," concluded Leonardo, looking at Michelangelo, Salai, Melzi, Einstein and the two popes. The two popes were disinterested, and were instead eyeing the light beyond the Pearly Gates with envy.

*****

"Well," said Saint Peter, "Now comes the moment of truth. Who makes it beyond the Pearly Gates and who doesn't."

Saint Peter touched a red button on the wall beside the Pearly Gates, and all of a sudden, a black hole opened up creating a whirling chasm exactly where the two popes stood.

"No, no!" yelled Julius. "I'm too important to be sucked into nothing." Likewise Leo hollered, "I was the head of the Church, the first in line for Heaven. We're both too important to be sucked away like this!" But despite these papal objections, they both slipped into the event horizon of the black hole, and were stretched out and vanished into the Abyss never to be heard from again.

"As the first among the lineage of popes," commented Saint Peter, "I've always wanted to say this to a few of my colleagues, 'you are excommunicated from Heaven forever'!" So for Julius and Leo there was no bang, not even a whimper when they were sucked out of sight.

Salai ever inquisitive about wrong things stepped too close to the spinning vortex. He was starting to be sucked in.

"I don't want to go there," he yelled. "I'm sorry for all I've ever done...well most of it anyway."

Leonardo had no thought for himself. He stepped forward to grab hold of Salai's pink tunic. "I need help," yelled Leonardo to the others. Michelangelo and Melzi stepped forward to give a helping hand. Einstein set himself in motion. He pitched in and grabbed part of Salai's tunic and yanked. They all pulled together, and with a mighty heave-ho, they got Salai free from the sucking power of the black hole.

"Hey," griped Salai, "you ripped my tunic." Then he smiled and nodded to each and everyone of his friends. "Thank you," he said.

Leonardo pointed to Salai's ripped tunic. "You'll have to get that fixed. I like your choice of colour, though. Gives you a certain 'je ne sais quoi'."

He then turned his attention to the black hole. Ever the scientist, his curiosity was piqued by such a phenomenon, but he did not venture closer to its spinning power. The vortex was turning counter-clockwise. *Now why was that?* he asked himself. *Why not the other way around?*

Before he took his next breath, the hole snapped shut with the popes somewhere inside forever. Salai could have been there too, so easily a victim to the unknown forces of the universe.

Out of the way of danger, Leonardo asked himself again: *Why did this black-hole spin counter-clockwise? Maybe for a counter-productive life?* That was as good a theory as any. He was so glad that the vortex had not claimed Salai. But on the other hand, he thought, *Good riddance to bad popes.*

Saint Peter said, "Alright people, the show's over. Let's get down to business, the business of Eternity." He expressed gratitude to Leonardo, Michelangelo, Melzi and Einstein for saving Salai from a fate worse than death. "You were Good Samaritans saving Salai from the brink of damnation. Greater love hath no man...well, you know the rest of the story."

Saint Peter instructed the archangel, "Give Michelangelo a helping hand, will you? He's still a work in progress. And by the way, take Salai under your wings too."

Raphael smiled and nodded. He felt like hanging out a shingle, *The Psychiatrist Is In - 5 cents.*

All of a sudden the Pearly Gates shimmered and melted away into another dimension, and Leonardo, Michelangelo, Salai, Melzi, and Einstein took on new bodies of light. Leonardo thought he not only heard but saw music, the Music of the Spheres. Einstein imagined himself playing a pretty tune on his old violin. They all made it to the other side of eternity into the light, except for the two pontiffs who were lost in the Abyss, who presumed all along that they were the ones who deserved Heaven more than anybody else.

*****

# Coffee-break wth Harry Rittenhouse

*Last scene of all,*
*That ends this strange eventful history,*
*Is second childishness and mere oblivion,*
*Sans teeth, sans eyes, sans taste, sans everything.*
*(As You Like It - first publ. 1623)*

The beginning of December is a drab month for seniors because there's not much to look out at from their windows at the United Mennonite Seniors' Home in Vineland. It looks cold out there. I made a bee-line this morning to Tim Horton's and bought a chunky chocolate chip cookie and regular medium coffee for Harry Rittenhouse. I ordered a French Vanilla and a cheese croissant for myself. Harry was in his usual pose, snoozing in his easy chair, head down on his chest. The minute I woke him, his eyes focused and his mouth gaped open with mock surprise. Judy had given me a gift card so I could get her dad something from Timmy's, while she and Wally (Marjorie's dad) were off on a cruise in the southern Caribbean. My chore was to visit Harry a couple of times a week to see how he was doing, so Judy wouldn't have to worry. Harry is 102.

Harry worked for many years at Vineland Growers in Jordan. In old pictures, he sported a good set of biceps and had the physique of somebody who was used to working physically. Big wrists, strong hands. He loved hunting and fishing.

It was only last year that he had to give up his walker. He has to be pushed to the dining room now in a wheelchair. He wears Depends and has "to be toileted" by the nurses. The past year has been more than embarrassing for Harry; it's been extremely traumatic because he can't walk anymore and his memory is shot. Harry has a witty and dry sense of humour which still pops out now and again despite his short-term memory loss. He's quite philosophical about things: "There's nothin' much you can do about it!" It usually takes Harry half the visit to remember my name, but at last, he does. We go through a ritual.

"Hi Harry. You keepin' out of trouble?"

"Not if I can help it."

I hand him his coffee and cookie. "Who's payin' for it?"

"Judy. She told me to take care of you while she was gone."

A young nurse comes in with a hot chocolate. She sees the coffee and decides to leave the hot chocolate for later.

"They take good care of me here," says Harry, "If it was any better, it'd be a nuisance."

He laughs at his own joke. He remembers now that Wally and Judy went to the Caribbean for two weeks. "I don't like travelling myself," he says.

"Can't be bothered with it."

He's been all over Ontario, hunting and fishing, and that's enough for him.

"Up northwest, around Essex County, and way above Muskoka."

He used to take his dog Bing with him on these excursions. "The best dog I ever had."

He looks at two photos of himself on the window sill. One at the age of 33 with Bing. Harry's sleeves are rolled up showing the nice biceps he had as a young man. Then there's the photo of himself with glasses when he hit his 100th birthday. I tell him, that he doesn't look a year older than 99. He chuckles.

Whenever Harry starts feeling down because he can't remember things, I change the subject and that usually works. He takes his situation in stride. "What day is it?"

"Tuesday," I say.

"Well, it don't matter anyhow," he says. "It's all the same to me."

"I'm anchored here," he grumbles. "Life sometimes hands you stuff you don't got no choice in."

But the old spark still occasionally surfaces and Harry has a certain twist of phrase or a pithy comment that's just a treasure. I remember asking him one time:

"How're you feelin' Harry?"

To which he replied without blinking an eyelash: "Ain't got no toe-tag on me yet!"

He considers himself lucky because the nurses there are pretty good. "I don't need much," he says.

I point to him, "You got warm booties on, you're wearin' a sweater and got a cookie in your hand. What more can you ask for?" He finds that funny.

I bid my goodbye and tell him that I'll drop in again on Thursday. I enjoy my visits with Harry, despite his occasional drifting off into a regret about his memory. The easy going man that he once was always come out in some way or other and he throws out little phrases that are pure, pure gems.

I remember when the Rittenhouses, Harry and Gert, sold their old house on Victoria Avenue some years ago and auctioned everything off because it was time to make the move into the seniors' home.

They had a little apartment unit together there at the United Mennonite Home and seemed to enjoy it. Then Gert had a bad fall giving her serious head trauma. She started showing signs of dementia after that and started mixing things up. She had to be moved to one of the rooms on the opposite wing of the home without Harry.

Gert had mood swings. Harry made it a point to visit her every day and he'd shuffle down the corridor each morning with his walker to her room. It's strange how you get separated by old age and health. You're a married couple living together for so many years and then you end up in separate rooms in the seniors' home like you're strangers. Gert, died several years ago. I think she was 95.

"The best wife in the whole wide world," says Harry.

I wouldn't mind aging, if it wasn't for the pain.

I used this line with Harry once: "You know, things would be a whole lot better if we didn't have these problems." That elicited a chuckle from him.

"You got that right!"

Before I turned to go, Harry started nibbling on his Timmy's cookie. It crunched.

"You still got your own teeth, Harry? I asked him.

"Yeah," he said, "but this thing is as hard as pineboard!" To make his point, he rapped the cookie on his tray with a solid thud.

"Yep," he said with conviction, "as hard as pineboard!" And he nibbled some more on his cookie. He burped, and said, "That tasted good twice. The first time and the last time." I chuckled and closed the door.

I left Harry's room and walked down the hallway into the sitting area on the second floor to catch the elevator there. The 42" TV screen was on but nobody was watching it. A lady sat asleep in her wheelchair with her head drooping on her chest and her mouth wide open.

I got a birthday card recently [for not being near Harry's age]. "You know you're getting older when 'Everything hurts and what doesn't hurt, doesn't work'."

What can I say about getting old? W.C. Field's little quip on his gravestone reads: "On the whole, I'd rather be in Philadelphia."

*****

# *Mom Passed Away*

**Monday, January 16, 2012 @ 10:00 a.m.**
**By Her Son, John Hartig**

**words 977**

Another chapter of my life is closed. My mother is dead. Mom died just shortly before 1:00 p.m. at the *Trinity Home* in Kitchener, just two days ago. I've been meaning to write something because that's how I usually "let things out." These are my Monday morning ramblings, my Monday morning blues...in words.

My brother, George, phoned on Saturday at 1 p.m. to tell me the news that "Mom passed away." She was 92. I had no tears, maybe that would come later at the Funeral Home on Tuesday evening or at the church on Wednesday morning. I just felt a gentle sadness.

At about 6 p.m. on Saturday, I thought, it's been 4 hours now. Mom was still alive today. I didn't want to roll back time; I wouldn't want to freeze time at a quarter to 1 to prolong the tiny life she still had at that point. Mom was skin and bone. She had not spoken for over a year. She refused to eat anything in the last month. I wouldn't want her to continue in such a state just to have her keep breathing. I don't think she'd want that for herself; I know I wouldn't.

I remembered mom, 3 years ago, at my sister Renate's 60th birthday party celebrated at the Concordia Club in Kitchener. She was up and dancing with Nick.and of all things, she was whistling to the music as they danced. Mom loved whistling. She still recognized us then. Well, that all disappeared a year ago. My brother, George, said she drifted in and out of awareness and often didn't recognize him, even though he and his wife, Shelley, visited regularly every week.

I was so glad that I drove to Kitchener a couple of days before mom passed away, on Wednesday. I stayed all morning and most of the afternoon. The weather was unseasonably warm, at about 5 degrees, no snow! Can you believe it? January 11! Everything was green. Lovely drive to Kitchener. The noise of the trucks on the highway was still buzzing through my head when I walked to my sister's room at the Trinity Home. My sister is in the same Home as my mom because she's handicapped with Multiple Sclerosis. The law of the universe did not hand her a blessing. We're all dealt something, I guess, at different times.

In a way, it was a blessing that I made it to Kitchener on Wednesday and not Friday. On Friday, it snowed, dangerous road conditions. Also the doctor had given mom a needle to sedate her, so she would not feel any pain through her last hours.

I didn't feel guilty that I brought my Star Trek novel, The Better Man, and read while I sat with mom on Wednesday morning. I broke off the reading to look out the window from mom's third floor room at the shriveled plants in the garden below. The sun would occasionally peep through the clouds. I spoke to mom intermittently: "The sun is shining outside the window, mom. I'm glad I visited you today. It's Wednesday morning. Everything still looks green. I'm glad you're my mother. I just had a lovely visit with Renate downstairs. Nick is here. George is going to visit on Saturday or Sunday with Shelley." Of course, all that was said in simple German.

Mom was born in Banat, now a part of Serbia. She was a Danube Schwabian [née Ginter], of Germanic descent, outside of Germany. She spoke 5 languages, which probably got her out of tight spots during World War II. She was separated from her Yugoslavian husband during the war and everyone thought he was dead. Mom fled to Austria as a refugee where she met my own father, Michael Hartig, who in turn was a Saxon fleeing Romania and the Communists. I was born in Austria. My half sister, Nellie [née Isailowitsch], from mom's first husband had the dark and beautiful features of the Slavic race. I loved my big sister dearly.

I kept reading my Star Trek novel and occasionally told mom about the weather or about the old family photos hung on the walls around her little room. The nurse brought in a glass of cranberry juice. I've always found the staff at the Trinity Home very caring and thoughtful. It can't be an easy job. The nurse let me put the straw in mom's mouth. Mom took forever to suck the juice up. It moved up the straw, then fell down again, up the straw and down. Finally, there was enough suction to get the juice into her mouth. Success in little things! By the time she was through, the glass was mostly empty and the nurse was pleased. They record these things.

I had a bowl of soup downstairs in the tiny cafeteria, which was also the entrance to the home and the foyer. I sat down by the pastor. I visited Reni once more and told her I'd go up to mom's room and probably stay until about 2:30 p.m. so I could get on the highway before the huge onslaught of traffic would hit the roads.

Mom opened her eyes twice during this visit. Once in the morning when I talked "at her" and once in the afternoon. Her left eye was clear and it glowed with recognition. Her right eye was blind due to macular degeneration. She said no word but I know she recognized me during those two times when she opened her eyes.

Well, it's a chapter closed now in our family history. How glad I was that I had visited mom last Wednesday and that I told her I was glad she was my mother.

*"Ich bin froh dass du meine Mutter bist."*

\*\*\*\*\*

# The Passing of Wilma de Jager

**Wednesday, Feb. 19, 2014**

They were neighbours for some 10 years, Jan and Wilma, a Dutch couple in their late 70s living in the house right across the street from us in Vineland. I'd heard that Wilma was in the Shaver Hospital, going downhill fast. I'd only found that out yesterday evening at the Loaf of Bread supper, so today would be my "mitzvah", my good deed, as my Jewish neighbours down the street would say.

I used to cat-sit for Wilma and Jan whenever they took a notion to hop in their car and drive to Tennessee or Florida. Jan had the wanderlust and he loved to drive somewhere, anywhere every year. They would also book a yearly flight to visit relatives in Holland. Jan sported a personal license plate, Huzum, the name of his home town in the old country. Their accents were Dutch, as thick as molasses, despite all these years in Canada. Every year, Jan showed me where the cat food was inside the foyer, so his chunky pet would not starve. [Man, that cat was fat!] It meowed incessantly whenever it heard me open the door and rattle with the scoop inside her food bag. The cat reminded me of Wilma, solid and chunky and rolly-polly. Jan was a stick of a man with a concave stomach. I joked about him being underfed. He laughed, padding his thin tummy, "Not enough doughnuts, eh!" He and Wilma liked going to McDonalds because the seniors got a discount there on muffins and coffee. Jan claimed, McDonalds coffee tasted better than Tim Horton's. Whenever they came back from holidays, they took me to McDonalds as a treat, for watching their house and their cat.

Last autumn, they put a for sale sign up in front of their house. It was gone in no time. Before they moved, Wilma was diagnosed with a brain tumour. Everything seemed to come at once. The house was sold; Wilma had brain surgery. The relatives helped them move. A young couple replaced them. I hardly see the new young couple who pretty much keep to themselves. Jan and Wilma left no forwarding address. I often wondered how they were doing. Then the news came sort of off-the-cuff from another Dutch couple at the Loaf of Bread supper, "You knew Jan and Wilma? Did you know that...?" So, I earmarked Wednesday for my dropping in at the Shaver Hospital, thinking I'd squeeze a brief visit in before the puck was dropped at noon in the Olympics in the game between Canada and Latvia.

Wednesday morning was such a sunny day, a clear blue sky day, a good day for a quick hospital visit. I put a Toonie in the parking meter for a one hour stay. I shouldn't be more than that. The receptionist pointed to the elevator and said, "Second floor, room 219." The door was ajar. Crowded room. Sons and daughters were gathered around her bed. I spotted Jan's gray hair. He was bent low, sitting next to the bed, holding her hand. Wilma's breath was heavy; she was rattling. Two of the sons spotted me just outside the door. I motioned for them to come out. They were teary-eyed. "I would be interrupting, wouldn't I?" I asked. "Yes," they said. "Later, tell Jan that John Hartig, his neighbour was here." "Yes, we remember you." "Thanks," I said and left. What a time to visit! I didn't know it was that bad. I headed to the car in the sunshine. I had 45 minutes left on the ticket and gave it to the guy who had just parked next to me. He'd been fumbling for change and placed his Bible on the hood of his car. He thanked me and put the ticket inside his dashboard. A young fellow. I wondered with whom he intended to pray. Maybe it was Wilma; maybe it was her pastor? I didn't pursue a conversation. What was my intention that morning? To ask Wilma if I could make a McDonald's muffin and coffee run? Chit-chat about the weather; about the hockey game?

I drove back down the hill at Brock University and noticed the cluster of students hovering around the bus stop heading up to classes. They all had their futures ahead of them, whatever that would be. I got home just in time for lunch and the start of the first period in the hockey game between Canada and Latvia. Canada won the game 2-1, not an easy win in the third period. Later that afternoon, it rained. And later that evening, after supper, Jan and Wilma's son phoned:

"Wilma passed away this afternoon. We thought we'd phone you because you made the effort to come out."

"I'm sorry," I said.

"It was quick," he said. "Funeral arrangements have not been made yet." He'd let me know. We said goodbye.

I thought I'd sit down and write something about this sunny and yet so rainy day. There must have been a rainbow somewhere.

*****

# Winning the Lottery

**Short Story**
**by John Hartig**
words 4,939

Chapter 1
*Sgt. Benton Wright Heads East*

One day, at the beginning of April, Sgt. Benton Wright got a registered letter in the mail from a law firm in Hamilton, Ontario. The letter named him as beneficiary of Aunt Sophie's estate, an aunt he rarely met but who left him $10,000,000. He had to look twice at the amount because it was in the millions, not in the thousands! Even in Canadian funds, that was a lot of money. What could he do with it? He had no use for such a huge inheritance. He had a job as an RCMP Sergeant, running a little outpost in Crooked Harbour, Newfoundland. He was young and he was happy with just the way things were.

He heard that Aunt Sophie was an avid purchaser of lottery tickets and last year she had actually won a huge fortune. He also heard that people who reaped a sudden windfall like that often lost it quickly because of unwise spending and greedy friends and relatives who seemed to come out of the woodwork.

He didn't let anyone know about the letter but he took a leave of absence from the police department for several weeks 'for personal reasons'. He left Const. Boo in charge since Boo outranked Const. Laroche simply by years and not by brains. He was sure they'd get along while he was gone. He had to straighten out this lucrative mess in Ontario. Doggone OLG [the Ontario Lottery and Gaming Commission]!

He booked a flight with the pontoon plane out of Crooked Harbour on a Friday evening in April, and then he transferred to a WestJet flight which zipped him from Deer Lake to Toronto. He rented a car in Toronto because wheels were obviously needed to get to the lawyers' offices, which were listed under the triple name of, 'Dirkson, Dirkson and Dudley'.

He also might want to see the sights a bit. Maybe take in *Phantom of the Opera* at *The Princess of Wales Theatre* in Toronto. Usually Sgt. Wright wasn't one to take in any kind of musicals but he liked the story line and he thought the experience would be a treat. Besides, Const. Laroche might be impressed with his new taste for something which was culturally refined.

*Dirkson, Dirkson and Dudley* were happy to get his business and to arrange all the necessary paperwork for the transfer of funds. Sgt. Wright had decided on the plane about what he would do with all that money. He would keep $1,000,000 for himself, for a rainy day. Then $4,000,000 would go to the Sick Kids fund in Hamilton and another $4,000,000 to the Mennonite Central Committee to help out with the Syrian refugees. He earmarked the remainder for lawyers' fees and maybe a pay-off to Aunt Sophie's other nephew, Maurice Barrow, who was currently living in Hamilton and was unemployed. Maybe the money would help him get on his feet.

He hadn't heard how Aunt Sophie died. She was only 69. Apparently, an intruder had entered her apartment looking for cash, maybe influenced by her television interview over winning the lottery. The money didn't do her any good; she was killed by a blow over the head. Her apartment was ransacked but no cash was found, except maybe coffee money in her purse.

Aunt Sophie had made sure she saw *Dirkson, Dirkson and Dudley* right after her winning and also made out a will. The only nice relative she could think of was her nephew out East whom she had met a couple of times. He seemed like such a decent kid and told her all about his ambition to become an RCMP officer. "Why?" asked Aunt Sophie. Young Benton answered, "Because you get to ride a horse." Aunt Sophie was expecting him to say, "Because you get to wear a gun." She liked him for his answer.

Since Sgt. Benton Wright had another three plus weeks to spend in Hamilton, he figured he'd do something else than just go see *The Phantom of the Opera*. He had a murder case to solve here. He needed to interview people, take notes and put this jigsaw puzzle together, not because he was a cop but because Aunt Sophie demanded justice. Of course, it helped that he was a cop. Being an RCMP officer, he had jurisdiction all across Canada to investigate and bring a murderer to justice.

*** 

He was glad that the musical in Toronto was on the very next day. That schedule meant he still got the bragging rights to a cultural experience, and then once that was out of the way, he could concentrate on finding his aunt's killer. When he sat back in his seat at *The Princess of Wales Theatre*, he drew in the rich lyrics written by Andrew Lloyd Webber. He thought the words were poignant and applied to his aunt on some level:

Think of me, think of me fondly
When we've said goodbye
Remember me, once in a while
Please, promise me you'll try

He had to get justice for his Aunt Sophie. She had been nice to him when he was a kid. He was determined to look for motive, means and opportunity. Who would do such a thing? Why? How? When? Show proof!

He understood that big city cops sometimes just wanted to clear cases. It was a matter of cutbacks and overload. Toronto and even Hamilton's murder rates seemed to be skyrocketing from year to year. All that was foreign to someone from Crooked Harbour, a relatively innocent town which was still waiting for its first murder to happen.

*Give me a little town and country roads any day*, thought Sgt. Benton Wright. But for now, like a hound on the scent, he started sniffing around for clues. He checked in with the local authorities and got permission to look around Aunt Sophie's apartment. Once inside, he put on rubber gloves and scanned the premises carefully. A soapstone figurine, an eskimo carving of a walrus, rested on a cabinet in the living room. Drawers still littered the floor where the murderer had feverishly looked for cash from the big lotto winnings. Aunt Sophie knew better than to take out big sums of cash, so she had sought out legal advice about her lottery money right away. The culprit had even checked under Aunt

Sophie's mattress and left it tumbled on the floor. Nothing of value apparently had been discovered. The murderer smashed the mirror on the dresser and then left in disgust. He was a man with lots of anger seething inside of him.

# Chapter 2

## *Setting the Trap*

Sgt. Benton Wright remembered Shakespeare from his high school days, now that he had given expression to a cultural side of himself in the big city. He knew he could be sophisticated when he needed to be. But he usually hid that aspect of himself; otherwise people might think he was a snob. Like the country and western singer who was asked if he could read notes, his answer was, "not enough to hurt my music any." Sgt. Wright's cleverness came out on its own, expressing itself naturally and not learned, as a supersleuth when he was on a case.

He recalled the *Hamlet* play wherein Polonius is determined 'by indirections to find directions out'. He liked that line, so he had to be smart, even devious, about talking to people who might resent or want Aunt Sophie dead. He thought about the 'mouse trap' scene in *Hamlet*, and hopefully taking hints from it, he might catch the guilty rat within it. So, the sergeant started compiling a list of people who were the most likely suspects and those who were the most unlikely ones in committing the murder.

There was his other Aunt Mary. There was Maurice, his cousin. There was Larry, the neighbour and Aunt Sophie's coffee buddy, Audrey. He needed to go through the process of elimination. The lawyers, *Dirkson, Dirkson and Dudley,* were obviously struck off the list, since they had probated the will and were happy with their fee. Aunt Mary was off the list too, since she was suffering from Alzheimer's disease and restricted to a seniors' home at the age of 82, way past her prime for scheming and dreaming about riches which she could never use. Aunt Sophie's coffee buddy, Audrey, seemed like a harmless old biddy, as long as her fixed income gave her enough petty cash to go to *Tim Horton's* twice a week. When Audrey heard about Aunt Sophie's demise, she lamented, "Now who do I go for coffee with?" She had suffered a stroke recently and her left arm was out of commission, too useless to deliver a decisive blow to Aunt Sophie's head. That left Larry, the neighbour, and Maurice, Sgt. Wright's cousin.

***

Sgt. Wright knocked on Larry's door.

Larry de Groote had no locks and opened his door wide. There stood a man who looked like the spitting image of Walter Matthau in pajamas. He was 6'2" tall and had no self-consciousness about his dishabille. His face looked wrinkled and friendly, kind of like a big teddy bear, with drooping jowls and eyes which seemed amused. "You must be the nephew!" He said.

"Why yes, from out East."

"I heard you were asking about your aunt's death."

"Yes, how did you know?"

"I have the same lawyers your aunt had. In fact, when she won the money, I recommended them to her."

"Why would an impoverished guy like you need a law firm?"

"Don't let looks deceive you. When I die, I'll leave a couple of million to the Salvation Army. Sadly the need for their Out of the Cold program is not going away any time soon."

"Can I offer you a cup of instant coffee and cookies?" asked Larry.

It was midmorning anyway, so Benton Wright accepted. They talked leisurely about his Aunt Sophie. "Nice lady," said Larry. "A pleasant person, though she did have an obsession about buying lotto tickets. She always said she was going to win the big one."

"She died from a blow to the head, some burglar or other?" asked Sgt. Wright.

"That's right, from what the police said."

"You weren't home?"

"Nope. Grocery shopping. Saturday afternoon is usually when I head out. Then I have a coffee at Timmy's with the boys. Sometimes your Aunt Sophie would join us. It was just last Saturday, she didn't show up."

"Any ideas?" asked the sergeant.

"Yes. Maybe that other nephew of hers, Maurice."

"Why's that?"

"They had an argument about the money after she'd won. He figured he wasn't getting his fair share. I could hear them arguing through the wall."

"It wasn't his money," observed Sgt. Wright.

"Yes, but he had none. What he had, he wasted in nightclubs and bars. He had no job and he figured being a blood relative, he deserved something more from her."

"Have the police looked into that?"

"I'm sure they have or will. Some of the cops in Hamilton may not be too bright but eventually they get around to it. They're just a tad slow because they're overworked."

"Maybe I'll hurry them along or at least help out a bit."

When Larry and the sergeant finished their little chat, the sergeant was sure he could check Larry off the list too. He exited the teddy bear's door, leaving the old timer behind smiling and waving goodbye in his pajamas. If instinct was right, the fellow was harmless. Thank goodness, the sergeant didn't have to deal with a grumpy old man!

\*\*\*

The next stop was back at the law firm of *Dirkson, Dirkson and Dudley*. Sgt. Wright had a private talk with the head of the firm, Mr. Dirkson. He figured it must have been Dirkson Senior, the first Dirkson on the list, since he was elderly and wore red suspenders. Nice touch for a lawyer. Benton could see him stretching those suspenders in deep thought, coming up with his next point in court.

"Yes," admitted the elder Dirkson, "our other client, Mr. Larry de Groote recommended your Aunt Sophie to our firm. We handle a substantial estate from him too, although we can't disclose the amount due to privacy issues."

That said, Sgt. Wright was assured that Larry had no real motive for doing away with his aunt. He had money of his own. That left only one other real suspect, Maurice Barrow, his cousin. Sgt. Wright had phoned the young man a bunch of times but got no answer.

"If you ask me," said Mr. Dirkson pulling on his suspenders, "I'd say the wind is blowing in your cousin's direction. He barged into our office accusing us of fixing your aunt's will. He left in a huff and said he'd get lawyers of his own."

\*\*\*

Sgt. Wright decided to go to the man's apartment, and in some unobtrusive way, stake out the place. He nursed his coffee in the hallway and stared out the back window at the empty alley. The building was run-down and housed a lower class of people, certainly lower than where Larry or his aunt lived.

Soon a young man, about 25 years old, came up the stairs or rather dragged himself up the stairs. He looked a bit wobbly. He was tall and wiry, almost as tall as Sgt. Wright himself at 6' 4". But he looked half the weight, skinny as a rail, with a face that was indeed lean and hungry looking, shifty and narrow like a weasel.

"Hello cousin Maurice," said Benton.

"What the f***! What do you want?" responded Maurice.

"Haven't seen you in a long time. I need to find out a few things about Aunt Sophie."

"Why? Don't you read the newspaper?"

"Sure! But I want to find out who killed her."

At that remark, Maurice's eyes widened and he seemed to sober up.

To allay suspicion, he seemed to suddenly soften his tone, saying, "Alright, come on in."

Maurice unlocked the door. There was a keychain on the inside, actually two, because the apartment building was probably prone to burglaries. Whom could you trust if it wasn't the neighbours? But judging from the building, maybe the neighbours were not trustworthy either.

Benton Wright scanned the room. Dirty dishes in the sink, a neon print with a black background of a matador facing an angry bull hanging over a ratty couch, some Lego trucks and plastic airplanes on top of the stereo set. The one and only cabinet in the room had a soapstone carving of a polar bear resting on it. Aunt Sophie had a match of that kind of artwork in her room but of a walrus.

"Present from Aunt Sophie?" asked Benton.

"Why as a matter of fact, yes," replied Maurice. "She gave me that when she returned from her cruise in Alaska a couple of years back. You're not her only nephew, you know!"

Maurice excused himself; he needed to go to the washroom desperately after having drunk beer at the Western bar and grille, all afternoon. While he was gone, Benton inspected the statue of the polar bear. There was a brown stain on its head. Benton pulled out a plastic bag from his pocket and scraped a bit of the stain into it with his Swiss Army knife. A small knife and a plastic bag were always handy if you're in the middle of sleuthing for clues about your aunt's demise. The sticker under the soapstone read, 'Property of Sophie Barrow'. Now why would Aunt Sophie not have removed the sticker if she freely gave Maurice the statue as a gift?

Maurice came out of the washroom. "I've got a migraine," he said. "I'll have to usher you out the door. Have a nice trip back East." Benton didn't feel the comment was very friendly as he headed out the door. He heard two chains lock behind him, and then some hard-rock music turned on loudly from the stereo set inside. Did he really have a migraine? He wondered how many complaints Maurice got from the neighbours about loud music. Some headache!

# Chapter 3

### *Springing the Trap*

Some police departments are touchy about the police from other jurisdictions butting in on their territory. The lead detective, David Weisman, wasn't sensitive about that at all. He had a soft spot for the RCMP because his dad had been one before he transferred to a detective's job in the big city. Detective Weisman was proud of the family tradition of generation upon generation choosing policing as a career.

He welcomed the young RCMP officer into his office. Only a week had gone by since the young man had arrived in Hamilton introducing himself as the law enforcement from Crooked Harbour, Newfoundland. "Crooked Harbour?" asked Det. Weisman. "Sounds like a big megalopolis."

"Oh, it keeps us busy with settling down rowdy teenagers and arresting the usual town drunk," said Sgt. Wright. Det. Weisman couldn't help but feel both amused and respectful. After Sgt. Wright cleared the air about why he was in Hamilton, the detective said he'd be more than willing to cooperate.

"We'll do anything we can to bring your aunt's killer to justice," he added.

Sgt. Wright explained that he needed a favour. "I have a scraping here from a certain statue which is in the possession of a suspect on my list," noted Sgt. Wright. "I want to see if the scraping matches Aunt Sophie's DNA."

"Where did you get the sample from?" asked the detective.

"The head of a polar bear statue which my suspect, in fact, my cousin Maurice Barrow, said was a present from our aunt. I suspect he's lying."

"Maurice Barrow? He's one of our suspects too. With two other murder cases under investigation, we just haven't had the manpower to interview Mr. Barrow yet."

"I can appreciate that," said Sgt. Wright, "Hamilton isn't like my mini-megalopolis at Crooked Harbour." The older detective chuckled over that remark.

Det. Weisman said, "The best we can do is get your results from the lab within the next day or two. Once we have that, we'll be in touch."

"It would be great if we caught Aunt Sophie's killer by the end of the week before I leave for home."

"Well, if that motto is correct about the RCMP, you should get your man by then."

They both chuckled. Det. Weisman offered Sgt. Wright a doughnut out of the box on his desk. The sergeant smiled and took one. "Thank you kindly," he said. The two talked hockey for a bit and the chances of the Maple Leafs rebuilding their club into a winning team. 1968 seemed so far away. It was about time again for Toronto to take the cup.

Det. Weisman commented, "Maybe after a few more trades? I think Mike Babcock is doing a fine job on the coaching end!" Sgt. Wright commented wryly, "We should ask Don Cherry for his view. He should have the answer! He seems to know everything anyway. We should ask him."

"Yeah, that's why he gets the big bucks and the chance to wear those flashy jackets on TV," said the detective. Sgt. Wright swallowed the last bite of his doughnut and headed for the door, nodding to the older man as a thanks.

\*\*\*

The next day, Sgt. Wright got a phone call from Det. Weisman. The scraping in the plastic bag did indeed match Aunt Sophie's blood type and DNA.

"We need to put a solid case together now," said the detective. "We've got a witness who overheard your aunt and Maurice arguing over the inheritance. We've got Maurice barging into the law office making accusations. What we need now is a search warrant for the man's apartment to get hold of that statue. We also need you to set up another meeting with your cousin. Call it a sting."

The detective explained, "You could go in wired. See if you can rile him up, and who knows, he might just say something which would incriminate him."

Sgt. Wright agreed. Det. Weisman would get a search warrant that very afternoon. As the sergeant headed for the door, the Det. Weisman said, "I love it when a plan comes together."

"Now, where have I heard that line before?" asked the sergeant.

"From an old TV series, *The A-Team* actually," said the older detective. "You had to live in that era to appreciate the saying."

While Det. Weisman got busy arranging for the search warrant, Sgt. Benton Wright got some legal papers together at the law office of *Dirkson, Dirkson and Dudley*. In fact, he was going to have similar papers drawn up anyway, before Cousin Maurice was ever suspected of anything. Benton intended to bequeath half a million dollars to his cousin, hopefully to get him back on his feet. Now, with a case building up against Maurice, those very papers were going to be used as bait to trap the killer.

*＊*

Sgt. Benton Wright waited in the hallway like last time. And like last time, Maurice staggered up the stairs.

"You again!" Said Maurice in an unwelcoming tone. "What the f***! What do you want?"

Benton had a momentary déjà vu. But he wanted a different outcome from this meeting with his cousin. A confession would be nice.

"I was thinking of sharing some of my good fortune with you, cousin," said Benton, "but I need a few papers signed."

"Well, come in," said Maurice like he had flipped some personality switch. "So, your guilty conscience got the better of you? How much money do I get? Where do I sign?"

"Half a million," said Benton as he walked through the door. They headed straight for the kitchen table. No offer of coffee or cookies.

"Half a million doesn't seem like much when you're the one who's getting nine and a half mil," countered Maurice.

"Well," said Benton, "you sign this and you've got half a million with no strings attached."

"We should've split the inheritance 50-50," asserted Maurice. "You're not the only nephew, you know."

"Well," said Benton, "you weren't her favourite, and that makes a difference."

"What the f***! She hardly ever saw you. You were never around."

"Maybe that's why Aunt Sophie got a chance to get to know what you were really like."

"What? Because I was around and always bugged her for a handout?"

"You had great marks in computers. You could have done something with your life, instead of pissing your money away in the pubs."

"You're such a goody, goody!"

"You had a choice. We all do."

Benton walked towards the cabinet upon which the statue of the polar bear stood. It looked so out of place in this apartment amidst all the clutter and the Lego trucks and toy airplanes resting on top of the stereo set. Benton took hold of the statue.

"Put that down," commanded Maurice.

"Why?" asked Benton. "Was this what you used to hit Aunt Sophie with?"

"Damn you. I should never have let you in."

"Well, was it?"

"Yes," admitted Maurice in a fury, "but you'll never prove anything."

"I don't need to," countered Benton, "the court will decide that. You'd better have a good lawyer."

"At least, I'll have the money for a good one," said Maurice. He still stood at the table with pen in hand and the legal papers in front of him, and in his mind, he had already signed the papers and collected half a million dollars. Benton took the papers and ripped them up.

"Even signed, these papers are useless," said Benton.

In his anger, Maurice grabbed the statue of the polar bear and poised it ready to strike Benton. Detective Weisman burst through the door at that very instant, gun in hand and two police officers came barging in behind him. The detective's voice was deadly calm, "Maurice put that down."

Detective Weisman handed Maurice the search warrant and then handcuffed him, hands behind his back. The police officers bagged the statue for evidence. Det. Weisman read Maurice his rights. At the end of the necessary spiel, he said to Benton, "All's well that ends well."

"I'm grateful for the rescue, even though I think I could have handled a skinny runt like my cousin, myself."

As Maurice walked out the door in handcuffs, the skinny runt turned toward Benton and sneered, "Aunt Sophie always liked you best." The line sounded faintly familiar, maybe used in an old comedy skit on TV from years ago. Benton shot back a ready reply to his misguided cousin, "Maybe the reason for being our aunt's favourite was that I made the right choices in life. You didn't."

# Chapter 4

### *No Place Like Home*

*Yes, all's well that ends well*, thought Benton Wright. He was grateful, but not for going back to Newfoundland, rich, but rather for finding justice for his dead aunt. He had another meeting with Mr. Dirkson of *Dirkson, Dirkson and Dudley*. Benton wondered what Mr. Dudley did, or if he even existed? Why do so many law firms come up with three names?

The sergeant drove to Aunt Sophie's gravesite during the last week of April, before he caught the plane back for Deer Lake. He bowed over the large stone already erected there. Bought and paid for through the law firm with part of the lottery money. The inscription read: 'Again, I tell you, it is easier for a camel to go through the eye of a needle than for someone who is rich to enter the kingdom of God.' [Matt. 19:24] *You're right about that, Aunt Sophie*, thought Sgt. Wright. He peered into the white sky. It was raining lightly. Angels shedding tears? Before he turned to go, Sgt. Wright left a bouquet of flowers on the grave stone.

He used his cell phone to let the police department in Crooked Harbour know he was coming home early. Const. Laroche answered with a cheery, "Benton!" He asked how they'd gotten along without him. She answered teasingly, "Oh, quite well. We hardly missed you." He wondered if he wouldn't have preferred a little admission to some hardships there for the time he was gone. Then Const. Laroche made him feel much better by confessing,

"Boo and I did really miss you, Benton! We're glad you're coming back home."

***

Air Canada headed east. Homeward bound. Sgt. Benton Wright would be in Deer Lake within three hours. He had sprung for the more expensive non-stop flight. He ordered a Black Russian drink once he was seated and comfortably in flight. The drink was an occasional luxury he allowed himself. Ironically, he did not realize that the drink was a favourite of Principal Brazeau's back home. He paid the stewardess and gave her a nice tip. Finally, he was in a mood to open Aunt Sophie's letter to him. She had left it with the law firm, writing it shortly after winning the lottery. Benton read the first few lines and smiled.

Dear Benton,

You are my favourite nephew. I'm leaving all my worldly possessions to you. I have no children of my own. If I'd ever had a son, it would be one like you. If you remember, years ago, I asked you why you wanted to become an RCMP officer. I thought you'd say something like, I'd get to wear a gun. Instead, you said you'd get to ride a horse just like the RCMP. I've always liked that gentler side of you.

Your Cousin Maurice created quite a row after I won the lottery. He thought he could just demand 'his share' because I'm old, but I've consulted with a law firm about dispensing my money the way I want.

Money can bring out the worst in people. You get to see the true faces hiding behind the masks. The only ones I trust now are you and my neighbour, Larry. I've written Maurice out of my will, though I was willing to make him a millionaire. But he'd only drink the money away.

I have to caution you to be on the lookout for people who double deal, who undermine others and who cheat to get ahead. One of my favourite writers has been Dorothy Gilman. She gave this advice to a young man in one of her books, a young man much like you, which I want you to keep in the back of your mind as you deal with people in your profession as a policeman.

> "You can never tell about people. They wear masks, you know, they're like icebergs showing only what they please, and they die full of secrets. You'll be blessed, Andrew, if you come to know – really know – just a handful of people in a lifetime."
>
> [p.67, *Thale's Folly*, by Dorothy Gilman, Ballantine Publishing, 1999]

Keep on the right path, Benton, and hopefully someday, you will meet a nice girl and settle down for your old aunt, so you can pass on the better part of our family's genes. That's the real inheritance.

Your Aunt, Sophie.

Benton folded the letter reverently and put it into a pocket of his carry-on bag. He could feel that the closing of the letter might have read, 'Your 'favourite' Aunt Sophie'. Benton sipped some of his Black Russian. He felt relaxed. He hadn't been greedy about Aunt Sophie's money, so he wasn't going back to Newfoundland as filthy rich as he could have been. He was grateful that he had a good job and good friends to go back to.

*****

# *Jean-Marie Leclair*
## *1697-1764*

A Novella

## An 18th Century Murder Mystery
### The Unsolved Murder
### of a Violinist and Composer

## Copyright © Author: John Hartig
## First Edition 2019

Jean-Marie Leclair

# Synopsis

Jean-Marie Leclair was an 18<sup>th</sup> century violinist and composer who founded the French school of violin. He was stabbed to death either on October 22<sup>nd</sup> late at night, or October 23<sup>rd</sup> early morning, in 1764, when it was still dark. His body was found in the vestibule of his home which was located on the seedy side of Paris.

No one was ever accused or arrested in the case, despite strong suspicions. It could have been a nephew who was envious of Leclair's success with the violin, playing in King Louis XV's Orchestra. It could have been his ex-wife who made money out of publishing and printing his manuscripts.

This novella follows the clues in the list of suspects. It also follows the life of the man and describes the time in which he lived. It weaves a tale where nothing was proved and no arrests were ever made. An unsolved murder mystery of the 18<sup>th</sup> century!

Until now!

*****

# Chapter 1

## Coffeehouse Chatter
## October 24, 1764

The usual crowd was drifting in: Denis Diderot, the Montgolfiers, Voltaire, even Leclair's old violin rival, Jean-Pierre Guignon, who was now collecting a pension for his long years of service in the Royal Symphony and the Royal Chapel. The King himself was not there. Word got around that Louis XV would at least be represented by his aide at the funeral.

Within the week and following months, news and gossip would spread among all the coffeehouses throughout Europe that Jean-Marie Leclair, once chief violinist and composer in the King's court, was dead. It would be a hot topic for some time, not because a talented man was dead, but rather because of how he was dead. Assassinated, stabbed in the back three times.

The news was of course a perfect topic for coffeehouse discussion about how or why Jean-Marie Leclair was murdered. It was the sort of thing that titillated people. But the chatter would not last long in these gossip circles. After all, Leclair was only a minor luminary in the music world. His time had come and gone. He was already 67 when he was so callously murdered. Others, younger, were waiting in the wings. They had already been chomping at the bit to race out onto the musical stage. Leclair, in hindsight, had missed his chance.

During the height of his powers, he had been too proud to care about catering to Kings and Queens to ensure a name for himself in the annals of musical history. Then, as he aged, those younger, more spry and indeed, more talented, were shrewd enough to market their names and their fame through the cultivated patronage of Europe's Kings and Queens. The new luminaries in 1764 were Haydn at age 30, and an even younger, Amadeus Mozart, at the age of 8, beloved of God.

Voltaire clapped his hands to warm up as he came through the door of the historic Café de Procope, shivering out of the cold. Winter came early to Paris that year. It was bright and chilly that morning on October 24, 1764, giving thought to those who could afford it, to head south to their villas on the Côte d'Azur. Voltaire broke into a warm smile as he spotted his coffee companions. He held his chin imperiously high, hailing the waiter for his usual order of "le petit noir". He also asked for a slice of torte with his coffee.

He felt effusive, as if today were any different than any other day in which he felt effusive. "Did you hear about Leclair?" he asked.  "The man was murdered last night, stabbed to death. Whatever his ambitions in life, they now lie in the dust. He will no longer give us melodious Sonatas and Concerti with which to brighten our world. 'Dommage. Très dommage!'"

Voltaire sat down next to Diderot, laying out the details: "Stabbed in the back, not once but three times! What a coward the culprit was! He could at least have faced the man. The police are now seeking the felon who appears to have gotten clear away."

Diderot shook his head in sadness, "France has a lost a gem. I remember just last month discussing with him the value of my Encyclopedia, which is my ambition in life to collect all knowledge of all mankind in various volumes. I pray to Heaven to have enough time to finish this project. Jean-Marie Leclair asked me if there was a market for such a thing. But after a pause, he relented, saying he did see value in it, after all, for any man who wished to educate and improve himself. Leclair admitted to his own penchant for self-improvement, editing and then re-editing his musical scores until each note was weighed and placed so meticulously on his score that it became musical perfection. He confessed that he even burned some of his failed manuscripts because they were not good enough."

The Montgolfiers each sipped their strong coffee, and munched thoughtfully on a piece of cake. They weighed their words carefully among these august and learned companions because compared to them they were only boys. They lived off the proceeds of their lucrative paper manufacturing business. Joseph-Michel was only 24 years old, and his brother, Jacques-Etienne, a mere 19. They gave deference to these older companions, but occasionally, drew up enough courage to have their say. Joseph-Michel asked, whether Leclair had been a nice man, or if he had enemies, or if indeed, he could be considered a gem in the coffers of France's musical history?

Jean-Pierre Guignon, once the King's premier violinist, offered his opinion, "Yes, Leclair was indeed talented but he had an infuriating personality." Guignon recalled, "Back in 1734, the King gave him a gold-plated pocket watch, since Leclair had dedicated several compositions to him. Leclair had a habit of pulling out this watch at rehearsals and saying, 'I see, by the King's watch, that I have three more minutes to sit in my first violin chair before we commence rehearsal...or he would say, 'I see by the King's watch, that I have just enough time to get to my scheduled appointment with the King'."

Guignon continued his recollections of Leclair: "I admit he was an accomplished violinist, much like myself. We agreed that we would share the first violin position in the Royal Symphony, and alternate that honour every month. He went first, but when it was my turn the following month, guess what the scoundrel did? He quit the symphony just so he would not have to take directions from me because he considered himself superior."

That was almost 30 years ago, and the resentment still smoldered in Guignon's heart. Guignon looked his companions fully in the eyes and affirmed, "I swear by heaven, however, that I did not kill the man for an old resentment. I've had a steady job in the King's employ all these years and have earned the respect of my fellow Parisians, playing first violin in the Royal Symphony and then in the Royal Chapel. I have been content with my accomplishments, and now enjoy a good pension."

Guignon took a moment and finally commented that, with Leclair's instability and unreliability, history would soon forget the man. "Perhaps he will be remembered more for the way he died, than for the value of his works."

The Montgolfiers sipped some more coffee, took another bite out of their torte, and then, finally spoke to defend the dead man who could not be there himself. "You are speaking ill of the dead." said the younger brother. "Even if it were true, you should treat the man more kindly because he had the misfortune to die such a cruel death."

"Maybe France has indeed lost a gem," continued the older brother, "who is to say what Leclair might yet have added to our musical history?"

Voltaire cut in: "Maybe he would have added nothing, certainly judging from the way he was going." He chuckled cynically and added, "As usual, the Montgolfiers are full of hot air. Next you will make Leclair out to be a benign saint or a national hero. A gem indeed! You two need to stick to your ballooning. Perhaps you can see to it that mankind will indeed fly before the end of the century."

The older Montgolfier, Joseph-Michel, reposted: "That indeed is a challenge within our grasp, and we will make it so, mark my words. Do you not agree, little brother?" Jacques-Etienne nodded his head. The older Montgolfier continued, "I see us flying above Paris skies before the century is done...and that, dear Voltaire, is not hot air!" Voltaire's eyebrows lifted, admiring Joseph-Michel's spunk. He simply uttered, "I can hardly wait." The Montgolfiers were indeed successful in a piloted flight over Paris in 1783. That was 19 years after Voltaire's brazen challenge and Leclair's death.

The group enjoyed the exchange immensely and ordered another cup of "le petit noir".

After a pause, Guignon asked, "So, who is going to the funeral tomorrow?"

He let the group know that the ceremony itself was to be at The Church of Saint-Laurent on the Ile-de-France. "Burial will be right afterwards. I intend to make an appearance at least for the eulogy inside the church. But I don't want to stand out in the cold for the burial." Everyone agreed: "The ceremony it is then," Voltaire agreed, suggesting that everyone meet back at Procope's Café afterwards in order to warm up with a lovely slice of cake and coffee. "You know," he said in reflection, "If France were ever to go to war again, it would have to be with coffee and cake served at the front."

*****

# Chapter 2
## Ile-de-France, Church of Saint-Laurent
## October 25, 1764

The church was huge, ornamented with spires and great columns. Large stained glass windows let in colourful light. The massive structure, like all the beautiful cathedrals in Paris was paid for by weekly donations from the coins of the poor, as well as the more lucrative gifts from the nobility of Paris. The incentive to pay for those great churches which reached the skies was incited by the fiery tongues of priests who said that the passageway to heaven was secured by how much you gave to the church.

On the morning of October 25, 1764, the attendance inside the church was sparse. One might say that this was a sign of the very few friends, if indeed any friends, that Leclair had. The coffeehouse group was there, the family, and the ex-family. Yes, there were indeed a few friends there, as well as Leclair's former landlord, Monsieur Legras. The King's coach pulled up to the front entrance, the coat of arms, boldly displayed on the doors of the coach. Louis XV's aide stepped out, meeting the priest at the door with his regrets from the King who was elsewhere attending to important matters of State.

Despite the cold, a cold which bit the skin, some comfort came from the fact that the sun shone brightly down upon this sad occasion. The King's aide slipped an envelope [full of money] into the priest's hand. Whispering, "With the King's condolences and gratitude". Inside the church, the sun also had an amazing effect through the stained glass windows so that people's faces were bathed in a myriad of soft colours. Radiance and iridescence shone above the head of Jesus. While the attendees stared at the stained glass windows and at the streaks of light coming in, they concentrated on the demise of the deceased in quiet whispers.

Voltaire couldn't resist. He leaned over to Guignon in the pew and remarked. "We've got to stop meeting like this." Only a month previously, Rameau had passed away in early September, just 13 days shy of his 81st birthday. That timing surely eclipsed the news of Leclair's untimely death. Voltaire added as an after-thought, "Leclair's murderer could have at least had the courtesy to kill the man later, so as to give Leclair a chance to enjoy fully the sole announcement of his untimely death."

Guignon remarked, "I was at Rameau's funeral only last month at St. Eustache. He was a strange one, an old man truly cantankerous. Irascible, critical and generally hard to get along with. Maybe all geniuses are that way?"

"Not me!" countered Voltaire with a self-indulgent smile.

"Well, he was irksome anyway, and a miser too. They found a bag full of 'Louis d'or' gold coins in his room. Maybe he thought he could take it with him! Bribe Saint Peter at the Pearly Gates, you know, like the Catholic Church seems to practice with their indulgences." Both men chuckled. Voltaire said, "All this heavenly bribery does not concern me. I don't believe in the same God as the Catholic Church." Guignon was pleased, "Ah, a Deist after my own heart, but I admit, there is something to be said for ritual and religious ceremony in society?"

The priest was not amused with all this chattering in the pews, which to his ears sounded like the buzzing of bees. He harrumphed and asked for respectful silence. "Let us have kindly reflection and forgiving thoughts about the departed soul," he announced, and he bowed his head. No one spoke. The crowd seemed to sink into a pensive mood more appropriate to this occasion of a great composer's passing.

Jean-Marie Leclair, at one time, had been one of the most famous violinists and composers in all of France. No one knew who had killed him. What coward had stabbed him in the back three times? What were the police doing to catch the culprit? Jean-Marie Leclair was only 67 years old. Who knows what other great works he could have written for posterity?

The priest highlighted Jean-Marie Leclair's accomplishments. He called him the "French Corelli" and the "French Bach". The priest pointed out the wide range of Leclair's talents, starting out as a dancer; and later pursuing a career as a virtuoso violinist, and finally, making a name for himself as a composer. Leclair wrote numerous Violin Sonatas for one and two violins, Trios, Violin Concertos, and one opera, Scylla et Glaucus, a tragedy in five acts.

The priest's eulogy briefly touched on all these points, as if these praises were prayers raised to God to allow Leclair straightaway into Heaven, for the excellence of his soul. The Eulogy was closed with an appropriate mention of the King, "The King sends his condolences and his apology that he could not be here, attending to other matters of State."

Shortly, some men in the church got up and headed toward the coffin, grasping its handles and then ceremoniously marching their burden outside into the churchyard where the hole had been prepared, open and gaping, waiting to take in Jean-Marie's earthly remains. The ceremony was short and sweet, thankfully short, because it was so cold outside. The priest blessed the casket, sprinkled holy water on it, and then the coffin was lowered into the ground. Nobody threw flowers in, or any scoopfuls of dirt.

At least the great musician left evidence of his work outside the grave to show the world that he had actually lived and created something. Jean-Marie Leclair left behind printed copies of many Sonatas and Concerti behind, which were reprinted in many libraries around the world. But how many times were they played and praised? That question was held at the mercy of an uncertain posterity and the hazards and the trends and tastes of time.

Meanwhile, the former landlord, Legras, schemed about how he could get his title back to the little house on the Rue Careme-

Prenant, so that he could resell it. He had done well the first time with Leclair, selling at twice the profit, since Leclair was desperate to get clear of his wife. Ah, a wife, the jewel in your crown, or the stone! Monsieur Legras wondered whom he could line up next to flip his hovel to in that disreputable part of "le Marais". The ex-wife wondered if there were any other extant manuscripts left in the house, which she could get her hands on, so her engraving company could print them.

Clear sunlight shone on the very tiny group huddled around the plot of dirt outside the old church. The coffeehouse companions had already filtered away. Sunlight almost seemed to bless the remaining few who stood in silence around the grave. The priest nodded to those few who remained, that they were dismissed.

That left only the grave diggers with the priest, waiting for his other nod to proceed with the drudgery of shoveling dirt into the grave. The priest left. The gravediggers were alone with their work, eager to get it done and get out of the cold. Bruno hesitated, "Now that the priest is gone, what about digging the grave up again and checking Leclair out for valuables. Maybe a ring or a watch? Maybe his violin is in there?" Jacques was none too keen. "Earlier today," I visited my old friend the coroner. Leclair lay naked as a jaybird on the table. I rifled through all his clothes. No rings, no watches, nothing! I heard that the violin was smashed at the neck by the killer, so there is nothing to take away, if we dig up the grave again."

Bruno looked disconsolate. Jacques said, "There's nothing for it old buddy, but get the work done here before we get drowned in the grave with the downpour that I see coming from the east."

They kept up a routine shoveling of dirt into the grave, periodically tamping the dirt down with their big boots, and then adding another layer of dirt with the objective to bring the grave to ground level before the big downpour. When they were at the top, they patted down the loose earth above Jean-Marie Leclair with the flat of their shovels, so that he would be secure until the second coming of Christ. "Don't worry about tromping the dirt down too hard and loudly," said one grave digger to the other, "he can't hear us anyway. He's deaf."

All in all, it had been a lovely October day, though nippy. A hint of clouds was blowing in from the East which threatened to make the air even colder and more biting. The Procope coffee klatch were more than relieved to get back into the warmth of the Café and  back to the comfort of  a nice slice of torte and a hot cup of "le petit noir".

"We have good topics to discuss," commented Voltaire. "Death and dying, God and eternity, and oh yes, our very troubled Catholic Church," he said.

*****

# Chapter 3

**The Crime Scene**
**October 23, 1764**

Jacques Paysant, the gardener, was walking to the house in the early morning of October 23rd to pull some dying shrubbery on that fateful day of Jean-Marie's death. The first bite of an early winter was in the air. As the worker came up the walk, he saw something suspicious in the vestibule of the little house. The front door was open and a man's boots were sticking out. The gardener cautiously got closer and realized the full importance of what he was seeing, his employer lying face down within the vestibule. The man's white wig lay disheveled and somewhat dislodged off the man's head. Paysant realized that his employer was stone-cold dead. Strangely enough, his first thought was, not about the horror of the scene, but about how to clean up the man's wig? There was blood on it. "Now it's ruined!"

Over the past six years, Paysant had held this part-time job here at Leclair's little house on the Rue Careme-Prenant. He was used to seeing Leclair take little walks, adorned with a white wig, a fashion of distinction for the gentry of the time. Paysant had seen many men with wigs come and go to and from the little house over the years, because after all, his employer was still a respected musician in Paris. But the gardener kept his opinion about wigs to himself, and gave deference to these lofty visitors whenever they graced the doorway of Leclair's little home. Paysant privately sneered at them behind their backs because they assumed a haughty air as if style truly made the man.

Powdered wigs became fashionable when Louis XIII first wore one back in 1624 to hide his baldness. Before long, the perruque was all the rage among the upper and middle class men in Europe, as a fashion statement, and not just to hide a receding or graying hairline. Men of quality in 18th century Europe lined up like peacocks to distinguish themselves as a superior class from the working poor, like the gardener. Styles and length of wigs even mirrored the level of society among nobles and people of culture.

Paysant pictured how absolutely ridiculous this trend was. He would never wear a wig to work, where his curly hairdo would get caught in the vines and shrubbery of his daily chores in the garden. He often chuckled at the outrageous thought of himself in a wig. His employer, of course, wore a perruque because of his higher station in life, and his distinction as a composer and a virtuoso violinist. Well, thought the gardener, "I suppose the man has earned the right to wear a wig. He is educated and has talent. And he is respected and recognized in society. I'll grant him that."

But if it came to hard labour with his fingers, Leclair would always say, "Let the gardener do it." The gardener harbored a private attitude of reverse superiority though, sneering down at his betters behind their backs. Openly, Paysant dared not show his disrespect. After all, this was 18th century France, and one must not mock one's betters.

Paysant snapped his attention away from the bloody wig. He took another cautious step towards the opened door. A few miscellaneous objects lay strewn about around Leclair's body, within the vestibule, a book of some sort and a musical script not far from his hand. Paysant saw the nasty stab wounds in and around the man's neck, three of them, glistening dark and wet. He asked two questions: Who did this? And Why? He shook his head in disbelief, backtracked and called for help. His work for the day was done.

Instead of his neck, some sources have said Leclair's stab wounds were in the back. The point was that Leclair murdered and dead!

Three police officers were assigned to the case: the Lieutenant of Police, Antoine-Gabriel de Sartine, and two lower level policemen, Monsieur Gentilhomme and Monsieur Lebrusque.

They concluded that the assault happened either during the night of October 22nd or sometime in the early morning of October 23rd when it was still dark. "Maybe we'll never find the killer," said one of the officers.

Unfortunately, the murder weapon was missing. That might have been a key piece of evidence for tracking down the owner. But then, The Lieutenant of Police, Antoine-Gabriel de Sartine, knew that things were never simple in solving murder cases. "How inconsiderate," he thought, "of the killer not to leave us the murder weapon."

Budgets had always been a problem for the police in Paris, probably everywhere in Franc. Money! Money was also used to bribe police officers because the Parisian system was corrupt. De Sartine at least was a man of integrity, and the men under him respected him and loved working for him. Unfortunately the members of the "Garde" were mostly soldiers from the provinces, and had little loyalty to Paris itself, but they did have loyalty to someone like de Sartine. Strict and fair.

Once you got to be a sergeant of the "Guet Royal", you got to wear the blue "justaucorps" which was a tight-fitting jacket with silver lace, a white feather in the hat, and red stockings, while the ordinary soldiers wore gray with brass buttons, red on their sleeve, and a jaunty feather in the hat and a bandolier, as part of the uniform.

Both Gentilhomme and Lebrusque were sergeants, wearing police blue. They took some pride in that. By 1750, there were 19 posts of the Guet in Paris, each post manned by 12 guards. Their uniforms gave them clearances to scenes of a crime, and people got out of their way. Police responsibilities up to this point included monitoring bread prices, keeping traffic moving in the crowded streets, settling disputes, maintaining public order, chasing robbers and muggers...and of course, arresting murderers.

When the three officers went to the house, they had no trouble gaining access. The vestibule door was already open, and the interior door had been smashed. The former landlord met them there "in case they needed to be shown around". He had heard from somebody who had heard from somebody what had happened here, probably the gardener's grapevine. The landlord, or former landlord, was not just snoopy. He hovered around the premises with the hopes of getting his house back so he could resell it. Leclair and he had an agreement that Monsieur Legras had access to the house in case anything ever needed fixing. Leclair disdained physical labour and preferred paying somebody a couple of "livres" to use hammer and nail. When he first moved in, the roof leaked, and later shelves were required to be built in his study to store his precious manuscripts.

"Lieutenant," asked Gentilhomme, "do you think the landlord could have done it?"
The Lieutenant of Police answered, "Even though the man is greedy, he looks too dumb to do this kind of thing."

So the three officers looked around, checking out the walkway and the vestibule still blocked by the body. They skirted around Monsieur Leclair and entered the house. Lieutenant de Sartine noticed the bowl with coins in it, in plain view on top of an escritoire, or small desk, by the inside doorway. "Interesting," he thought.

He walked to the bedroom and ventured to peek under the bed. He saw the chamber pot under there. It smelled. "Gentilhomme," he called, "why don't you take this thing outside. I saw a shovel in the backyard. Why don't you bury the contents at the back in a corner somewhere? Leave the chamber pot outside for M. Legras, to dispose of." Gentilhomme wrinkled his nose at the chore, obediently stooping down to retrieve the chamber pot, which was unfortunately full. "Are you sure this isn't evidence?" commented Gentilhomme holding his nose. This only gained him a frown from his superior.

After some searching, the Lieutenant steepled his hands and puckered his lips in deep thought, "It appears that theft was not the motive here. We also found a bag of money under the mattress, and when we scrutinized the shelves in the study, all the man's manuscripts seemed to be intact. The violin broken at the neck and the bow snapped in half, both lying on top of the harpsichord, indicate obvious rage. The harpsichord itself is untouched. Other things indoors do not seem to be disturbed."

The Lieutenant commented, "Leclair lived simply but was not poor. His dwelling place seemed to be a deliberate lifestyle." He asked himself why this was so. "For the life of me, I cannot understand why a man of modest means would prefer to live this way, here in this hovel, in the northern part of 'Le Marais', in a part of Paris that everyone knows is dangerous."

Lebrusque, the next officer in line [with some brains to his credit] offered an opinion. "Well, maybe the man was a recluse or a bit of a rebel, living a bohemian lifestyle, determined to live without ostentation, but rather to live frugally like a monk." The Lieutenant nodded. "Strangely enough, that makes sense," he said. "Lebrusque, when you're right, you're right."

Gentilhomme remained silent, open eyed like an owl. He was merely the "yes man" in the group, a nice fellow enough, but one who did as he was told. "Someday, he will go far in the bureaucracy," thought the Lieutenant.

They had gone through everything in the house, and came up with nothing. No real evidence, nothing that the murderer left behind. "It appears this was a pure crime of passion," said the Lieutenant, "Perhaps revenge or envy. The violin broken at the neck and the shattered violin bow speak volumes."

The Lieutenant had two other officers stand by with a coach from the coroner. They lifted the body into the coach and drove off, after de Sartine had one more quick inspection of the walkway, the wounds and the vestibule with the book and manuscript which were dropped in it. He wished that someday whatever the killer touched in the house could be somehow linked to the killer himself. "But someday is not now," said de Sartine dismissively to himself.

\*\*\*\*\*

# Chapter 4

Antoine-Gabriel de Sartine and the two sergeants went back to the police headquarters to discuss the facts. At that time, the police headquarters was called the Maréchaussée, not the Gendarmerie, which came later during Napoleon's time. De Sartine invited the two sergeants into his office. He sat behind his desk with steepled hands in serious concentration. The two sergeants sat on chairs facing their boss. De Sartine took a deep breath before he outlined the facts of the case as he saw them, and the plan of attack. He lit his pipe. He asked Sergeant Gentilhomme to take notes and make a list.

"Here are our suspects so far. We must start with the people who are readily available to us, and then there are those who, of course, are unknown, like a prowler or a hidden mistress." De Sartine drew on his long years of experience in the city's police force.

- first, there is the gardener, Jacques Paysant, who discovered the body
- it could be that one of Leclair's brothers, did the deed. They also were musicians,
- Leclair's own 40 year old nephew, Guillaume-François Vial, son of Leclair's sister, Françoise, was a very likely suspect. He aspired to becoming a great violinist like his uncle who refused to promote the young man's career, and this sparked jealousy
- the ex-wife, Louise Roussel, made a good candidate. She owned the engraving business which made money out of printing Leclair's musical scores. Apparently the business had come on hard times lately since Leclair and she divorced.

- then there is the possibility of a "rôdeur", a prowler who did Leclair in, though with the viciousness of the stabbing, a personal vendetta was more likely
- lastly, it could have been an angry mistress or a prostitute though this is doubtful because of the brute force of the stabbing. If it were a female, she could have hired a man to do the dirty work, which of course, would make the investigation more complicated?

"We have our work cut out for us," commented de Sartine. "We may never know who our killer is. We don't have the murder weapon. We do have perhaps two clues left at the house." De Sartine hesitated and puffed on his pipe, blowing out smoke that drifted leisurely to the ceiling like his thoughts. He asked, "Are you taking notes, Gentilhomme?" The sergeant fidgeted with his notepad, "Yes, Lieutenant, I have jotted down points as we go, for you to review later."

"So," continued the Lieutenant, "Whoever it was who broke through the inside door to gain access went in to look for something, but what? Theft seems unlikely since there were coins left so obviously in a bowl on the small desk, and of course, under the mattress. What is interesting, however, is that Leclair's violin lay broken at the neck on top of the harpsichord, as was the bow snapped in half. The harpsichord itself seemed untouched."

The Lieutenant continued to puff on his pipe, "It was rage that did this, rage aimed at Leclair and his most prized possession, the violin. Our killer did away with both, the violin and Leclair himself. Who would be so angry with the man? We saw that the man's books and manuscripts were still neatly stacked on the shelves in his study. Even the book and the manuscript he dropped when he was killed were left at the scene, though somewhat stained with blood."

"Are you taking notes, Gentilhomme?" asked the Lieutenant of Police. "Yes, yes, Lieutenant de Sartine. Every word." Although he did not mean every word, except point form and only the barest minimum. It didn't matter anyway because the record of Leclair's broken violin and his shattered bow never made it past the French Revolution. Gentilhomme's meticulous note taking went up in smoke as the citizens of Paris stormed government buildings, emptying desks, drawers and burning any papers they could find in 1789.

De Sartine expelled another puff of smoke. With finality, he said, " So, let's see what we can do about finding our killer! Lebrusque, have you brought in the gardener for our first interview?"

"Yes, Lieutenant de Sartine, the man is waiting ready for questioning."

"Let's get to it!" said the Lieutenant dismissively.
Jacques Paysant, the gardener, was escorted into a little room at the Maréchaussée. He was a big oaf of a man, a beefy peasant with a little head and small piggy eyes. He looked and acted dim. He entered the interview room hat in hand trembling. Officer Lebrusque equaled Paysant in stature, and stood within the small interview room, intimidating the gardener with his own big size. Lieutenant de Sartine directed the proceedings quietly. Gentilhomme was asked and said yes to note-taking.

"Why would I kill my employer?" objected Paysant. "He was my source of income and he always paid me on time. I would not kill my own living." The Lieutenant saw the logic in this and with confidence made the interview short. "We are merely doing our jobs," said the Lieutenant, "I'm sorry this happened to your employer. It appears you have lost not only your employer but also some of your income. Your protestation is duly noted, however. Make a note of that Officer Gentilhomme."

"Yes sir," said the officer, as he scribbled away. "By the way, are you left-handed or right-handed?" asked de Sartine. "Right-handed," responded Paysant.

The Lieutenant cautioned Paysant, "We will let you go for now, but please, stay in Paris where we can reach you if we need to get more details." Paysant bowed his head in acknowledgement and was glad to get out of there with hat in hand. He was already known to the police at the headquarters after being brought in for several brawls at the La Dame Chantante, his favourite tavern. After he left the Maréchaussée, a sudden thirst hit him. He needed a drink.

"We have him on record," said de Sartine. "He has a habit of dropping in to our building on a regular basis for matters of minor misdemeanors, basically drunkenness and brawls. Well, what do you think Sgt. Gentilhomme?"

"Yes sir," agreed the Sgt. most readily. "He likes his drink alright and his fights, and once he has a glass or two of wine, if he is our man, then he might just want to brag about it to his companions. We will keep an eye on him. I already sent the word out to our informants at La Dame Chantante and other taverns around the city, just in case he has a loose tongue."

"The only thing I see that the gardener has going for him," said the Lieutenant, "is that he is the one who brought the crime to our attention. I don't think the man is clever enough to stab his employer in the back and then cover the crime up by calling the police. That just brings attention to himself. He is also right-handed, and the attack was apparently carried out by a left-handed man."

De Sartine pointed out that the burly gardener easily had the physical power to dispatch of his employer, with three vicious strokes to the upper back and neck. "The first blow," said the Lieutenant, "was delivered from behind, smashing the upper clavicle in two, close to the neck. This incapacitated Leclair, and already put an end to the man's violin playing career. The second blow came in at the side of the neck, severing the man's aorta. There must have been arterial spray everywhere, as is evidenced by the drenched book and manuscript of music which Leclair had in his hands. Then the third blow almost severed the man's spinal chord just below the neck. I don't think Leclair died instantly but it must have been a horrific realization for him to be dying."

The Lieutenant told his officers that Leclair was probably turned over immediately after the assassination. "It could have been that the killer shared a few words with Leclair face to face before the man died, and after that, the assassin turned Leclair back over again onto his stomach, and dragged him into the vestibule to hide the body. The criminal was even fastidious enough to grab the book and manuscript from the walkway and throw those into the vestibule, as well. "

"And how do you know all that," asked Sgt. Gentilhomme, not wanting to be left in the dark.   "Because there was a big pool of blood on the walkway and a smear that ran into the vestibule. The way I see it, the victim fell face down on the walkway, and then was turned over on his back bleeding profusely from his wounds in the upper back and neck." "Brilliant deduction," said Sgt. Gentilhomme. He was forever willing to ingratiate himself with his superior, whereas Sgt. Lebrusque shrugged his shoulders, not bothering to think in "deductions".

The Lieutenant continued, "There must have been immense strength in these blows, perhaps fueled by sheer anger. The gardener certainly had the strength, but a woman generally would not be capable of digging a knife so deeply into a man's neck. And then to drag the body into the vestibule to hide it until morning! If it was the ex-wife or a mistress, then she must have hired some man, which would make our case more complicated."

At the end of these speculations, the Lieutenant said, "I think our gardener, however, must remain on the list, just in case, and must remain available for further questioning." He added, "After all, the gardener has been imprisoned twice before. He is a recidivist. I am not happy with his testimony about when exactly he discovered the body, and where he was the night before."

154

"Uh, Lieutenant de Sartine, what's a recidivist?" asked Gentilhomme.

"Why, a convicted criminal who keeps doing  the same old crimes," said the Lieutenant.

"Then, I guess I'm a recidivist," confessed Gentilhomme. "I come home every night and head straight-away to the tavern for a game of billiards with my buddies and a cup of wine."

"What does your wife say to that?" asked the Lieutenant.

"She said, I'll never reform." They all laughed. At least, Gentilhomme wasn't a convicted criminal; just a policeman needing an outlet after a hard day's work. He liked his vices, and for all three officers, those were acceptable faults, not crimes. Their vices made their jobs as police officers bearable and sane; otherwise there would have been no release from stress, and who knows, without that, they might have become criminals.

De Sartine sadly reflected on Leclair's demise, "Right from the first blow, Leclair's violin career was over. The man would never recover full mobility. What a tragedy for all those years of practice. A unique talent utterly destroyed." Gentilhomme scribbled more notes into his book as his superior ranged freely over his thoughts, openly and out loud, so that a written record of every detail could be kept on file. Gentilhomme had such neat handwriting, and he was meticulous in his note-taking.

Lebrusque was eager to get on with the investigation. "Sir, the Leclair siblings are next on our list. Three of them are also accomplished musicians. I have procured the use of several rooms for these interviews to keep these men separate."

"Then let us proceed," said the Lieutenant. He gestured towards Gentilhomme with a sign to bring his scribbling pad along.

Lebrusque pointed out to his superior that there were actually two Jean-Marie Leclairs, the older brother, called "l'aîné", because he was older, and Jean-Marie Leclair, the younger, called "le frère cadet". The older Leclair was 67 at his death, and the younger brother was 61 years old at that time. Despite their age difference, the brothers had been getting along quite well together, always had been since childhood.

Jean-Marie Leclair, the younger, was born in 1703, 6 years younger than his older namesake. After his brother was murdered, he outlived his older namesake by 13 years, reaching the venerable age of 80 at the time of his own death in 1777, which, was still not bad when the average life expectancy for a man in the 18th century was 41 years of age. Perhaps "le frère cadet" was a likely suspect because he seemed more competitive than the other brothers, and in fact, did achieve some minor success in a musical career, publishing a few meager pieces for two violins and one vocal piece of no account.

"Why should I be jealous?" challenged Leclair, the younger. "I loved my brother.
He was the other half of my soul. We played duets together when we were children." Jean-Marie Leclair, the younger, looked uncannily like a copy of his dead brother, similar build, and similar face. "I always admired my older brother," he swore, "and in fact, that goes for all my other brothers too."

The other two brothers pretty well said the same thing about each other. Pierre Leclair was 55. Benoit Leclair was 50. They loved the older Leclair and aspired to be better musicians because of him. "He was our inspiration; he gave us a goal," said Pierre. "He was my big brother; we looked up to him," said Benoit. When the interviews were over, the Lieutenant looked at each of his officers and shrugged his shoulders. "Who could argue with such a role model?" he said. Both Lebrusque and Gentilhomme agreed because they each had their own brothers, with whom they admittedly fought, but whom they dearly loved anyway. Whenever one of them got into a scrap around the neighbourhood, the other ones would bail them out. That was blood relations and what it meant to have family loyalty.

"We've interviewed the gardener and the brothers, so far," said de Sartine, "I will dismiss the gardener for now, for being too stupid, unless he spills something in the tavern other than his wine. Besides he is right-handed. Likewise I will dismiss the three brothers for loving the deceased brother too much. Blood among brothers is thicker than water, and we will respect that, for the moment. They are also all right-handed."

Gentilhomme flipped his notebook. "Next on the list we have Guillaume-Francois Vial. He is Leclair's 40 year-old nephew, reportedly jealous of his virtuoso uncle and resentful that his uncle did not promote the nephew's career." "Ah," said de Sartine. "Nepotism, or rather the lack of it. No support for a slack nephew who never was a favourite of Leclair's anyway. Pure and simple. We have motive here, and possibly an opportunity if Vial was in the city for those two days during which the crime was committed."

When the nephew was called in the next day for the interview, all three officers were amazed at Vial's size, a huge man with enough apparent strength to plunge a knife deeply into any man's neck. The nephew's face looked young and innocent despite his 40 years. But he stood large and tall, 6' 4", with a broad back. The Lieutenant was impressed, thinking to himself, "I suppose not all violinists are the artsy and delicate type!" He also wondered how a violinist with a penchant for fine notes could find himself in such a massive body capable of extreme violence? The Lieutenant raised his eyebrows, and silently wondered, "And this is a violinist?" He judged that only the gardener and possibly Sgt. Lebrusque were equal to this man's huge stature and strength. How could such largeness be capable of touching the heartstrings of the soul with the mellifluous tones of a violin? Here stood one large contradiction. A giant who had a sweet gift, and as the police shortly found out, a foul mouth. Vial also insulted the nose, since he smelled badly.

He could have left his body odor outside the door of the small interrogation room. All three officers smelled it. "Worse even than our Superintendent!" thought de Sartine. Body odor was a commonplace occurrence during Leclair's lifetime, and was generally accepted within reason.

Everybody covered up their smells with other smells in those days, using perfumes and powders. Full body bathing was not practiced because it was a luxury. Plumbing and servants carrying water buckets cost money. Also a belief was common that bathing in warm water was not healthy because it opened up the pores which let disease in. A moneyed household would install a scented fountain for their dinner parties, or supplied each room with a "smelling box" that contained a sponge soaked in vinegar-based fragrances which masked the unpleasant odors emanating from the city streets. Maybe the only good thing that came out of this era was that France soon dominated the international perfume industry.

After the initial shock of the man's size and smell, the officers soon faced another contradictory shock, the minute that Vial opened his mouth. There was no sweetness and light in his words, only a torrent of acerbic fluency of cursing, the mastery of which surprised even these seasoned officers of the police. Perhaps the production of sweet melodies and a gentle soul did not necessarily go together.

Vial let loose a string of invectives which expressed strong objections to being here at the Maréchaussée headquarters for questioning, questioning about something Vial absolutely and categorically denied. How dare they! Several other invectives pursued the first.

When the man finally settled down, Lieutenant de Sartine said, "Well sir, welcome to police headquarters. These are my fellow officers, Sergeant Gentilhomme and Sergeant Lebrusque. Have a seat."

# Chapter 5

**November 2, 1764**

The officers had a prearranged system. Good cop, bad cop. Gentilhomme was the good cop, looking innocent enough with his notepad. Lebrusque was the bad cop, using his big size and stern demeanor to intimidate. Lieutenant de Sartine was the referee.

"Reports tell us that you did not get along with your uncle. Why was that?" asked Lebrusque.

"It was obvious," said Vial with a sneer. "The old fellow did not give me a letter of introduction to the King's court, confirming that I was a gifted musician quite capable of playing both first and second violin in the Royal Symphony. I am a man of some considerable talent, you know!"

"The lack of a recommendation. Is that why you killed your uncle?" asked Lebrusque.

"Certainly not!" objected Vial, standing up as if slapped. A gentle hand from Officer Gentilhomme guided Vial back down into his seat. Lebrusque on the other hand preferred grabbing Vial and straightaway beating a confession out of the man. But as he had been often told before, by his stern minded superior, "We simply cannot do that. We need to be professional. This is 1764, after all!"

Vial looked convincing, "No, I swear that I did not lay a hand on my uncle. His endorsement could have meant the world to me. Why would I kill my ticket into the King's court?"

"Had you ever laid a hand on your uncle before?" pursued Lebrusque.

"Well, maybe there was that one time when I grabbed him by the lapel. He turned his back on me and said that my playing was at best mediocre. He called my talent minimal, and that I should practice for hours like he did when he was young."

"Perhaps, he was right. Practice makes perfect," commented Lebrusque. "But then what do I know about music, though I do know about hard work."

Lieutenant de Sartine cut in. "You are a healthy man, and I imagine, you like your drink and your women. Did you not frequent the taverns, especially La Dame Chantante?"

"Yes, I like a drink now and then," admitted Vial.

"And what about women? Instead of sawing away at your fiddle at home like a good boy to get your uncle's approval," asked Lebrusque.

"Now hear!"countered Vial. "Before you accuse me of the easy life, you need to look at my uncle's habits. He frequented prostitutes and had a mistress after the divorce from his wife. Maybe you need to look into that, and maybe that is the cause of his untimely death, not me!"

"Duly noted," said de Sartine nodding at Gentilhomme. "Make a note of that."  "Yes sir," said Gentilhomme.

"Where were you on the night of October 22nd and the early morning of October 23rd ?" asked Lebrusque.

"Why, probably at my usual haunt, La Dame Chantante, on the 22nd until the early morning, and then I rented a coach home because, as you know, the streets are unsavory during those hours in the early morning walking home alone. I slept it off until noon the next day, had a little lunch and then practiced my violin diligently until mid-afternoon."

"Sgt. Gentilhomme," commanded the Lieutenant, "Make a note so we can check his alibi out at a later date." Gentilhomme made a note.

The Lieutenant advised Vial not to leave Paris, in case there were further questions. "Do not fly south like the birds unless we issue a warrant for your arrest. By the way, are you right-handed or left-handed?"

Vial was confused, "why, I am ambidextrous. I am a very talented man, you know."

Lieutenant de Sartine lifted his eyebrows toward Gentilhomme to make a note of that. He said then to Vial dismissively, "You may go."

Vial rose with obvious disdain for the local constabulary. "Why don't you look at the ex-wife instead, or the mistress," he shot back in response.

When the unpleasant nephew was gone, all three officers wiped their brows in relief, and let out a sigh. "Well, good riddance to bad smells," said Lebrusque.

De Sartine complimented his team. "Good work," he said. "Perhaps, Guillaume-François would have trouble in the King's Symphony not only because of his personality but also because sitting beside him would be unbearably smelly."

Lebrusque commented, "He is some piece of work, and is so full of himself that he obviously over-estimates his own abilities."

"Aren't we all somewhat like that?" judged Gentilhomme. The other two officers smiled.

"Now let's line up the ex-wife for a little chat," said the Lieutenant. "However, if we are to do good police work, we need to do a background check on all our suspects. Why don't we grab some of our city records and bring them over to the Café de Procope, in more conducive surroundings, over a pleasant cup of coffee and a slice of cake. Wouldn't you agree our work would be more palatable there?" Needless to say, Gentilhomme and Lebrusque liked their boss. He had such good ideas.

Gentilhomme, as the "Yes Man", was the one who carried a box of files into the Café de Procope. De Sartine looked for a corner table where they could spread their work out, and sip coffee quietly, while they sorted through the files and solidified facts in their heads. Lebrusque went to the counter to order the coffee and cake. Diderot, Voltaire and the Montgofliers looked on from the other side of the room, and whispered to themselves.

"According to our files," said Gentilhomme, "Leclair married for a second time, Louise Roussel, in 1730. She owned a lucrative engraving business, and prepared all of Leclair's compositions for printing from Opus 2 onward. They were married for 28 years, apparently their happiness only falling apart over the last several years. It seems that Leclair struck out on his own to get rid of a nagging wife who was going through menopause, who no longer enjoyed intimacy, and who argued with him constantly about whose money was whose.

According to a neighbour, Leclair confided in him that he wished to be rid of the wife, so that he could live alone in an apartment or a little house, and finally have his own freedom. He said he wanted to have independence and cultivate female relationships on his own terms, even if it meant getting a mistress or a prostitute. The neighbour said Leclair wanted to spread his wings. He finally purchased a small house on his own, though it was from a seedy landlord, Monsieur Legras, who promised to repair things for a small fee each month if any work needed doing. Somehow things always came up, spring or winter repair, the leaky roof, drafty windows, and the uneven cobble stones in the walkway. There was always something! Which Leclair shied away from because he preferred that someone else's fingers got pinched. Leclair was no good as a handy man and liked to spend his time instead, reading comfortably by the fireplace, smoking his pipe, and of course, composing music at his desk or practicing the violin at all hours.

By the time they had drunk their second cup of coffee and disposed of their cake, the trio of officers concluded that the ex-wife was indeed a perfect candidate for the murder. She may not have had the strength, but possibly, one of her male co-workers could have been hired to kill Leclair with an engraver's tool from the shop, maybe a "bright-cut engraving tool" or a "knife graver" which could make deep cuts.

During the investigation of Leclair's whereabouts on the evening of his death, they found out that the man had been playing billiards at his favourite tavern with a friend who was also a musician. They had interviewed that friend first thing and found no reason for suspicion there. Just an amicable game of billiards which Leclair and the friend routinely played to wind down the day. The friend said that Leclair chose to sit for a while by the window and sit privately for a time sipping his wine and nibbling on cheese. Then he got up and left. The friend added one more item of note, Leclair's nephew was there in the tavern that night, sitting in the far corner seemingly entertained by the tavern's tipsy revelers. But then the nephew routinely did that and chose never to sit with his uncle, although he would occasionally play billiards and sit and gossip with other customers.

The police had something to go on by that time, in terms of background and persons of interest. Procope's coffeehouse actually made the investigation fun. The Lieutenant knew enough about managing people's productivity by including a few humane perks in the work. Now the next task was to actually interview the ex-wife. The Lieutenant suggested going over to her shop. That way, they could actually see all the instruments and engraving tools which were available to a potential murderer or murderess.

As the police sauntered out of the door at Procope's, carting away their files, the intelligentsia in the room whispered amorphous things about the departing presence of the police. The Lieutenant of Police, Antoine-Gabriel de Sartine, only smiled as he shut the door of the coffeehouse behind him.

\*\*\*\*\*

# Chapter 6

**November 4, 1764**

The three officers stood at the door under the sign of "Louise Roussel, Engraver" in the Rue Saint-Jacques. De Sartine turned to Gentilhomme and said, "Why don't you do the honours and knock?" A big iron door knocker faced them, shaped like a large treble clef. "Hmm," wondered Gentilhomme, "I wonder if it plays music when you knock?"

When Gentilhomme did as he was told, it was Louise Roussel herself who opened the door. She eyed the three men up and down and realized they were not there to bring her business. She was curt. "What do you want?" she asked. Lebrusque countered, "As the ex-wife of the recently deceased M. Leclair, we need to interview you, Madame. We are the police."

"Ah, the boys in blue!" she said.

The lady made them wait for a moment or two, just to show them she could. She was past working age, they judged, so she probably was not in a financial position to afford the luxury of retirement. Approximately, 65 years of age, judged the Lieutenant. She reminded him of an old crow, lean and thin, with a small beak extended from a wrinkled face. Maybe age had extended that beak somehow. "These must be the lean years," thought de Sartine. She finally let them in and guided them past her place of business, an assortment of engraving machines on the floor, and an array of cutting tools strung up on the walls. One large man was bent over scribing into a metal template. When he rose, he showed an evident limp.

"We also print musical scores," commented Mme Roussel as they went by her co-worker. She led them into her inner office and asked them to sit. The large man limped over carrying two chairs, one at a time, and then left.

"Now then," she said. "What can I do for you gentlemen in blue?"

Lebrusque got to the point. "Where were you on the night of October 22nd or the early morning of October 23rd?"

"I was sound asleep in my quarters upstairs," she said. "I find that arrangement economical, especially since my business has suffered a setback in recent years."

"Because your husband left you," asked Lebrusque tersely.

"Why yes," she confessed. "Because and ever since he left me."

"Why did he leave you?"asked Lebrusque.

"That dear Officer, is none of your business," she retorted.

Lieutenant de Sartine cut in. "Quite right Madam. For the moment, it is none of our business." He took over the questioning. "However, can you prove you were at home during the night of October 22nd and the early morning of October 23rd?"

"Only if sleeping with André is proof," she chuckled. "We are a couple. He likes older women. Just loves my blue eyes and my dimples, if you've noticed!" She called out, "André come in here, were we or were we not sleeping together last week on Monday, October 22nd and Tuesday, October 23rd?" He limped to the door and blushed. "Why, as a matter of fact, every day of the week!" he acknowledged with a broad smile. "There," said Madam, "my alibi!" And proudly she added, "One that is clearly 20 years younger than myself."

De Sartine backed off, not wanting to get into the business of their bedroom which was of no concern to him. When Madam realized that the Lieutenant was backing off somewhat, she relaxed. Tears rose in her eyes. She took a breath and talked about her former husband. "I did love him you know." She reminisced, "Those were good years when we first started out."

She explained that a woman goes through changes, and when her menopause hit, she felt moody and argumentative. She also did not feel attractive and so was disinterested in her wifely duties to her husband in the bedroom. "That's when the marriage fell apart," she said, "we slept in separate bedrooms." Madame explained that her husband started going out at night to taverns. He preferred Le Coq d'Or, a higher-end establishment, not like La Dame Chantante, which served a lower class of people. They went through 7 years of uncertainty and insecurity like this until he got the notion to trundle off to Holland with his violin, to leave the country, and leave Louise and daughter Little Louise behind in France with the business while he cavorted around with lords and ladies at the court of the Princess of Orange at Leeuwarden.

He became a changed man, a different one who needed love and pity when I first met him, when his first wife took ill and died. Louise confessed that it was difficult to keep her business' finances solvent after he left because he'd visit Paris now and again and then be off back to Holland or heaven knows where. "After more years since he went to Holland, we finally divorced in 1758. He was a career husband married to his violin, and my little Louise needed a father who was never there." She added, "For old times sake, however, he brought me his future compositions to help out with our business and our living.

"I kept my business going with other small commissions," she said, "but found it convenient to move in with a Monsieur Chavagnac on Rue du Four-Saint-Germain after our divorce. It was funny that a former patron, the Duke of Gramont, offered my husband the chance to move into his very own luxurious house, so that my husband could live with some dignity and respectability...and what did he do? He rejected the offer and decided to find his own place to live...in a dark and tiny, run-down hovel close to the Saint-Martin's canal. Can you imagine living by the canal on the dirty side of town, north of Le Marais? How completely insane is that, for a violinist to lower himself so? If he ever got into a brawl with a street thug, can you imagine the damage he could do to his delicate hands? My husband had some crazy notion about independence and living freely. He did not wish to rely on anybody's charity, and wanted to make it on his own, with his own talent, with confidence that his talent would pull him out of his financial problems."

Madame added as an after-thought that Leclair wanted to try out a libertine lifestyle; eat the poison fruit, so to speak, and enjoy other women before he died. "That's when he looked for prostitutes, and eventually a mistress," said Mme Roussel, with indignation. "I was no longer good enough for him."

"Madame" we know what happened to him during those unsettling years but what about you? Louise Roussel explained that her business almost went bankrupt, much of it as a result of her spiraling into years of menopause, but somehow, she kept her business afloat, and as her spirits lifted, she found that her business slowly got better. "I managed," she said, "with bumps and scrapes, as it were, but I survived."

She explained, "I know I've had financial difficulties; I've had them before. But Monsieur Legras has approached me recently to sell him the title of that little house back, north of "Le Marais". My husband still kept me in the will. There are some belongings which I wish to retrieve there, and I also wish to publish some more of my former husband's works which I have discovered in the house. I see light at the end of the tunnel."

Madame Roussel said she found her talk with the police most refreshing, and the Lieutenant especially kind. She never talked so much to police officers in her life. André had been listening at the door like a guardian angel. He got the hats and coats for the officers as they made their way to the door.

As the trio walked slowly past all the machines and the sharp tools, they judged that none of them seemed sturdy or wide enough to slice through a man's shoulder blade, even with the application of tremendous force. They were tools for artwork, scrolling and cutting fine lines in blocks of wood or metal for the printing process.

They each shook Madame's hand and walked out the door with the feeling that Madame Louise Roussel was indeed on the way up again and that indeed she had not perpetrated the crime, especially with a cripple at her side. It was clear that Madame Roussel's paramour, André, was not agile enough to run up behind Leclair and subdue him quickly with three forceful stab wounds in the back. The Lieutenant wished them well and hoped the business would soon improve.

As the door closed to Louise Roussel, Engraver, Gentilhomme nudged the Lieutenant's elbow, "Well, what do you think?" The Lieutenant said, "No murder weapon there. If we look at Leclair's body and match the wounds to a knife or sharp object we will find that the width and depth of the wound most likely came from a broad bladed trade knife. Almost anyone in France could carry one of those for self-protection at night. It could even have been a Katar, a knife favoured in India. We do not have the resources to look into every possibility. I am at a loss. Who is next on the list?"

Gentilhomme flipped the pages of his notebook. "How about the mistress or a prostitute? But how do we find her?"

"Well, gentlemen, we won't do that just sitting here!" said the Lieutenant.

*****

# Chapter 7

**October 22, 1764**

Leclair did not like walking home alone from Le Coq d'Or at night. Most nights he did not even go to the tavern, but when he did, he hailed a carriage to take him to his little house in the northern part of "Le Marais". Carriages hovered around the taverns in Paris late at night, like vultures swooping in circles to scoop up clients, the prize being a fare and  sometimes a tip of an "Écu au bandeau de Louis XV", which in silver currency was a handsome pay for one night's work for getting a drunken patron home without mishap.

There should have been a carriage visible down the street tonight, but none was this night. And yet, it had been a recorded fact, that there were more than 10,000 carriages for hire in Paris by 1750, the first taxi-cabs. But tonight? Nothing! "That's a nuisance," Leclair thought. He did not have the patience to wait, so he started walking instead.

Jean-Marie Leclair was ready to spend the "Écu" because he was not feeling that well. He confessed out loud, "By God, I must have had a good 5 glasses of wine in me this night!" He murmured, "Quaffing that much in one night will ruin my day tomorrow for practicing my fiddle.  But I did it to myself. Nothing like an old fool."

He remembered a lot of sitting in the steamy tavern, looking at women, with an obvious intention of picking one up, a "femme fatale" which would give him one night of pleasure; it really didn't matter which one; he wasn't particular...but the opportunity came and went since he was too inebriated and too smelly to perform an "art d'amour" even if he were able to sweet-talk one of the women to come home with him. While he drank in the tavern, maybe his fifth glass of the night, he thought he spied his nephew, Guillaume-François Vial, sitting in the far corner, studying the scene with a shrewd eye. Maybe his nephew was there to beg for a letter of recommendation again to get into the King's Symphony. Leclair was tired of these repeated entreaties. They were becoming tiresome. Leclair turned his back away from his nephew, once he confirmed that the big man was actually there. He faced the window instead, and concentrated on eating his slice of cheese and piece of bread in peace.

The talk in the tavern was tiresome too, more complaints about the increased taxes on wines, and the threat to use the hundreds of "guinguettes" or smaller taverns springing up around the outskirts of Paris like fireflies. Wine cost a third of the price there than inside of Paris. Perhaps Leclair would not have to run into his unwelcome nephew in one of those, whereas Le Coq d'Or was a more habitual haunt for both himself and Vial. Although wine, cheese and bread cost more, at least he could rub elbows with a more refined crowd.

"Still, I really do need to find a different watering hole," thought Leclair. He sneered in the direction of his nephew, thinking, "He is not that good a violinist anyway. He should be at home practicing his fiddle, even in these late hours, rather than wasting time here drinking wine in a noisy tavern." Leclair's eyebrows rose with the sudden realization that this advice could apply to himself as well.

Leclair had had enough. The women seemed to have their eyes set on younger men tonight. He finally decided to stagger towards the exit, stepping into the fresh air of the night. Leclair looked for a coach to hail, flashing a brand new silver coin, an "Écu au bandeau de Louis XV". There were no takers down the street, tantalized by the sight of the coin because they had all been taken by other drunken clients, so no coaches were in sight. Therefore, Leclair pocketed his coin and staggered slowly in the direction of his home in the Rue Careme-Prenant. "Oh well, I've got more money for wine next time around," he said to himself, and promptly vomited on the nearest lamppost on the street. The lamplighter for these street lamps which were fired by oil was just finishing his rounds, not happy to see Leclair desecrating and then leaning against his precious lamppost. Who would clean up the mess? He ignored lighting this particular lamppost, and spit towards Leclair in disgust. "Merde!" he said.

Somehow by the grace of God, or the twinkling of the stars above, Leclair got home to his own walkway on the Rue Careme-Prenant. He was near his door when he suddenly felt a heavy blow to his back, a solid hit which was piercing and sharp. His right hand went up to reach back to his left shoulder, wondering if a rock had hit him. Some prank by a thug? As Leclair keeled over, a second blow smashed into his neck. He heard bone crack back there. "My god," he grunted, "I've been stabbed! How ever will I practice tomorrow?" He felt a third blow in the back of his neck, and he keeled over, paralyzed. Finally he fell face first onto the cobble stones. So close to the door of his own home. He dropped his book and also the musical manuscript which he clutched in his left hand. That manuscript sketched out the plan for a new Concerto, one in the key of E Minor, Opus 16. It would be quite lovely. It would never be heard.

After the first shock, Leclair realized he would never play violin again. "Oh my beautiful Concerto," he lamented, "unfinished, and gone forever just like dust."

Someone grabbed him from behind and turned him over. "Who is it? What is happening?" He faced the night sky. He could see the distant stars twinkling high above, so delicately like the runs of an arpeggio on the keyboard. But the hateful eyes of his killer blocked the stars, and stared down on him, face to face. The eyes mocked him. He only saw those cold eyes, colder than the night sky. "Yes, I recognize those eyes," he thought, "I never thought you would do this to me."  The lower half of the killer's face was covered by a black shawl, like a road agent's disguise.

Leclair stared into those cold eyes and wanted to know, "Why?" But he already knew; it's just that he did not think he'd do it.

The voice said, "You've had your time, old man. Now you must get off the stage for young men like me to claim the fame. That is the order of things, and the way it has always been."

The culprit turned Leclair over again onto his stomach. He wiped his bloody hand on Leclair's overcoat, and as he did so, he felt the man's pocket watch. It was gold-plated. Why not take a memento? He snatched the watch and chain, and then got up with a nod of satisfaction. He took a deep breath and looked up at the twinkling stars himself. He raised a clenched fist to them, and said, "It is my turn to inherit them." He spit upon Leclair, as the man lay dying. He then sheathed the dagger and pulled Leclair into the vestibule, leaving the door wide open. He picked up the blood-stained book and the blood spattered manuscript, and threw them into the vestibule beside Leclair's dying body.

Leclair was not even sure if it had been the nephew, so drunk and shocked was he. And as he sank further into oblivion, the thought crossed his mind whether all of this was only a dream. After all, how could he be dying? His head swam, and he seemed to be floating far away up and up, beyond the last glimpse of the distant stars. But how could that be? He was lying face down in the vestibule, and that was absurd. "My Concerto!" he groaned, "unfinished. So much to do. This breaks my heart."

There lay at his side a book, Rameau's "Treatise on Harmony Reduced to Its Natural Principles" [1722]. The book had fallen open on a blood soaked page which suggested ways in which to approach harmony and make it work. Beside Rameau's work lay a sheet of music with notes scribbled hastily on the page like chicken scratching, an incipient plan for a new Concerto. At the top of the spattered page was written, "Violin Concerto in E minor by Jean-Marie Leclair". One could hardly read the notes because of the blood stains. Which were the notes and which were the blood stains? The killer hadn't bothered looking at these objects which he carelessly tossed into the vestibule beside Leclair's dying body.

The time was one minute to midnight. Jean-Marie Leclair would never hear the cathedral bell toll 12, and he would never live to see the new day and the new sunrise of October 23rd 1764.

\*\*\*\*\*

# Chapter 8

"I feel really good. It's been a great rehearsal," said Jean-Marie Leclair wiping his brow. It was October 23$^{rd}$ , 1715. He was 18. His dance partner, the ballerina, Marie-Rose Casthanie, had worked up a sweat too. She wiped her hands on her colourful frock, and then dabbed her brow with a lace handkerchief patterned in floral designs. She was much older than Leclair but still quite slim and attractive.

She did not wear a tutu, of course, because that fashionable item did not make its appearance until 1832 when Marie Taglioni wore a gauzy white skirt cut to reveal her ankles at the Paris Opera. Baroque dancers back in 1715 made up for spectacle on stage by wearing colourful silk gowns, feathers and lace like the nobility; the men wearing three cornered hats, fancy coats with shiny fringes and pantaloons and stockings that covered the calf, all very colourful, gaudy and fluffy.

Ballet had taken France by storm ever since The Sun King, Louis XIV, had taken a small part in a ballet at the age of 14 where he represented the rising sun. It had become a tradition now to have fancy Balls at court featuring amateur and professional dancers. The Academic Royale de Danse was created in 1661 and now that Louis XIV had died at the age of 77 in 1715, the tradition continued more popular than ever in the courts of the nobility. The Lyons Opera was busy rehearsing for a Ball which was coming in several weeks hosted by the Duke and Duchesse of Lyons before the Lenten season.

Marie-Rose looked admiringly at Jean-Marie attired in his cocked hat, red double-breasted coat, and maroon pantaloons. She imagined his body underneath, lithe and muscular like a whippet. "Your steps were impeccable today," she complimented him. "I do not know at which you excel the most, the dance or the violin?"

"Neither," he joked, "I love them both equally."

Marie-Rose was still stunning, especially to a 19 year old. He felt special since an older woman found an interest in him. She stood there in front of him like a queen, regally outfitted in a fluffy blue silk dress, narrow at the waist with lovely folds billowing out beyond her dancer's narrow feet. Her coiffure puffed up above her head, held in place by a decorative hair comb shiny with pearls. He was only somewhat less resplendent wearing a white wig, pony tail at the back, his head topped with a red cocked hat, of the three corner style. His coat was pink and his pantaloons maroon. They looked like human peacocks, proud, iridescent and precise. After all, they were dancers dressed to catch the eyes of an admiring audience in the 18th century.

Both of them had been retained as professional dancers at the Lyon Opera. They were rehearsing a Gavotte, as well as a Rigaudon, the Rigaudon requiring more energy because it was a sprightly dance, whereas the Gavotte required elegant precision. Occasionally, Jean-Marie doubled as a violinist for the Opera but was not paid double, because he was on contract. Four of his seven siblings, however, were retained as musicians by the Lyons Opera and thus added extra money to the family income.

The Duke and Duchesse will be pleased," said Jean-Marie to his pretty dance partner. They were in love. He would be 19 next year, of marriageable age, already having had his parents' blessings. Perhaps, his parents had second thoughts though about his union, especially to an older woman, but then the father gave in, "Let him make his own mistakes." The mother secretly lamented, "I see black."

"Come let's go for another round," he said to Marie-Rose, "the Rigaudon still needs some more work."

Unfortunately, there is little history recorded on either Leclair or his bride-to-be at this point, not until they got married in February 1716, after which Jean-Marie started to make his mark as a dancer and musician of remarkable talent. Jean-Marie must surely have excelled in the art of dance because in 1722, a mere six years after the marriage, he was hired as first dancer at the Turin Opera. Yet, he remains an enigma because his marriage paper described him as a "braid maker", neither dancer, nor musician.

The next decade of their lives was rather unsettling because they did not stay in one place for long after their marriage. The stay in Turin, after 1722 was about a year. In 1723, the couple moved to Paris. Then within another three years, in 1726, the couple moved back to Turin. Then, in 1728, they bounced back to Paris. All of this must have been hard on the wife, especially an older wife. In 1728, Marie-Rose Casthanie died. There are only a few mentions of her in the history books. Two years after his first wife died, Jean-Marie married his second wife, Louise Roussel, in 1730, in Paris. She published and printed Jean-Marie's musical compositions.

It would be interesting to read between the lines and create some drama, a real story with dialogue  between Marie-Rose Casthanie and Jean-Marie Leclair during those dozen years after their marriage with all the moving around they did. What might have been the real story if one applied an imagination beyond the bare facts. What did they feel? What did they think? Did they argue? What did they discuss over dinner? How often did they make love?

*****

Jean-Marie Leclair was born in Lyons, in East-Central France, May 10th , 1697. He was the eldest of eight children [another documentary says seven children]. The father, Antoine Leclair, was indeed listed as a "braid maker" by profession and apparently Jean-Marie did indeed learn this trade, among several others. The father was also described as a haberdasher by trade, who relaxed by playing the cello in his off hours. He and his children would presumably be called upon to play for various church functions and events in the city of Lyons, and occasionally be paid a bit of money.

Just to jump ahead somewhat, it is interesting that Lyons was the home of other famous people, like the Lumière brothers, Auguste and Louis, who invented the cinema or "cinematogaph" in 1895. But jumping back to 1697, one might say the other invention which Lyons was famous for was producing Jean-Marie Leclair, a genius of the 18th century, who had a combined talent in dance and in the violin.

Nothing is mentioned of the Leclair matriarch. But the father, Antoine, with his non-descript wife, produced eight children, four of them musically gifted, and as young children, ready to provide the neighbourhood with the joyful noise of their instruments. The family lived crowded above their haberdashery shop. There were three girls and five boys.

The family included the oldest, Jean-Marie himself, born in 1697, then, Jeanne, b. 1699, Francoise 1701, Jean-Marie, "le cadet", [in English, the younger] 1703, Francois 1705, Antoniette 1708, Pierre 1709, and Jean-Benoit 1714. Four of these children became musicians, two of them making a minor mark on musical history. Pierre published a book of duets in the same year that his brother was murdered, 1764. Jean-Marie, the younger, also published works for two violins and a vocal work of no account.

It is interesting that Johann Sebastian Bach in Germany was fruitful in the number of his children, outdoing Antoine Leclair 8 to 20, with an amazing 11 Bachs becoming composers.
Maybe there is something to a crowded family developing music as part of their survival skills. There could be heated debate here about Nature versus Nurture, genes over upbringing. If one studied the lives of the Leclairs and the Bachs, a person of common sense would say that the outcomes in both sets of children was a happy mixture of genes, as well as upbringing. It's

the academics who like to argue percentages, of which influence was the more dominant, which is not relevant to the weaving of this novel.

Compared to his father, Antoine, it is ironic though, that Jean-Marie Leclair only had one child, a daughter out of his two marriages, a daughter named Louise, who was not only named after her mother, but also became an engraver just like her mother, ignoring any musical gift from the father's side. The younger Louise later married a painter, Louis Quenet, thus putting a dead stop on Leclair's musical gene pool.

*****

# Chapter 9

After kissing Marie-Rose Casthanie goodbye outside the door of the Lyons Opera, Jean-Marie Leclair walked home in a world of his own, light-headed and in love. His father, Antoine, had provided well for his family by 1715. Each of his children could follow their own dreams, provided they helped out with the family business. The haberdashery was thriving. "We Suit to Please," boasted the sign above the door. The haberdashery was known for its decent reputation of quality and honest service. The shop stocked a wide array of men's clothing, accessories and repair kits for coats and dresses. The shop sold needles and thread, sewing notions like buttons and ribbons, and advertised that pantaloons, frocks, coats and dresses could easily be altered, or made new, made to measure.

All the children had become adept in the trade. Jean-Marie even described himself as a "braid maker" and haberdasher, just like his father.

The mother was in demand as a seamstress and made all items of clothing for the Lyons Opera and the little theatre in the city, as well as for the ladies and gentlemen of the aristocracy who staged Balls and special events in the mansions of Lyons. In short, business was booming for the Leclairs and they had the man-power to handle it with their eight children.

Yes, Jean-Marie was on top of the world. He had a loving family, huge talent, and a sweetheart [even though older] who adored him. He went home in a cloud.

"I'm home Papa, shouted Jean-Marie," as he sauntered in the door. "Good," said the father, "Go hold the cloth for your mother then."

Since Jean-Marie had been born in 1697, Papa Leclair had made substantial renovations to their domicile. The haberdashery where they worked and stored most of their wares was downstairs; the family lived and slept upstairs in a large space divided in three. The boys' bedroom, the parents' bedroom [which was also subdivided by a curtain for the three girls], and then the living quarters where they visited, practiced their instruments and ate their meals.

The downstairs was heated by a large fireplace, which always needed to be replenished with wood as the winter months approached. This need was already felt; now that October had descended upon this East-central part of France. It was a chillier October than they were used to. The family heated the upstairs with a modern German stove which took some maneuvering to get into the center of the living quarters upstairs because the stove had to be taken apart and then put back together again. Jean-Marie was useless at the task, but Papa Leclair figured it out. The family was snug and warm when they practiced their instruments there in the evening and visited before going to bed by 9:00 p.m. It was too bad that the Franklin Stove did not come on the market 25 years earlier, being invented much later by Benjamin Franklin about 1740. It was popularly called the "Pennsylvania fireplace", incorporating the basic principles of the heating stove. Papa Leclair could have afforded it back then, instead of purchasing the bigger and more cumbersome German stove. The main thing was, that the family did well financially and they were comfortable in their living quarters, summer and winter.

Their daily routine was simple: early to bed, early to rise. They worked 12 hours each day. They retired at 9:00 p.m., got up at 5:00 a.m. Had tea, bread and a piece of cheese, practiced music for two hours until 7:00 p.m., had bread with an egg for breakfast, if they were lucky, and then opened the shop by 8:00 a.m. to start making clothes for the nobility. By 9:00 a.m. the shop was open for business. By 1:00 p.m., they closed up shop for two hours for a lunch-break, until 3:00 p.m. They would be back at work until 6:00

p.m. and then have the shop cleaned and everything put away by 7:00 p.m. or so, when they had a late supper, called a "souper".

The only one exempted from this daily routine was Jean-Marie, the elder, because he had progressed so quickly at dance and at the violin that he was in demand for various pageants, plays and ballets put on by the Lyons Opera. The best part of this was that he was actually paid for something he loved doing.

Meanwhile, the rest of the family faced the same routine each day, but neither the parents nor the children minded because they got to play lots of music during various breaks, and in the evenings they enjoyed each others' company, because unlike many working families, money was not an issue and they got along.

Now this did not mean that the Leclairs had an abundance of time on their hands where they played nothing but music. They did their chores like all the artisans and shops strung along the street adjacent to each other. Papa Leclair made sure that he had a broom and a bucket of water standing outside his shop, so one of the boys could sweep wayfaring urine and other unsightly stuff further down the street to the next shop. This was all a co-operative effort silently agreed upon by all the shops. However, if one shop happened to be recalcitrant and didn't do their bit, occasional inflammatory remarks could fly. It might take a while to get friendly again until that neighbour did his bit again in front street maintenance. No underground plumbing existed at the time to do a more efficient and civilized job of disposing human waste.

Papa Leclair's customers were ladies and gentlemen of the nobility, or the wardrobe mistress of the Lyons Opera, from whom they got lots of business, especially since their son, Jean-Marie was one of the key dancers and an orchestra member for the theatre. But there was only so much they could do about urine control, considering how everybody in the 18th century disposed of their waste.

The front of Leclair's "Mercerie" [haberdashery] could not avoid unwanted things floating down the street. Urine on cobble stones was a problem not only for his shop, but for all the shops down the street. Monsieur Frugé's "Boucherie" [meat], Madame Vincens "Boulangerie" [bakery] and Monsieur Franchessi's "Fromagerie" [cheese], even Monsieur Levesque's "Menuiserie" [carpentry], and Monsieur Bourassa's "Maroquinerie" [leather], all sported a broom and bucket outside their doors.

Urine could cause unsanitary damage to the bottoms of the flowing gowns of high-class ladies. Papa's broom and bucket just outside his shop were a sure sign that this was a store to come to because he was serious about keeping things clean for his clients.

At least, wealthy ladies had the means to have fringes and trim sewn into the lower edges of their dresses. These were washable fringes and needed to be replaceable because dresses which dragged along the cobble streets as ladies walked along, unfortunately soaked up the inevitable urine. It was a stinky time, the best of times and the worst of times. And dresses were brought into the Leclair haberdashery on a continuous basis to be cleaned and to be fixed.

Wealthy ladies who entered the Leclair "Mercerie" also asked Madame to make dresses with fine silk, so finely woven that it kept the fleas out. Ladies of the nobility could easily afford most anything, and Mme. Leclair did not mind the extra work or the extra money for cleaning or repairing the filthy outfits which were brought into the shop. Often the ladies would walk out of the store with an unexpected purchase of a brand new dress which was the latest rave. Because the Leclairs were middle-class, they could not afford to dress in high fashion themselves, but they could supply the materials for that, and so the Leclairs grew rich, if but slowly, on their own terms.

*****

# Chapter 10

Sleeping arrangements in the Leclair household were simple. Boys on the one side upstairs, parents and the three girls on the other side, divided by a curtain. Little Jean-Benoit slept with the parents because he was only one.

The boys had two "closet-beds" on their side which were enclosed furniture units with a door. After a four week trial period, it was decided that each of the older boys would sleep with a younger brother to keep them from being silly at night. Jean-Marie, the older, was 18, so he took Pierre who was only 6. Jean-Marie, the younger, was 12, so he took Francois who was 10. This arrangement kept a lid on the silliness at night. Because of the nature of boys, the two youngest ones poked each other if they slept together and made a big deal if somebody farted. It was understood that chatting quietly was tolerated before everyone settled down for the night, but not when silliness occurred. However, by the time the door to the closet-beds was closed, and sleep overcame them, the whole family was snug as a bug in a rug, even during the winter months. Their mattress was thick and fluffy, filled with hay, and so was their top blanket.

During the first four week trial period for the sleeping arrangement of the younger boys, the complaints about farting was an irritating ritual every night, which kept everybody awake. Papa Leclair shouted a stern warning from his side of the room. "Stop it!" he yelled across the divide. If things did not settle down, the boys knew that a spanking was coming, which was a rare occurrence anyway, considering Papa Leclair's high tolerance level for nonsense in the household. If Papa ever brought out his belt, however, that was when tolerance ceased, and a capital offense had been committed. This hardly ever happened though, because just knowing that the belt was there, was enough to settle the boys down. Papa had only to say a word once and obedience followed like the sun breaking through the clouds. Papa and Maman decided to switch the boys around though after one month. The girls seemed to be more civilized at night, just naturally.

Occasionally, somebody had to use the chamber pot which was positioned just outside the closet-bed, located at its end. The chamber pot thankfully had a tight lid on it. Different children were assigned to empty the pot in the early morning for their week's "potty duty". The Leclairs were lucky enough to have made a deep enough runnel in their backyard for waste, at least away from the garden where they grew tomatoes and cucumbers every summer.

On the parents' side, there was another set of closet-beds, one for the parents and one for the three girls. Little Jean-Benoit had the privilege of sleeping with the parents until he was three, at which time he would migrate to the boys' side. By that time, Jean-Marie the older should be married and out of the house.

The wood panels on these furniture sleeping units was painted with colourful designs, so as to blend in as actual furniture during the day. Most people in the 18th century slept in a half-upright position in these closets because lying down was associated with death. Because of their littler size, the smaller boys were allowed some leeway to sprawl out in all directions at night. If there was a leg or sharp elbow that poked the older brother, the offensive body part could always be shoved aside. So sleeping was not perfect, but manageable.

A baker's boy would walk up and down the street each day and shout out, "Fresh Bread, Baguettes, Croissants", which had to be bought each day, or else the family would be eating dried out crusts. Papa Leclair always had a can inside the door filled with loose change to pay the boy. Occasionally he would buy "eau de vie" which was brandy from another street vendor, "for his nightly medicine".

The water bearer was yet another a vendor whose job it was to carry a bucket of water up and down the street, out of which he would scoop a measure of water for a fee. Public fountains also required a fee, and often fights would break out there between water bearers and domestic servants who were told to fetch water by the nobility.

All in all, the Leclair family lived well. And now their 18 year old son, planned to get married by the following year. "Ah," Papa Leclair thought, "1716 will be an expensive year." Maman thought, "I see black!"

*****

# Chapter 11

The family's basic diet was bread, meat and wine. Watered down wine, for the children. The big meal was afternoon lunch from 1:00 p.m. until 3:00 p.m. which involved "une entrée" of a mixed salad, soup, or some terrine or paté. "The main course was meat, if it was affordable that week, or fish, with potatoes, rice, pasta, vegetables and an assortment of cheeses, local of course. The next big meal was "le souper" which happened after 7:00 p.m., routinely the end of the day's work.

It was during those two big blocks of time in which home schooling took place in the Leclair household. Everybody took a quick nap at 1:00 p.m. Maman got up first and laid out the dishes and cut the bread, and prepared a plate of cheese, the salads and soups. Papa would corral the young ones, along with the older children and herd them toward the corner table for their day's memorization of languages and discussion of themes. The children asked questions like, "Were all Italians lazy? Were the English really rude and had no manners? Will anything good ever come out of Poland?" Papa would answer, "You must always keep an open mind. Do not dress everybody in the same cloth!" He would point out that the Vatican was built by the Italians. And as to the English being rude? "Why Handel chose to live there." As for Poland, "We must wait and see."

Papa Leclair loved his wine, and made sure that the family had plenty of it. Every few years he would make enough to last another few years. The first time when he made wine was before a big holiday when he put a "Signe Fermé" [i.e. Closed Sign] on the front window. He got baskets of grapes from the local farmer, a trade-off for Maman fixing the pants for the farmer and his children. Papa would begin the messy task of loading the grapes into the press and then cranking the wheel. A bucket would catch the juice. The whole haberdashery smelled rife for days, right up to the rafters, downstairs and upstairs included. Maman said, "I don't mind the taste of my wine, but to smell it all over our lodgings, with the children there, that's more than I can stand." So, in future Papa Leclair made a deal with the farmer to do the grape pressing out there on the farm. Papa and the farmer split the work and they also split the wine. Papa brought plenty of bottles home for the fruit cellar. He stored the wine bottles down there, in wine racks, and on shelves the carpenter had built. Papa also placed few staples of meat and cheese on those shelves. Bread was bought each day from the Boulangerie.

Papa asked Jean-Pierre, "le cadet" i.e. the younger, to go into the fruit cellar one day and bring up two bottles of wine. One was to go to the carpenter's shop down the street. Monsieur Levesque had agreed to build some shelves for the family to hold volumes of music. There would be a friendly exchange of a bottle for carpentry service rendered. The other bottle was to go to Madame Vincens at the bakery because she was ailing. Papa told his young son to tell her, "No charge." Bartering was a customary practice to avoid the exchange of money and to avoid taxes. Finding ways to avoid taxes in France became a national pastime.

People were usually generous with each other, bartering and sharing their skills, admittedly not just out of a good heart, but as a means to avoid taxes. Despite the growth of the middle-class, more and more poverty was noticeable, as were homeless people in 18th century France. They were called "les clochards" [the bums]. Paris seemed to be overrun, and Lyons was only a little better with rising poverty. All shops and houses had bars at the doors and shutters on the windows, which one can still see on houses to this very day in cities in France.

It would be wonderful to get a government grant to search tax records for the Leclair haberdashery through the 1740s to see how well the family was doing. But then those records stored at city hall were probably ribbed or burned up by the peasant mobs storming government offices during the French Revolution. Better yet, it would take a miracle in a time machine to track the prosperity of the Leclairs after Jean-Marie left home. Instead of making a living just out of the gowns and coats for Lords and Ladies of the Kingdom, did they diversify their sources of income to include military uniforms? After all, the thing which distinguished Napoleon's army from the Duke of Wellington's at Waterloo was the colour and cut of their uniform.

Likewise, one would wonder what really had changed in society, between those people in power and the poor. France's King Louis XVI was dethroned and decapitated. Emperor, Napoleon Bonaparte, took his place, in fact crowning himself...and the question remained, had anything really changed? At least, some professions had steady jobs, like metal workers for swords, guns and horseshoes, haberdasheries for uniforms and ladies' gowns and coffin makers, once those uniforms were shot to pieces.

So, Rich Man, Poor Man, Beggarman, Thief,  the social order seemed to remain constant, moving along in any century, despite revolutions and the search for a Utopia. King, Emperor, President or Dictator, what did it matter? Top dogs were top, and bottom hounds always seemed to fight with each other to survive.

Haberdashers, like undertakers, were always employed. Somebody had to make those splendid uniforms with fancy buttons, epauletted jackets and hats with feathers, so one army could tell the difference from the other arm, so they'd know whom to kill. There is room for justified cynicism here about political movements and the masses through the French Revolution and beyond. One thing is clear, the Leclairs would have done very well indeed in peace or in war. They were blessed and lucky to make such a good living in the first half of the 18th century.

France got into a huge mess in the War of the Austrian Succession which lasted from 1741 to 1748, a 7 year war. It was an involvement where prized colonies were lost, and equipment, men, horses and uniforms cost lots of money in a foreign campaign. It did not help either that alliances kept changing during that time period. Louis XV and his 90 year-old adviser, Cardinal de Fleury, were too weak to argue against the vested interests of their courtiers. The national debt sky-rocketed to 2,200 <u>Million</u> "livres" in 1763, just one year shy of Jean-Marie Leclair's ignominious murder. Jean-Marie of course didn't care about his country's woes by that time because he was dead!

The Royal Court was already squeezing the lower classes dry, hence the growing masses of poor people. How do you pay the debt? Who will pay for it? The King looked to the privileged classes to remedy the situation by taxing them more. But this was difficult to accomplish!

The privileged classes ran the "parlements" of the kingdom. They had paid for and owned their positions or inherited them for life and were considered irreplaceable, which of course, made the whole bureaucratic structure corrupt. The privileged classes did not want to pay for the debts of a losing war.

It wasn't until 1771 when King Louis XV showed enough backbone under his Chancellor Maupeou to exile members of the corrupt "parlements" of Paris to the provinces and to replace them with salaried officials. The Abbé Terray began tax reform for the King and by 1774 had the budget almost balanced. That's when King Louis XV died of smallpox, and a weak Louis XVI took over the throne of France. The new King, dominated by his courtiers, ran the country back into debt. Educated men did not remain silent, and openly criticized the government and the King.

Diderot and d'Alemberti continued to work on a collective project with 150 contributors to print their "Encyclopédie" which criticized "l'ancien régime" of corrupt customs and religion, arguing that society would be better off served by Reason and not a King.

In this context, Jean-Marie Leclair's family life and his teenage years, 1710-1716 [when he got married] were indeed blessed years. The family had it good. By the time of his murder, October 1764, Jean-Marie's country was so deep in the hole, that anybody with a brain could see that a revolution was coming. One wonders how much a society can take before it explodes? It took 25years, however, after Jean-Marie Leclair's assassination, i.e. in 1789, for that social explosion to go off. The guillotine took the lives of King Louis XVI and Queen of France, Marie Antoinette, as well as many nobles, dukes and duchesses, who had ironically made the Leclair haberdashery rich.

Bastille Day, July 14$^{th}$ , became a national holiday for future generations. They thought they had gotten rid of the ills of society. The old order was swept away, the new order came in. The King was gone, Napoleon marched in, not as King but as Emperor, and it should be noted, an Emperor who crowned himself. The question remained, did any of this solve anything?

The point, in retrospect, is that Jean-Marie Leclair and his family were lucky to have made their living in the first half of the 18$^{th}$ century. Yes, Jean-Marie Leclair could have picked a better part of Paris in 1758 to buy a house. He might not have been stabbed to death if he had lived in another part of town He might have had a longer life, and more years of productivity as a composer before the French Revolution ever happened. But that speculation, like the question about whether The French Revolution could have been avoided at all, is a lovely discussion for academics over a cup of coffee. It could be an interesting question to pursue which a generous government grant could pay for, no?

*****

# Chapter 12

There was something special about little Jean-Marie Leclair when he was three years old because his eyes lit up when Papa played his cello. The child swayed back and forth to the music, and was annoyed when Papa stopped. From there on, Papa permitted the child to sit and play at his feet, both Leclairs, father and son, swaying in time to the music. That was the turn of the century, 1700.

When little Jean-Marie was a little older, about 5, his father stopped him and told him to put his baby violin down for a moment. Jean-Marie looked at his father as if he had done something wrong. "You did something clever," his Papa said. Jean-Marie did not know what, but he smiled bright eyed because little boys love getting praise, even if they do not know what for.

Mozart has gained an undeserved reputation as a child prodigy for composing the tune to "Twinkle, Twinkle Little Star" at the age of 5.  The tune was actually a French melody, "Ah, vous dirai-je, Maman," published in 1761.  The English lyrics came later in 1801, published by Jane Taylor. Mozart probably swayed to the music that his father, Leopold, played but "Twinkle Twinkle Little Star" is one credit for little Mozart at the age of 5, which is false. He did write 12 variations to the simple tune when he was 25 years old, just for fun. The point here is that prodigies, like Mozart and his predecessor, Leclair, show their gifts early. That is why they are prodigies. Leclair displayed that gift way back in 1707 when he was 10 years old and even earlier.

At the age of 10, Jean-Marie already knew what he wanted to be "when he grew up". His father felt that the age of 10 was a magical number for gifted children where some imprint or impression naturally came to them which would make music their destiny for the rest of their lives. Jean-Marie Leclair knew that the violin was part of his soul. Father and son, by 1707, played duets together, their most favourite pieces being the minuets, gavottes and gigues, composed by Jean-Baptiste Lully, which usually accompanied dances and ballets at the opera.

When Jean-Marie found out that his hero Lully was not only a violinist but also a dancer, Jean-Marie's said to himself, "I should be able to do that." Thus Jean-Marie began his dancing career at the Lyons Opera, at the age of 10, volunteering in bit parts at first and more involved things later. He got lessons from his father's friends at the Opera because there was always a demand for little boys in their theatrical productions of "opéras comiques" and even in Lully's "Tragédie en musique". By the time Jean-Marie was 15, he had acquired skills as a ballet dancer and had bettered himself as a virtuoso violinist. Whenever he would play a solo, Jean-Marie's eyes would glaze over and he would be transported into another world. The dance became his second love, but he could never make up his mind which discipline to follow to make his living. He was only sure that being an artist, in either dance or violin, was what he wanted to do "when he grew up".

When Jean-Marie was 16, Jean-Phillipe Rameau came to town, spending a couple of years there between 1713 and 1715. Rameau was 30 years old, and at the height of his powers. Lully had been dead already for 26 years, stomping his foot accidentally with his conductor's staff during a performance for the Sun King, Louis XIV. He smashed his big toe which got infected and eventually caught gangrene. He refused to have his leg amputated, and so, stubborn as he was, Jean-Baptiste Lully died, taking all his talent with him to the grave in 1687. Perhaps there is something to be said for being replaceable. There are and were clever people born all the time. After Lully, Jean-Phillipe Rameau was one of them, and at a later date, Wolfgang Amadeus Mozart was another.

When Rameau made Lyons his home back in 1713 or 1714, he worked for the Lyons Opera, at least until 1715, during which time he contributed a few "grands motets" to the Lyons Concert. He gave a little performance as well so he would astound people with his virtuosity. The 16 year old Leclair was impressed by Rameau's flashy fingers on the strings and loved the show. He said to himself, "One day I will do that."

However, by sheer coincidence, Leclair and Rameau met earlier when Rameau first came to town in 1713. He swept into the foyer of the theatre with an air of importance, and upon spotting the young Leclair, Rameau asked, "Well, where is my dressing room?" Jean-Marie didn't know what to say, "Well, we don't have a dressing room as such. All we have is that back room there where everybody gets changed before we go on stage." Rameau patted the 16 year old boy on the shoulder patronizingly, and commented, "This is a real hick-town isn't it?" Jean-Marie was speechless, and finally replied, "I guess it is." He thought afterwards, "Paris must sure be some sophisticated city." Rameau was in Lyons long enough to actually see young Leclair dance in a ballet once, and also hear him play his violin briefly in a small orchestra. He said to himself, "That young man will go far someday."

Jean-Marie got married just three years after he met Rameau. He was 19 in February of 1716, and madly in love with Marie-Rose Casthanie, his usual dance partner in the Lyons Opera. His parents did not like the fact that she was so much older than he. But what are you going to do with a willful teenager? He brought Marie-Rose flowers every week, and she enjoyed the attention. He asked Marie-Rose's mother if he might call upon her regularly on Sunday afternoons. The parents always stayed in the room with them, engaging in frivolous conversation, except several times when the couple was allowed to stroll around in the back garden during the summertime. This was all under the watchful eye of the parents who stood at the back window which overlooked the garden.

Marie-Rose was self-conscious about her age. "I'm so much older than you," she said, "will you still love me when I'm 64? I will grow old and ugly before you do." He protested, "You will never grow old and ugly in my eyes." As a dancer, she had maintained her figure and taken care of her looks. Jean-Marie did not look or think beyond that. What he said as a teenager in love, said something good about his good intentions. But good intentions and promises are one thing when you are young, and another thing in real life, when that determination is tested as the years go by. One good thing is that the marriage lasted 12 years, until Marie-Rose died in 1728, and that for a young Leclair was, one would suppose, a respectable fact.

On the day of the ceremony on a cold, cold February day in 1716, the couple got out of their carriage in front of Saint Jean Cathedral in the old part of town. The gathering of special friends and relatives was small. They decided to go cheap with a small crowd, though they splurged on being driven to the church in a carriage. The reception was held in Marie-Rose's large home which was more spacious than the inside of the Leclair haberdashery blocked by aisles of clothing and sewing articles.

Marie-Rose's parents provided a substantial dowry, and the Leclairs matched that sum. Jean-Marie and Marie-Rose put the money into a down payment on a small house in the old part of town. Since the house was a fixer upper, they hired a handy man to repair the roof and build some shelves. Jean-Marie knew about the violin, dance and haberdashery, but he knew nothing about carpentry and using his hands on crude work. He knew enough to protect his fingers for violin playing, which afforded him enough money at the Opera to pay somebody else to do the manual labour. It was amusing that in his marriage certificate, instead of violinist, ballet dancer or lace maker, he put down "braid maker", same profession as his father.

The couple lived happily in their little home for 6 years and often visited both sides of the family alternating them for Sunday meals and chatting away the afternoons. No children ensued. Both mothers-in-law were disappointed. No grand-children! The couple were a career couple instead. They could have invented the word, "workaholic".

By 1722, Leclair got tired of the same old routine in Lyons. They had been married 6 years, and nothing was happening in his life. He was 25 and wanted to spread his wings, to grow and get famous and possibly rich.

"But I don't want to move," argued Marie-Rose.

"Don't you see," said he, "what a wonderful opportunity it is to move to Turin? They've offered me a job as principal dancer at the Turin Opera." This would mean not only moving out of the city but also into another country. Turin was the cultural centre of the Piedmont area of northern Italy. At least, they both knew the language, since educated people and the nobility in those days knew several languages.

She countered, "I like our happy home here. We've made it a comfortable place to come home to at night, even though it is quite small and modest. But it's ours and we can afford it."

Well, Leclair insisted. He wasn't getting any younger at 25. He accepted the job as "first dancer" at the Turin Opera. It was an offer he could not refuse. Besides she also had a job as a support dancer with the troupe.

The rest if the family stayed in Lyons and continued their lives as usual. Jean-Marie Leclair, the younger, was now 19, the same age as his older brother had been when he got married. At the moment, he had no thoughts about marriage himself, but he knew he was happy to stay in Lyons where he could build a good reputation for himself as a violinist and composer in his own right. Although he did admit to himself that he was riding somewhat on his older brother's coattails.

Meanwhile, the older brother reasoned with his wife, "Things will turn out alright, you'll see." They sold their sweet little house, having made it attractive after several renovations, which became a real selling point. They got a good price for their investment, and arranged for the big moving day. At least, part of the Turin contract provided that things would be packed up for them and moved. They would not have to lift a finger.

"It's nice to be wanted," said Leclair. So a new era opened up for them, even though that era involved anxiety, especially for Marie-Rose, being older, as to what the future would hold. "It's an adventure," said Jean-Marie. His crystal ball only saw opportunity, and not displacement every few years from town to town. Marie-Rose was a lot like Jean-Marie's mother who saw black. But then Jean-Marie wondered if all women were like that?

The bare listings of dates and events up to this period in 1722 for the Leclairs are sparse, but the chance for imagination around these facts abounds. One can easily fill in the cracks by creating details like a baby Jean-Leclair swaying in time to the music at his father's feet, learning ballet at the age of 10, the courting ritual to win his wife, the marriage ceremony and buying a little house, and even the pretended meeting between Rameau and Leclair in 1713. All of these "happenings" are fiction, and enjoyable literary inventions. Otherwise, we would have nothing to add to an 18th century murder mystery. It is unfortunate that details are so sparsely recorded in this man's life and that the murderer was never caught. Perhaps the murderer created his own hell on earth through a guilty conscience for the rest of his life?

*****

# Chapter 13

Recorded detail about Jean-Marie's life becomes more solid after 1722, after the move from Lyons, once he spreads his wings into new cities in France and Italy, and becomes famous. It was only after the age of 25 that he makes his mark as a virtuoso violinist and composer, when he decides to take his teacher Somi's advice to concentrate on his violin playing and composing and not his dancing. From then on there is more flesh in recorded history, but even in the last half of his life, there is still plenty of room for conjecture and a chance to build a fictional world around the hidden facets of the man's life and to invent a good 18th century murder mystery.

"And we didn't have to lift a finger," said Leclair staring up at the apartment which the board of the Turin Opera had provided for them. Mind you, it was not located on the posh side of town, but nevertheless, it was their new home.

"I miss our little house in Lyons, "said the wife. "Home is what you make it," replied Jean-Marie cleverly. "Home is where the heart is," he added glibly, "and that is with you, my dear." The wife felt like she was being patronized. Jean-Marie already felt, at the age of 25, that 6 years of marriage were dragging him down. Just that past February, they celebrated their 6th wedding anniversary. Time seemed to fly by so quickly. February! Why did they ever pick February to get married in?

After 6 years, he felt the stirrings of a secret unease. Deep down, he wasn't as fond of his wife as he used to be, though he still remained faithful. Marie-Rose wasn't stupid; she picked up on his cooling towards her. At a private moment, she faced him head-on and said, "Jean-Marie I know things have gotten difficult between us lately. I know we can't have children. But whatever you do, please don't hurt me." He didn't say anything.

Even though his main occupation was the ballet at this time, he felt less passionate about the art than in previous years. The more he thought about his violin, the less he thought about his ballet dancing. The more he thought about his violin, the more he yearned to be a published composer.

He felt like he was the featured headliner for the Tetra Regio of Turin under false pretences, and yet, he enjoyed the big title, "first dancer and master of the ballet".

He did not want to upset his wife, so he said little about his desire to publish his music. At midnight, he worked on his Opus 1 in the little back room by candle light. His Opus 1 was a collection of a few sonatas which danced around in his head. But the publication of these sonatas would have to wait, and remain an unrealized dream on the sidelines. For now, the ballet gave them their bread and butter, and satisfied his wife. She was also hired by the Turin Opera as part of the agreement, which brought in extra money. The wife followed along in Jean-Marie's shadow, quiet, submissive, and asking few questions. He seemed so forceful about his dreams and what he wanted to do. She was simply overcome by his youthful exuberance and his energy. Marie-Rose could live quite contentedly with how they made their living at the moment.

It was after a performance at the Turin Opera, that Jean-Marie received a note from a Monsieur Antoine Bonnier to come to his private box. M. Bonnier was a wealthy financier, holding the office of Treasurer-General of the Etats de Languedoc in southern France. M. Bonnier had connections in Paris, and with the provision that Jean-Marie take the financier's son, Joseph, under wing as a violin pupil, the father could make things happen for Jean-Marie in Paris. Jean-Marie's infatuation with Turin didn't last long, barely a year, when the Leclairs packed up and found themselves moving yet again to Paris, the City of Light, in 1723. There, Jean-Marie Leclair finally realized his dream for being published. He dedicated his Opus 1, his First Book of Sonatas for

Violin and Basso Continuo, to Monsieur Antoine Bonnier, who made good on his promise to connect Leclair with the right people.

There seems to be some discrepancy among sources about the years when the Leclairs bounced back and forth between Paris and Turin, but we will take the simplest one. Suffice it to say, that the infatuation with either city didn't last long, and within a few years, in 1726, Jean-Marie got up enough gumption to say to his wife, "My dear, we need to talk. The Turin Opera wants me back as 'premier danseur'. They've renegotiated my contract as master of the ballet for the theatre. I'm serious about taking the position. Besides you will get your old job back as an extra with the troupe." His wife said, "We could have saved ourselves a move by simply staying in Turin all along." Jean-Marie did not say anything to that.

Once back in Turin, they settled into a different apartment, within walking distance of the theatre. At last, it seemed like they had a life of calmness and composure. Leclair's spirit felt more complete these days, because now he was published.

He was so satisfied with himself knowing that his Op. 1 sonatas were in print. Leclair also composed some ballets which were used as postludes to two operas at Turin's "Teatro Regio Ducale" in 1727. Ironically and unfortunately these scores have been lost. So remaining in print and preservation of his publications was no guarantee to posterity. Perhaps a note about the notion of immortality.

Although he was not in Paris, the City of Light, he met some grand people in northern Italy. One of them was Johann Joachim Quantz, the great German flutist and Baroque composer who was in Turin doing a grand tour of Europe to promote the flute. Quantz was born in 1697, the same year as Jean-Marie Leclair. They had lots in common. Quantz had met Scarlatti in Naples and Handel in London.

After Quantz rubbed elbows with Leclair in Turin in 1726, he moved on later to impress the Queen of Prussia and then the Crown Prince, Frederick II, who decided to take up the flute. Quantz told the writer, Friedrich Nicolai, that he had to hide in a closet one time, when he was about to give Frederick a lesson, when the domineering father exploded into the room in an outrage because he disapproved of his son "tooling around on the flute."

"Complete waste of time," he shouted red-faced, "that infernal flute...and that Quantz!" Well, perhaps the words weren't exact, but the Crown Prince's father must have shouted something equivalent in German. This did not deter the Crown Prince, Frederick II, though, because he actually became quite a good flute player.

1726 also gave Jean-Marie the chance to improve his skills on his own instrument, the violin, while he earned his pay as a ballet dancer. At the grand old age of 29, Jean-Marie Leclair began taking violin lessons from Giovanni Battista Somis. Somis had been a pupil of the great virtuoso and Italian composer, Arcangelo Corelli. Somis was impressed with Leclair's musical talent. It should be noted that Somis also took on another violin student by the name of Jean-Pierre Guignon, who also figured in Leclair's life at a later stage in Paris.

While in Turin, Leclair showed his talents beyond merely dance and violin by dabbling in choreography for the opera, "Didone". "Didone" was based on the tragic love-story between Aeneas, hero of Troy, and Dido, Queen of Carthage. Leclair also squeezed in time for composition, for example, three intermezzi for "Semiramide", an opera by Giuseppe Maria Orlandini.

It was Somis who said to Leclair that he would do better to concentrate on the violin, instead of wasting valuable time dancing. One can imagine Somis putting his hand on Leclair's shoulder after a good violin lesson, "The violin will get you further and a career in it will last longer than in dance." There seems to be some discrepancy here whether it was 1727 or 1728 [or both] during which time Leclair headed for greener pastures in Paris. But it is clear that he did follow Somis' advice to make the violin his mainstay for fame and fortune. Spreading his name, meant moving between Turin and Paris. This must have been difficult on his wife who dutifully followed.

*****

# Chapter 14

Once ensconced in Paris, in 1728, though not specifically clear exactly when, we are informed that "soon" he travelled to London and to Kassel. In Kassel, Jean-Marie Leclair met Pietro Locatelli where the two of them staged a battle of the violins, French and Italian styles of playing, which people loved. Leclair's playing was angelic, marked by a beautiful tone, with rhythmic freedom. By contrast, Locatelli's playing was aggressive with a scratchy edge where he purposefully played "like the devil", perhaps a harbinger of the style adopted years later by Paganini. This was all showmanship and deliberately designed to entertain the journalists who wrote sparkling reviews for their papers.

During all this time, while Jean-Marie Leclair travelled and showed off, one wonders where Marie-Rose, his wife, was and what her thoughts were about the rising fame of her husband, and about whether he remained faithful to her. We do know that, coming back to Paris in 1728, Leclair published his Opus 2, which was a Second Book of Sonatas for Violin and possibly Traverse Flute. Now, he was truly published and famous!

This time, Leclair dedicated his music to Bonnier's son, Joseph, who inherited his father's money and hotel after the older Bonnier died. Joseph Bonnier became Leclair's new patron. Apparently, as part of the bargain, the young Bonnier wanted to continue in free violin lessons from Leclair, in return for which Leclair and his wife would get free lodgings at the Bonnier hotel. This seemed like an equitable arrangement, a perfect example of what goes around, comes around.

When the Leclairs were shown their luxuriant rooms in the hotel, they were awed by the opulence in each and every room, the furniture, the chandelier in the living room, the breakfast nook with large windows, the water closet even. M. Bonnier smiled and said, "You must be pleased?" Jean-Marie beamed, "We are, we are, and ever so fortunate!" "Well," said Bonnier, "my father was fortunate when he first started out as a financier, and as he always told me, by boy, it helps to have money. Remember money makes money." "Hmm," said Jean-Marie, "remind me to retain you as my financier." They both laughed.

The friendship with Monsieur Joseph Bonnier de la Mosson paid off in dividends, not only in lodgings, but also in networking with the big who's who. The friendship also gave Leclair a steady income in a pension from the young Bonnier's gratitude for teaching him the violin.

In the meantime, Leclair had other income. He performed twelve times as a virtuoso violinist for the "Concert Spirituel" which launched a new public concert series. His performances drew enthusiastic applause and he was asked back repeatedly to perform his own sonatas and concertos. The young Bonnier also opened doors for Jean-Marie's wife, so that she could get a job as a dancing coach in Paris teaching well-to-do young ladies in the art of becoming ballerinas. Mme Leclair was in her 40s by this time, less capable of springing about on the dance floor. Instead, she verbalized and pointed out to young ladies what needed to be done in a dance. The young ladies adored her and listened to the experienced teacher.

Not much is known about why or how the health of his wife degenerated, nor what the private situation of their relationship was. The bare fact we know is that the Leclairs moved back to Paris in 1728.

Jean-Marie might have already met Louise Roussel, by that time, and with his first wife, Marie-Rose, being older, less healthy and less capable, he might have sparked up some sexual interest in Louise Roussel. Perhaps, the fact that Marie-Rose could not have any children also gave him "leave", as it were, to let his eyes wander across the fence. Someone suggested that Marie-Rose did indeed get pregnant and might have died because of a difficult childbirth. It might simply have been just getting sick because she was older, and not having health care and poor meds, she went downhill and finally passed away. This was the 18th century!

Leclair was only 31 at the time, and had enough vim and vigour in him to let his eyes wander across the fence, sick wife or no sick wife. Whether he kept what he should have kept inside his pants is also a guess, as to how faithful the man was to his older wife, and to his marriage of 12 years.

But we cannot accuse him of being a philanderer at this time, because there are no records saying that he was one. Maybe a good case for philandering could be applied to his Parisian years after 1728, after Marie-Rose died. He was more famous then, more published, and moved around a lot from town to town. He also hobnobbed with the rich and famous, and they of course, afforded a different lifestyle and a set of mores beyond what the working middle class, like his parents, could afford. Money and success, and becoming a new bachelor, can change a person. Anyway, the seeds for a "transition" were already sown when Jean-Marie Leclair met Louise Roussel in her engraver's shop.

Louise Roussel was three years younger than Jean-Marie. In 1728, that age difference seemed to be a better match than with his own wife, Marie-Rose. Louise was 28 and Jean-Marie was 31. Marie-Rose's age was never specified in the history books, except that she was "much older" than him. Perhaps that age difference was 14 or 15 years, which would place her around 45? People in the 18th century seemed to age faster and die younger than what we are used to with our modern medicine and health care. It is also dubious that Marie-Rose would be pregnant at that age in those days, which would remove the argument that she might have died in childbirth.

Those things being said, Jean-Marie was attracted to a younger woman in 1728, one who looked fresh as a daisy. Ironically, by 1764 when Louise Roussel was 64 and when the police interviewed her as a possible suspect in her husband's murder, she had aged substantially and looked more like an old crow. But back in 1728, when Jean-Marie first walked into Louise Roussel's shop to ask about publishing his Opus 2 sonatas, he was smitten with a pretty face which far surpassed that of his wife. Louise Roussel on her part was not necessarily smitten by Jean-Marie's looks, even though he did look pleasant enough. She was more impressed by his obvious multi-faceted talents.

"Oh, a violinist...and a composer?" she asked.

"Well, yes, I'm guilty on both accounts, and maybe a third...I'm also a ballet dancer."

"My, my," she said coyly, "we don't get very many of those walking through the door. Let's see what we can do about getting your grand Opus into print. Number 2, you said?"

Since there are no records of Jean-Marie Leclair being a philanderer during his first marriage, we can say that he was faithful to his older wife. Though it seemed to be an accepted fact that men with status and money often had mistresses. But let's make Jean-Marie Leclair a somewhat nice guy. He was too busy with his work and composing to be distracted by dalliances.

Maybe his original family background gave him firm values from his Maman and Papa, and family life with his brothers and sisters. When Jean-Marie Leclair, at the impressionable age of 19, proposed to Marie-Rose, he was serious about his wedding vows. So, years later when his older wife started ailing after a few months in Paris, it seemed somehow like an extra betrayal, not to stay by her side. He couldn't live with himself if he were unfaithful at that time. Striking up an affair with Louise Roussel at this point, despite the intense attraction he felt for the woman, would be like stabbing Marie-Rose in the back. No, he could not, would not do it.

It is not certain if the first marriage had been generally a happy, though one likes to think so, because there are no records of friction or arguments between them. If one were to interpolate, one could argue that Marie-Rose might have been upset with her husband for being "a rolling stone", and moving from town to town every few years.

The wife might also have had her maternal instinct kick in, when she was still healthy, wanting something more in her life because she was childless. Not having children of her own and being an older woman, she might have asked her husband about adoption. She might have pointed out that Vivaldi might have been more prolific as a composer merely because he devoted his life to teaching orphans, as a service to God, in an all-female orphanage.

"Imagine what joy adopting an orphan or two could bring to our lives," she might have argued, "while we are doing the good work of Our Lord!" But these are speculations about their private lives and their feelings, something we know nothing about. Sadly, the only thing that is for sure, is that the couple had no children. The marriage could have been a happy one. It might have been a sad one. Who knows? Who knows if Leclair's mother's prediction, "I see black," ever came true about the marriage of that couple.

Thus, at the age of 31, we have the first part of Jean-Marie's life ending, wifeless and childless. A clean slate seemed to stretch ahead for the young violinist and composer when he lived in Paris in 1728. At least he played regularly at the "Concert Spirituel". It is a shame that there are so few records up to 1728 during the first 31 years of Jean-Marie Leclair's life. But at least, by this time, he was a published composer!

*****

# Chapter 15

Jean-Marie was required to visit Louise Roussel's engraving shop several times a week over the next two months. The shop was in the rue Saint-Jacques. He got there either by carriage or on a good day by walking with his walking stick as a sign of distinction. The visits were not just to finalize things about his Opus 2, but also to talk about other concertos and trios he had in mind for Louise's publishing house. Therefore, Jean-Marie had a legitimate excuse to get out of the apartment and go down to the shop and "confer with the engraver".

An acquaintance who had his artwork printed by Louise told Jean-Marie that, informally among friends, she was called "le petit moineau", The Little Sparrow.

"Why?" asked Jean-Marie.

"Her movements are so quick and precise, the way she gets things done, it is astonishing," replied the acquaintance. "Besides, everyone notices her pointy little nose which reminds one of a little bird." Jean-Marie made an internal decision never to call her Little Sparrow, certainly not to her face.

It seemed that affectionate friends had given her that moniker years ago, and she accepted it graciously as a compliment to her energy. Not that she couldn't be adorable like a little bird,  but those who knew her in business, knew she could be a bird of prey. Keen eye for profit and the deal; she knew how to talk to people and turn a profit. She was also good at the physical work of her engraving trade. Engraving was a skill highly prized by women in the 18th century. Her father, Claude, would have been proud to see his daughter make the business work at a time when women were supposed to be kept home making babies.

Louise noticed from the beginning that the dedication in the masthead to Opus 2 was to Monsieur Joseph Bonnier. "Oh, the financier?" asked Louise. "Why, yes!" said Jean-Marie. "A friend of mine, a violin pupil and my patron." This opened up a whole line of discussion about whom in Paris they knew who was anybody important. Louise brushed her hand over the manuscript and made a quick sketch for an idea of a masthead. She blushed as a thought popped into her mind. "I wouldn't mind sketching out your masthead," she thought, "and I don't mean this." Jean-Marie noticed, "Why, you're blushing!" She shrugged, "Oh, I always get worked up about work. Leave the masthead, I mean your manuscript, here with me, and we will figure something out by Friday."

Jean-Marie was entranced with the look of her pretty face. She had light blond hair, braided in a long pony-tail at the back, light blue eyes and deep dimples in her cheeks, which appeared like magic whenever she smiled. Jean-Marie found those dimples erotic. Perhaps the only fault he might find with her face was that her nose was pointy, like a little beak, but somehow that could be ignored because of her smooth skin, her full figure, and those dimples which could drive a man crazy.

"Oh, oh," he admitted to himself, when Louise Roussel first approached the counter and his eyes lit upon her smooth face and blue eyes, "here comes trouble."

He and Marie-Rose had lived in a protective bubble all these years. Nothing came from the outside to disturb their busy little world up until now. He had never experienced anything like this instant spark at the counter of the engraver's shop which brought temptation into his life like never before. He had always been able to put up blocks and concentrate on his violin playing and his compositions. But now there was something else. Perhaps it came with success and with the environment around rich people. Up until now, Marie-Rose and he had lived in a little world of their own, and had been reasonably content focusing on their work, i.e. mainly on his work.

His attraction for another woman was only afforded to a man who was physically healthy and had nothing wrong with him. In that respect, he could not identify with the other side, i.e. with his older wife's problems, who was suffering from ill health. Perhaps it was all the moving; perhaps it was simply that she was, after all, 15 years older than her husband. So while she pulled in her horns like a snail, he was bushy and spry like a fox looking for mice. Not that he did anything about it at the moment, because after all, he had a conscience, a responsibility and work to take distractions away. But on occasion, something in the recess of his mind when he put his violin down to rest, something yearned. Health secretly seeks out its own pleasures, and Jean-Marie entertained those thoughts with a belief that it was natural in the order of things, and that, if something happened, then he could not help it.

He tipped his hat to Louise's dimples and smiled when he turned to leave the shop. The bell jingled when he opened the door and left.

The carriage still waited for him on the street. On his way back to the apartment, he did not realize how difficult the next few months would be with his wife, whether he had the loyalty and the stamina to stand by her.

He barely stepped in the door at the apartment, when Marie-Rose complained, "We should have stayed in Turin. It's been hard on me." She took a breath and looked at him sternly, "I've had more hot flashes lately, and the gout has broken out again on my toes. A dancer with gout is finished. I am grateful for the coaching job at the girls' school of dance, but even that is getting too much for me. I'm sorry we ever left Turin and moved to Paris."

He said in frustration, "But Paris is where I need to be to be published and to be noticed."

She said, "I thought you cared about my needs too? Didn't we speak endearments to each other when we were younger, and you said, you promised, that you'd love me even when I'm 64?"

Again he looked at the ceiling and said nothing in response. He wished he did not feel trapped. That he was not here. Not with her. He was only 31 years old!

Jean-Marie wanted to run out into the street and yell. But no, he stayed in the apartment to listen to his wife run on about this and that and the other thing. How did they ever get this way?

Jean-Marie was convinced that Paris was where anybody who was anybody had to be to make his mark. Paris was where you get published so people would notice. Like usual, Jean-Marie listened to his wife droning on, adding to her list of ailments and dissatisfaction for just being in Paris. Why did they ever leave Turin or Lyons for that matter? Jean-Marie was not a happy man, and Marie-Rose had been noticeably looking sicker and sicker over the past two months. The City of Light looked less and less bright.

He looked forward to next Friday when he could confer with his engraver and get out of the apartment. Something positive to talk about, and some positive person to be with.

The door-bell jingled as he walked in. "Come to the back," invited Louise, "we can look at the proofs." They looked fine, the masthead looked fine, the dedication to Monsieur Joseph Bonnier was large enough, and his own name, stood out in an appropriate font, Jean-Marie Leclair, Opus 2, composer, 1728. He apologized to Louise if he did not seem as enthusiastic about the project as last week. He confided that his wife had been going through "the change" lately, hot flashes, and suffering from depression since her gout prevented her from dancing. "I do sympathize," he said to Louise, "how you can't be happy when you no longer do what makes you happy!" He needed a confidante so desperately...which meant not his wife, which over the next few weeks became Louise Roussel, more and more.

"Oh, you poor man," said Louise. "Is there something I can do?" She patted his hand, stroking it lightly, and locked eyes with him. Her smile broke forth with those attractive dimples. "No," he said, "the words of a friend will be enough, at least for now. I know there have been feelings between us, but I have a duty to my wife...you understand?" "Yes," replied Louise, "let us be friends...for now. It would not be good to bring a guilty conscience into an affair with me."

That is how things fared for a few months until Easter approached. By that time, Jean-Marie Leclair got published again. His Opus 2 took Paris by storm and the King's court eventually took notice of the new talent in town.

The meetings on Fridays came and went quickly. Jean-Marie had been practicing all morning in March. By noon, Marie-Rose told him she needed a break from his playing. He said he would go out to check on the progress at the engraver's on the layout of some more pages. They ate in silence and he walked out the door to hail a carriage. When he got to the shop, he was glad to see Louise. The day had been overcast and it looked like it would rain later on during the day. "Rainy days always get me down," he thought. It rained a lot in Paris. During March, with the onset of spring and Easter weekend, clouds clung to the Paris skies and the city seemed in store for rain and even more rain, that year in 1728.

*****

# Chapter 16

The move to Paris should have been one of joy and renewal for the Leclairs, a hopeful start for success. He was engaged at the "Concert Spirituel", one of the first public concert series, in the City of Light. His acclaim as an exceptional violinist was spreading throughout the city. The precision and refinement of his playing won him an enthusiastic following. He got what he wanted. Yet, his wife of 12 years was sick, too sick to share his joy, too sick to dance, and too sick to be a wife.

"You will leave me?" she asked.

"No, my dear, that is your sickness talking. I will not leave you."

M. Bonnier had seen to the medical expenses for Jean-Marie's wife. He paid for the doctor and for the medications. Leclair was ever so grateful to his benefactor. When Jean-Marie came home, either from his performance at the "Concert Spirituel" or from a practice there, he made his wife drink chamomile tea. Then he would rub eucalyptus oil on her back and on her chest. He was careful not to get any of the ointment on her nipples because that would sting.

"Do you remember when," he'd say, "when we did this for pleasure? We talked about love then and not plumbing." He chuckled; she didn't think it was funny. Sometimes he put some of the pungent oil into boiling water and made her hover over the basin with a towel to clear her breathing. But the situation was more serious, he realized, that it was not a mere flu or cold, or in her breathing. Once her ritual with the towel over the basin was done, he would carefully open the door and carefully toss the water out the door onto the street. This was a nightly ritual in the month of March. With his ministrations to her, he would always say, "Do you remember when..." Marie-Rose was not getting any better. The doctor prescribed making tea at night with Root of Valerian, adding a spoonful of honey with it, to help her sleep.

Jean-Marie was subdued and noticeably taciturn during his review of the new engravings in the print shop. He shied away from eye contact with Louise. She sensed his mood and accommodated him by going through the review that Friday in professional silence. He gave his nod of approval and said to her, "My wife is very ill. I will see you next Friday." The doorbell jingled as he went out.

During Holy Week, he had to play at the "Concert Spirituel" several times. It gave him some reprieve from the apartment. He fed his wife broth. They ate quietly, and then she said, "You will probably find another. I am sorry that I cannot share your success or your future with you." She hesitated, "But in the meantime, I want you to be faithful. If you do not come home tonight, things will never be the same again between us. Please, do not hurt me." Jean-Marie nodded. He guided her to bed. She rested her head on his shoulder. Her thoughts before she dropped off to sleep were, "When your own health and talent are taken away little by little, you get so dependent on others, too dependent. I do not know what I would do if he did not come home back to the apartment?"

Once she fell asleep, he kissed her on the forehead lightly. She had a fever, but he needed to escape the enclosure of the apartment. He put on his cape and hat, and quietly closed the apartment door. It began drizzling outside. He walked resolutely into the rain, heading for the engraver's shop. Jean-Marie sought refuge in the air, the rain and the long walk.

By the time he reached Louise's shop, the drizzle had become a downpour. He sought shelter under the overhang of an establishment across the street from Louise's shop, tightened his hat, and pulled up his collar. As the raindrops fell in rhythm, drip, drip, drip, off the overhang above him, he thought to himself, "Raindrops are so sad. They are like the sad beating of my heart. Perhaps someday, somebody will write a melody about raindrops.

But it will have to be the tap, tap, tap of piano keys to imitate the drip, drip, drip of those sad, wet raindrops dropping down in rhythm from the eaves. My violin does not have the nature to imitate raindrops like the piano does. Onomatopoeia, I think they call it, or the imitation of sounds in nature."

"Yes," thought Leclair sadly, "the steady tap, tap, tap of the piano keys. It will have to be someone else, a pianist, maybe in another time to capture the sadness I feel tonight under the wet, wet rain."

He stared at the light in the shop. Louise must be in. The attraction to find consolation in her face, a word of sympathy in her voice, a look in her eyes, to see her lovely dimples spring to life in her cheeks, was like a magnet. He resisted. He held himself back; he could not ring. He walked ponderously back to his wife in the pouring rain. Somehow he did not notice that when he left his little shelter, the sign above the overhang read, "Maison Funéraire". By the time he got back to the apartment, his wife lay peacefully dead. He cried with her hand in his. "In a way," he thought, "it was a good thing we did not have children."

Thus, sadly, in 1728, in Paris, the week before Easter, his wife of 12 years passed away. It was a small funeral, carried out quickly and sadly. Again it was a rainy day, with overcast clouds which perhaps mirrored how the spirit of Marie-Rose must have felt somewhere up in the sky, as it made its way into Heaven. Jean-Marie took the carriage home, sipped a glass of wine in the empty apartment to relax, and then made a sudden decision. It came like a bolt of lighting.

"The hell with it," he thought. He hailed another carriage, and instructed the driver to go to Mme Roussel's engraving shop. She noticed him coming and opened the door for him. "I saw you coming," she said, all smiles and dimples. He shook off his wet cape and hung it on the coat-rack. "You are lucky," she said, "I am alone. I had no work for my assistant today". She led him to the back room. "A glass of wine? And let's get you warm".

# Chapter 17

Jean-Marie was not a grieving bachelor after Marie-Rose died in 1728. Men in those days, maybe in any day, had affairs. Women apparently had to put up with that, and perhaps some of them had affairs too. It was accepted and a "modus vivendi" in some cultures. The only thing which could be said about Jean-Marie was that he held out until his wife passed away before he did anything about his desire for Louise.

Celibate was not a word Jean-Marie was familiar with after the age of 18. At least, he had kept his wedding vow to Marie-Rose until that Easter weekend. He knew the words loyalty and help while she was sick. No, he did not want to stab her in the back in a clandestine affair with Louise, while his wife was still alive. That kind of cad, he was not! And yet, if only his private thoughts could be read, and if one could look behind the scenes of his secret life, one could weave quite a story for the coffeehouses and tabloids of 18th century France!

Leclair was all of 31 years old at the time, and being a ballet dancer, he was quite fit, and he felt a need for a lover, a second wife perhaps, or both.

Louise shared a glass of wine with Jean-Marie in the back room as they held hands by the fire. He warmed up, and she comforted him in a way she always had wanted to. She put her hand on his thigh. They embraced. They agreed that for now, "this friendship with benefits", as they called it, would have to do. Some of the consideration was, of course, what society would think so soon after his wife's death. Public appearance was important. The other consideration was that each brought business and money into the relationship. Louise liked her independence. She had inherited the engraving business from her father, did quite well at it, and was proud to make it her own.

Jean-Marie and Louise Roussel were happy with their understanding. They "visited" each weekend, during the off hours, at the engraving studio. Meanwhile, Jean-Marie's music spread in popularity in the courts of the rich and famous.

Jean-Marie settled down to a new routine and in a strange way grew content now that Marie-Rose was no longer in his life. Jean-Marie got a dog, a little Shih Tzu puppy. At first, he was in a quandary as to what to name him. Lully. Rameau? Lully was dead so he might not mind. Rameau was still alive and that could be an insult. "Ah," Jean-Marie had an idea, "I will name the little scoundrel 'Monteverdi'."

"It will be a long name for a short little dog. How fitting!"

The dog seemed to be somewhat musical. He would sit and remain silent and sway when Jean-Marie practiced his sonatas in the room. "Yes, he has music in him," thought Jean-Marie. "This is a perfect match made in Heaven." A friend suggested that the dog's swaying was merely caused by the eyes of the dog following Jean-Marie's bow arm. But Jean-Marie preferred to think otherwise. "No, no, Monteverdi has the music in him!"

"Next you'll say he has perfect pitch too," said his friend.

"Why? Yes, he does!" asserted Jean-Marie.

"Never mind. I won't ask," said his friend.

That friend, of course, was Jean-Pierre Guignon. Both he and Jean-Marie had been advanced students of the great virtuoso and composer, Giovanni Battista Somis, when both of them lived in Turin. Somis still has a street named after him in Turin, "Via Giovanni Somis". The provenance, as it were, went back to Arcangelo Corelli, because Somis was a pupil of that great Italian master.

When Jean-Marie moved back to Paris he looked Guignon up. They had never really been close friends, but Jean-Marie made it a point of courtesy to drop in on him, and talk "old times" about their common mentor in the violin. So they visited and occasionally talked gossip at Jean-Marie's apartment once the wife died. That is when Jean-Marie introduced Monteverdi, his dog whom he was convinced had exceptional musical talents "beyond your average canine".

In the meantime, the dog, loosely called "Monte", on occasion, was getting so attached to Jean-Marie that he sat obediently at his feet while the master played or composed. "Monte" would only interrupt with a growl or give one bark for the signal that it was time for a walk, or if he needed to be fed, which the master would sometimes forget, if he was entranced in the middle of a musical phrase which needed putting down on paper.

"So, let's go out for your walk!" said Jean-Marie. The dog immediately perked up, seeming to understand the word, "Promenade." He looked upon his master with gleaming and adoring eyes. If the day was on a weekend, Jean-Marie ventured to walk the dog all the way to the engraving studio for a little afternoon delight.

In those days, carrying along a doggy-"do-do" bag was unheard of in France. Not until some 260 years later when France tried to clean up its act to make a clean impression internationally when Barcelona, Spain, a next-door neighbour, hosted the XXV Olympiad in 1992.

But in the old days, right up to the 20th century, dogs ran free, and when they had to go, they simply had to go, either on a bush, a tree, a lamppost, and sometimes in the middle of the street! When you are dealing with cobble stones, then the sticky stuff could get caught in all the nooks and crannies, and remain there for days until it dried up and or was washed away by a good rain.

A person always had to walk with an alertness underfoot in Paris, otherwise come home with doggy evidence stuck to one's shoes, and the chore of scraping things off with a stick before going indoors. With France's liberated attitude toward dogs, the country earned an international reputation among other nations as being a dirty country, especially on its streets. If you wanted to visit France, you had to watch out where you tread, and carry a big stick, not exactly in the meaning that Theodore Roosevelt intended!

Lampposts were Monteverdi's favourite repository or depository, whichever you prefer. Jean-Marie would look at the sky as if for musical inspiration while the dog went. He was glad that it was too early for the lamplighter to do his evening rounds, so the lamplighter would not notice what Monteverdi was doing.

Arguments could fly, if the lamplighter saw his beloved lamppost soiled upon and disrespected. And that occasionally happened too, whenever Jean-Marie took Monteverdi out for a brief nightly walk. Jean-Marie did not like a nightly encounter with the lamplighter. The lamplighter did not understand that a dog had to do his nightly rounds too! "If the man was that picky," thought Jean-Marie, "let him clean it up." Otherwise Parisians relied on a good downpour of rain and the passage of time to solve the problem.

Both the dog and the composer loved their regular routines. The dog felt good and the master got inspired.

Jean-Marie and Louise did not always transact their business in a slam-bam fashion. They shared feelings and often talked. He explained to her one time, "When I see a blank manuscript page, I want to fill it." He said, he experienced the same thing when he read the lyrics of a poem to himself. They would go through his head like a song, like music straight from God.

Occasionally, he thought about what he would do when he got older, having lived with an older wife for years. "I'd probably keep on doing the same thing," he confessed. "I will never retire. I'm too busy for that." He was happy that his old friend in Turin, Somis, had advised him years ago to give up dancing and to concentrate his talent on playing the violin and on composing music.

"The music is in me," he said to Louise during a private moment, "I do realize that I am blessed." Then he quipped light-heartedly, "Sure beats ditch-digging!" He added more seriously, "No, there will never be a day for me when the music will stop. I would rather die." Jean-Marie said this without thinking, that indeed the music would stop when he died. He merely meant that music was everything to him. He was in the same train of thought as Jean-Phillipe Rameau, his competitor and a 14 years his senior, who believed that music was everywhere in the air. We are the receptors and depending upon how fine-tuned our minds are we can receive the music of the spheres.

Jean-Marie also believed like Rameau that God was in everything and everywhere, not like some invisible white bearded Father in the clouds interceding on behalf of his creation. Deism was a belief that once God created creation, he did not interfere, which appealed to Jean-Marie, Rameau and also Voltaire's sense of Reason. Many intellectuals of the 18th century thought that this type of God made more sense than the God of intercession preached by the Catholic Church. One could argue that this line of thinking, of a non-interfering God, appealed more to intellectuals because they were naturally more cynical.

After Marie-Rose died, Jean-Marie promised himself he would visit Turin once a year, and renew his friendship there with Giovanni Battista Somis. His former mentor was also older than he was, like Rameau, but only 11 years older. Jean-Marie thought of him like an older brother, valuing his advice. After Jean-Marie struck up his arrangement with Louise Roussel, Somis said to him, "You have to watch out for her. She is ambitious, she has a career, and she knows her mind. If the woman is too aggressive, she is a woman of experience, not only in business but also in sexual matters." Somis was cautioning his former pupil about his sleeping partners, "now that you are a free man again".

"Gonorrhoea and syphilis were a common side effect of a libertine lifestyle and a hazard among artists," he warned.

"Zealous love-making with too many people can make you go blind," said Somis, "and I'm not kidding." Jean-Marie breathed a sigh of relief because so far, so good, he had had no symptoms of burning while urinating. "Louise Roussel," he said, "isn't that kind of girl." So, when Jean-Marie went back to Paris, he resumed his walks with his dog and a confident friendship with Louise, "with benefits".

*****

# Chapter 18

Louise Roussel and Jean-Marie did not have a respectable relationship, certainly not in respectable society, and certainly not in the eyes of the Catholic Church. It was a clandestine affair, as all such affairs needed to be in proper society, for having a mistress or a lover had its own code of ethics, and as long as it was not talked about, it could claim a private sense of decorum of its own. Such things among polite society could be tacitly tolerated, as long as everybody pretended it was secret. Now, that two and a half years had passed by since the death of his first wife, Jean-Marie and Louise had the social sanction to bring their relationship out into the open, since so much time had passed by, provided of course, they had the blessing of holy matrimony.

There was no rush, not even a thought, at first, about marrying each other. Their friendship "with benefits" was convenient, and assured their independence because they each brought money into the union. Jean-Marie quite enjoyed his long walks with his little dog, Monteverdi, on Saturday afternoons when the "Closed" sign was on the outside door of the engraving shop. These walks were regular like clockwork. Monteverdi was given a bone to chew outside the back room of the shop, and remained quiet knowing his master was on the other side of the door, moaning and groaning or whatever he was doing. Sex was not all there was to the affair; however, they often talked like friends, like lovers do.

"Why didn't you make a move on me earlier?" Louise asked one afternoon.

Louise spoke as a woman of her time, as a woman raised in the 18$^{th}$ century. She had always seen men as the aggressors. She wasn't shy herself about what she wanted, but she wanted to know why he didn't make a move. "I was waiting for you. After all, it's always been that way, hasn't it?"

"I suppose," said Jean-Marie stroking her hair while she lay on his shoulder. "But I could not be unfaithful to my sick wife at the time. It would have been like stabbing her in the back, secretly sneaking around when she was sick, when she was dying. I simply could not live with myself." Louise kissed him on the forehead.

"Have we found a magical island now?" she asked him.

"I don't think so. There are magical islands when we make money, when there are no wars, when we are healthy and strong, when we have new lovers...but no, there are no permanent magical islands. If there are, then I think, they are surrounded by the fires of hell, and we are lucky when those fires die down a bit even for a little time."

"That is cynical, Jean-Marie," she poked him.

"You want the truth or a wished-for dream?" he asked. "I do understand that we all have a need to escape the drudgery and pain of life...there is so much of it out there."

"So sad," she said, "like the dark clouds I feel gathering around Paris this late afternoon. Perhaps you want to stay the night?" Her actual living quarters were upstairs above the engraving shop.

"It's an agreeable idea," he conceded, snuggling closer. The dog snuffled outside the door. Jean-Marie opened the door and threw him another treat. He was glad he brought plenty of treats this afternoon. Monteverdi could bark so loudly out of tune when he was unhappy.

There was also something else that the couple was equipped with, in plenty of supply. Condoms. It was agreed that Jean-Marie would bring his own, and he had plenty extra for tonight, in fact plenty extra for every visit.

Condoms in the 18$^{th}$ century were available in a variety of qualities and sizes. They were either linen treated with spermicidal chemicals or "skin", made of bladder or intestine softened by treatment with sulphur and lye. France was a rather open society about sex and what goes on in people's lives. So condoms were sold at pubs, barbershops, chemist shops, open-air markets, and at the theatre throughout Europe and Russia. Casanova in the 18th century was very innovative for his time period by using "assurance caps" to prevent impregnating his lovers. Jean-Marie was no Casanova, but he knew how to use a condom.

As double insurance, Louise kept diaphragms and spermicidal douches by her bedside upstairs with a ready supply of creams, gels, film, foams and suppositories. She knew how to use them, and kept a few supplies downstairs in the cupboard of the back room, in case of spontaneous love-making.

Historically, birth control was always the woman's responsibility, not a fair fact, but it was so. In their affair, Jean-Marie bore some of the responsibility by bringing condoms for his afternoon's pleasure. The least he could do.

The problem with sex is, especially if you talk, share feelings and stay the night, is that you become bonded. That means you identify in things beyond sex, and one can call that love.

That bonding was occurring between Jean-Marie and Louise over the two and a half years in which they had their secret affair. One New Year Eve went by 1729 and then another 1730.

New Year in France was celebrated more than Christmas in the 18th century. While the public celebrated the New Year with food and drink and family, Jean-Marie and Louise spent December 31, known as "la Saint Sylvestre", hunkered down in quiet seclusion within the confines of the upstairs rooms of the engraving shop. Louise missed not celebrating the feast with the rest of her larger family.

"You know," she confided during New Year's Eve of 1730, over a glass of wine, "it would be great to have other family come over to the shop next Saint Sylvestre and celebrate with us openly." This was as clear a hint about marriage she could muster for her lover of two years. Jean-Marie stared at her, "Let me think about it." He kissed her deeply, drank some wine, and said, "Let's have more cake before the midnight hour strikes at Notre Dame." The impressive Emmanuel bell that dates from the 1600s rung out its ringing across Paris as the couple toasted good fortune to each other for the following year January 1, 1730. "Perhaps family would come over next year," thought Louise, "with all her heart, and I can bring Jean-Marie out in the open. Maybe he will play the fiddle for us to bring in another year then."

The wedding took place on September 8, 1730. Jean-Marie Leclair was 33 years old. It was now two and a half years after the death of Jean-Marie's first wife. Louise and Jean-Marie felt they had waited long enough. The match seemed to be made more in heaven than with his older first wife, after all Louise was three years younger than Jean-Marie, and she had blue eyes, a pretty face and dimples which could light up a room.

New Year 1731 went as expected. It was indeed the best New Year that either one of them had ever celebrated. The larger family came over to the shop. Everyone felt in a festive mood, and brought food and drink. They patted Jean-Marie on the shoulder as they entered; embraced him and kissed him on both cheeks in the traditional French greeting. They brought their food and drink to the table already laid out with plates and cutlery. He was one of the family.

They took their plates and made a beeline for the breads, cheeses, meats, paté, oysters, and foie gras. They drank wine and champagne, and told jokes, some of them rife and ribald. Soon Uncle Gaston, the first to finish his multi-course menu, hors-d'oeuvre, soup and entrée, ignored the fish and sorbet and eyed the desserts with a child's delight: pot de crème, crêpes, opera cake, custard tart, poire belle hélène, and the box of cherry chocolates. As the evening went on with the initial food and drink, they urged Jean-Marie to play something. He joked that he would not play the violin that evening, but the fiddle, treating his new family to traditional French folk tunes. Uncle Gaston teased Jean-

Marie that he would specifically save a piece of "opera cake" for the august violinist in the group. "I will hold you to that," joked Jean-Marie, patting Uncle Gaston's ample tummy.

At midnight, the bells in the towers of Notre Dame rung out that Saint Sylvestre. New Year had arrived, 1731! Louise was so happy. Jean-Marie was red cheeked and smiling broadly from all the drinking and playing he did. They were not only celebrating a New Year but a new life together. Jean-Marie was 34, and Louise was 31.

*****

# Chapter 19

The marriage, and Jean-Marie's career, seemed to go splendidly for at least 3 years, at most 5 years. You can safely say several years of happiness. Louise had her steady job printing her husband's compositions and those of other musicians, plus there were the engravings and prints of various artworks. Jean-Marie had his pension from his patron, the financier, M. Bonnier de la Mosson, as well as the remuneration he received from his performances in the city's concert series. The couple continued to enjoy life, each other and success. But like the Parisian weather, there was always a cloud in the silver lining.

First, a spark of good fortune! In 1733, he was named "ordinaire de la musique" by Louis XV, quite an honour from the King's orchestra. Then, in 1734 he was appointed "Premier Symphoniste du Roy", not a bad title for the son of a haberdasher. That meant he was now concert master of the orchestra.

Well, the honour had to be recognized, especially when you get such a title from King Louis XV. In gratitude, Jean-Marie Leclair dedicated his set of sonatas to the monarch [one source says Third Book set, another source says Opus 5 set]. Whatever you call it, the Third Book was a milestone for violin virtuosi of all levels, perhaps similar to Paganini's Capriccios. Sere de Rieux made a note about the importance of the Third Book : "Leclair is the first composer who, imitating nothing, has created something fine and new, something that is distinctively his own."

King Louis XV called his first violinist into court one day and presented him with a gold plated pocket watch which had the King's image and coat of arms engraved on the inside. Jean-Marie bowed with delight and proudly retreated from the King's presence. "I shall keep this forever," he thought.

This was all fine, if Jean-Marie Leclair were the only rooster in the hen house, but an old acquaintance of his soon flexed his musical muscles, Jean-Pierre Guignon, who had his eye on the top spot. Threateningly, the man had talent! He, like Jean-Marie, had been a personal violin pupil of the great Giovanni Battista Somis back in Turin in the old days.

Both Jean-Marie Leclair and Jean-Pierre Guignon competed for public acclaim and notice from the King. They both performed in the King's orchestra, as well as the "Concert Spirituel", the city's concert series.

Similar to the earlier musical jousting between Locatelli and Jean-Marie, which was in fun, Jean-Marie and Guignon squared off, but in earnest, during the concert series to show who was the best violinist! M. Marc Pincherie was an eye-witness, reporting that there was no clear victory. "Their performing styles differed profoundly, Leclair's being more precise, more technically delicate, more cerebral, while Guigon's was more colourful, more fanciful." It should be noted here that references in various sources about Guignon's name vary in spelling, sometimes found as, Guigon. Perhaps the variation is due to his original Italian name being Frenchified. Guignon did become a French citizen, however.

Historical footnotes aside, the two couldn't stand each other. Louise, at home, noticed that her husband was growing more moody and withdrawn by 1736. This musical animosity had also been brought to the attention of the King.

An aide, who knows all and hears all, told Louis XV that certain sparks were flying between the two violinists both in the Chapelle and in the Chambre du Roi. The King agreed that perhaps the competition could be settled with a compromise, so that the two men could take turns being concert master.

"Your Highness," said the aide, "how can two grown men be so childish?"

"Well," said the King, "you should see some of my elder statesmen!"

"Then, who shall take the first turn as first violin?"

"How about a toss of the coin?" suggested the King.

"Your Majesty, if you permit, I have an old souvenir, a Louis d'or, from the old days..." said the aide.

"No, no, you keep your souvenir," commanded the King, "let us use my own coin, minted just last year, a silver Écu of myself. You call it, heads or tails. Heads is for Leclair going first for first." His Royal Majesty chuckled at his little quip.

"Heads," said the aide, "your image is so imposing whenever it comes up."

The King flipped the coin, caught it and put it on the back of his other hand. It was heads indeed, with the regal head of His Majesty staring out into destiny. "Jean-Marie will be first violin this month! So be it!"

"But," asked the aide, "is there a permanent solution? To whom should the first violin honour go then?"

The King said, "To the strongest." He added, "Let them play it out to the end...and I do not mean the music!" The King chuckled and smiled with amusement, enjoying the personal drama among his staff. He enjoyed toying with them.

The other members of the orchestra did not enjoy the tension between the two men, and some of them did not know which one of them to follow when they were playing. The music suffered. Perhaps the King did not care. His enjoyment was the personal drama and the court gossip. But all that did not matter, because Jean-Marie Leclair had had enough by 1736.

When Guignon's turn came the next month to be concert master, Jean-Marie was damned if he was going to take lead instruction from this second fiddle. He packed up his violin, walked out of the rehearsal and resigned from the King's service. He never performed in the public concert series again at the "Concert Spirituel". His pupils, however, continued to play there and perhaps were a living legacy there to the teaching skills of their volatile violin teacher. According to one source, their names were Pierre Gavinies and L'Abbe le Fils.

Jean-Marie was sending out feelers for work outside of France. His home life was also in shambles, falling apart not only because of friction at work, but because of rising personal matters involving his wife, Louise.

As to the man's virtuosic abilities, historians are inclined to compare him with Bach, or certainly musicians above Guignon's caliber. Perhaps he wasn't as great a giant as Bach, but nevertheless the man was great. He needed and wanted respect for his talent. Musicians world-wide recognize him for his musical sophistication, his knowledge of harmonies and ochestral writing.

Jean-Marie Leclair is played world-wide in modern times by people no less than, Itzhak Perlman and Pinchas Zukerman accompanying the piano in a Trio by Jean-Marie Leclair, Sonata No. 5, or virtuoso Henryk Szeryng playing the Leclair violin Sonata in D major, Opus 3 No. 3. Where is Jean-Pierre Guignon in all this? He remained a musical glimmer in history, whereas Jean-Marie Leclair became a star.

Francois Filiatrault, went so far as to say, "We are tempted to call him, for the technical power of his skills, the French Bach."

*****

# Chapter 20

The private lives of Louise Roussel and Jean-Marie Leclair are difficult to pin down in terms of what exactly happened there and when. We know that by 1734, Jean-Marie was living on the Rue Saint Benoit, near the Abaie Saint Germain. That obviously meant he had moved out of the house and gotten himself a new location away from his wife's engraving shop.

It's always sad when a loving relationship disintegrates, sometimes the fault of circumstances, clashing personalities, strains about career and money, and sometimes nobody's fault, where you just fall out of love. Maybe with them it was all of the above, ending with falling out of love, but maybe never not quite!

The first sign of bad things to come came with the dog's death. Shortly after Jean-Marie was named "ordinaire de la musique" by the King in 1733, Louise forgot to close the door to the shop and inadvertently let the dog out. Monteverdi scampered out into the street at the exact moment that a speeding carriage passed by hitting the poor little dog with a wheel crushing its poor little chest. Monteverdi gave out one yelp and then expired. Jean-Marie was angry with his wife. They found a little piece of earth in the back yard by a tree to bury their musical hound in. No matter how many times she apologized for her carelessness, Jean-Marie turned away from her and sulked.

Things improved, however, when Jean-Marie was made "Premier Symphoniste du Roy" the following year in 1734. But after that lush appointment, tensions at work in the orchestra mounted. Guignon made suggestions about the choices of music and even criticized Leclair's dynamics.

Jean-Marie exhibited irritable moods during rehearsal times and he took those feelings home to his wife. He sulked and occasionally said snippy things. They just came out; he didn't mean them. She retreated to her work in the back of the shop. On his part, he had found a private studio somewhere in Paris where he could saw away at his fiddle to work off his frustrations.

It's not exactly clear when little Louise was conceived or finally born, but sometime during this difficult period, Louise Roussel took on the big-bellied look of pregnancy. Jean-Marie was furious. He was not in the mood to be a father. "I thought we agreed that our careers would come first. That our careers were the only thing. You had all your contraceptives to prevent a pregnancy. What went wrong? Or was this deliberate?" This crushed Louise.

Jean-Marie relented somewhat, and in a spirit of compromise said, "Fine, if it's a boy, it will be fine." He was hoping that a son would mean a legacy where he could teach the boy all he knew about the violin. "But," he threatened, "if it's a girl, I'm divorcing you." They stopped sleeping together from that point forward, and he moved out of the house into his own little apartment. "Been there, done that," he thought to himself, sipping a glass of wine late at night. This time he had no little Monteverdi to console him through his lonely nights. Occasionally he picked up a lady of the night if he had the urge to be with somebody. He remembered to use his condom or "assurance cap". Those were used primarily, not for contraception, but to prevent catching a sexually transmitted disease.

When the baby came, it was a girl. Louise named her, Louise. She too became an engraver like her mother. She had no inclination towards music, and if she did, it was not encouraged by the mother. Louise fashioned the little girl into a miniature of herself. When she grew up, she married a painter. Jean-Marie had nothing to do with the girl.

And so, Jean-Marie opened the page to a different chapter in his life. He closed the book on his life with Louise. It was him and his violin against the world.

By 1737, Jean-Marie was 40 years old, and Louise was 37. The Little Sparrow was still energetic, quick in her movements, and still looked pretty with those blue eyes and dimples, despite some facial lines. Jean-Marie was getting a furrow in the forehead and a little paunch around the tummy.

Now, that the reality faced him, Jean-Leclair dragged his feet about a divorce. In fact, it didn't happen until 1758, in another 21 years!

It is difficult to say why they let this action slide so long, either out of apathy, no respect for government documentations, maybe a little lifeline, holding on to someone you once loved? It took 21 long years, and by that time, Jean-Marie was 61 years old and Louise was 58 when they finally divorced. Both of them were white haired, walked with a stoop, and facially, they were getting wrinkled.

Although they drifted apart, mostly because of circumstances and understandable tensions at work, they were never really spiteful towards each other during all this mess, after Monteverdi died and even while that battle was going on with that insufferable Guignon. They certainly were not enemies. Even after Jean-Marie moved out, they found ways of working together because they were still tied by business interests and they somehow respected the affectionate history they had together at one time.

Louise Roussel published and printed Jean-Marie's compositions from Opus 2 onward. There were a total of 92 works published through to Leclair's Opus 15. Many for violin as well as several theatrical productions, including one opera. Strangely enough, despite their personal clashes after Monteverdi died, Louise and Jean-Marie reached a civilized agreement where her business would still publish all his works, even after their separation.

But perhaps the slowly festering problem lay in the fact that both of them were such high-strung people, stuck in and married to very demanding careers. There was no room for children, at least not on his side. How ironic, he coming from a family of 7 siblings, although one source says 6 siblings.

\*\*\*\*\*

# Chapter 21

As early as 1734, Jean-Marie was sending out letters of introduction to various courts and heads of state throughout Europe, not being happy with his working environment at the Chapelle and in the Chambre du Roi, especially with Guignon there. Haydn apparently made a remark, something to the effect, where Mozart is, there Haydn cannot be. But that was praise from a friend, nothing like what Leclair and Guignon experienced when they were occupying the same space together.

It was also strange how the death of Monteverdi, his little dog, poisoned Leclair's home life. He just wouldn't let it go, blaming his wife.

So letters went out to various nobility and to fellow musicians alike throughout Europe, as early as 1734, letting it be known that Jean-Marie Leclair was looking for work outside of France. It's always a clever idea to send out "résumés" and letters of introductions, while still employed at home, especially under unfavourable conditions.

By 1737, Jean-Marie Leclair received an envelope with the royal seal of the Princess of Orange on it, from Leeuwarden. He would receive a warm welcome there.

He started packing: a huge trunk with clothes and all his worldly possessions. He would carry his precious violin in his arms. He had a comforter for his knees to rest his violin upon. He would be leaving on the 5:00 a.m. stagecoach which would head out of the City of Light, facing a 10 day rough ride ahead, first into northern France, then further north yet through Belgium and finally, if no wheel broke on the coach or a horse died, onto the Netherlands and Leeuwarden.

The coach would be stopping overnight at various inns. He could sight-see by sliding back the shutters in the windows of the coach, but then he would have to cover his mouth with his handkerchief because of the dust or wear a bandana.

Jean-Leclair was 40 years old and still robust enough to make such a journey, unlike Mozart's mother who some four decades later was so stressed out by travel and a strange city, she got sick and died at the age of 37. That strange city was Paris. Mozart knew little French. Leclair was fortunate enough to be a fluently multi-lingual, and not so coddled by his parents in his formative years. In that respect, Leclair was a survivor and looked forward to the adventure of going to the Netherlands, all 540 kilometers to get there, better than a week-long trip, maybe 10 or 11 days. Unlike the Mozarts who travelled as a family, Leclair travelled as a single man, was still robust and also had money.

The stops were roughly evenly spaced, staying over at local inns for food and drink, and a good night's rest. The coach averaged about 50 kilometres per day, before they stopped at an inn for nourishment and sleep. The only cities of any note were Arras, on the second day, Lille, the last stop in northern France on the third day, then some unknown inn in some unknown town on the fourth day, then on to Ghent the fifth day, Antwerp on the sixth, some unknown inn and town on the seventh day [probably St. Annbosch], avoid the side trip to Rotterdam and The Hague, stop in Utrecht on the eight or ninth day, avoid the side trip to Amsterdam, stay in an unknown inn and unknown town on the ninth or tenth day, and finally kick the dust off the coach at Leeuwarden either on the tenth or eleventh day.

The schedule in 1737 was not rigid, depending upon rest for the horses and passengers, also the road conditions, weather and mechanical problems like broken wheels.

Leclair looked forward to Arras on the second day, because the city was known for its architecture and its history. It was once part of the Spanish Netherlands. He looked forward to tasting its wine.

Lille was nothing to speak of, but it was the most northern town before the coach got to Belgium. When they got to the border, Leclair enjoyed the look of the peaceful countryside. Belgium was known for its laid-back culture and its peace.

Heinrich Heine, the 19th century German poet and philosopher, reflected upon the nature of Belgium. He is reported to have said, "When the world ends, I will go to Belgium. There everything happens 50 years later." He also said with keen insight, "Where they burn books, they will, in the end, burn human beings too." He didn't know he was talking about his own country, Germany. But then Heinrich Heine was a German Jew and a visionary.

Jean-Marie Leclair did not know any of these things, either Heinrich Heine's sayings or the Weltschmerz of the Romantic poets. He merely looked out the window of his carriage when they got to Belgium and dreamed.

They should reach Ghent on the fifth day, the city known for its luxury cloths, and Leclair hoped great wine. Antwerp was on the itinerary for the sixth day, the city of finance and the diamond trade. Surely, there had to be good wine there! The seventh day meant another unknown inn in another unknown town.

The coach would bring Leclair to Utrecht and finally the Netherlands. Utrecht meant architecture again, stretching back to the High Middle Ages. The Treaty of Utrecht brought an end to the War of the Spanish Succession in 1713 between England and France. France was driven out of the Spanish Netherlands by this treaty, not a happy deal for King Louis XIV, the Sun King. Surely the town too had good wine!

The coach avoided Amsterdam. Leclair did not care for the art and architecture there. They drove on for the ninth and tenth days, stopping overnight at little towns. The food was good, as was the wine, and the bed was passable, without bugs. On the eleventh day, the coach drove into Leeuwarden, close to the northern coast of Holland.

What an adventure! A friend told Leclair, "As long as you keep your sphincter tight, you should be doing fine on the trip." They laughed at that. Leclair asked, "Is it true if you ain't Dutch, you ain't much?" There must have been some jocular equivalent to that saying in French at the time, pointing out the attitude of superiority one nation or race seemed to have over others. That was human nature!

Territorial identities, even within a country, were strong in the 18th century. Wars were fought on that basis. Leeuwarden was also known as Stadsfries, or the capital of Friesland within the Netherlands. It was also Protestant, welcoming Jean-Marie Leclair, a non-practicing Catholic from a Roman Catholic France. Even though Leclair was a Deist, he had no place in his life for religion, period! His religion was his violin.

Nothing is said about the origin of his violin, so it might as well have been a Stradivarius. He won it in Turin when his mentor Somis set up a violin playing competition at the Turin Opera. The two physical possessions which Leclair valued the most were, first his violin, and secondly, his gold pocket watch from King Louis XV. He kept his gold pocket watch safely tucked away in his big trunk for the trip, thinking that was safer than in his vest pocket if a road agent stopped the coach.

He told a friend once, "I wish I could wave a wand and turn all guns into violins. They would make a better sound than the gunpowder that takes a life."

Jean-Marie Leclair did not know it, but he soon found out that the Princess of Orange had problems of her own. He wondered if he had walked from one hornet's nest in Paris into another hornet's nest in Leeuwarden. Maybe all royal courts were the same?

His welcome was indeed warm. The Princess was not available at the moment, but her aide ushered Leclair in to have food and drink. He even offered Leclair an anteroom in which he could practice his violin before he entertained the Princess with his talent. Leclair had a slice of baguette with cheese and meat, a bit of wine, and then retired to the anteroom with his violin to warm up his playing. Even in the little room, the sound of his arpeggios and then his launch into one of his own concerti echoed out into the hallway. A servant passed by, mesmerized, and slipped the door of the anteroom slightly ajar.

"Sir," he asked, "you are playing without any music in front of you. Do you not read notes?"
Leclair chuckled and responded in perfect Dutch, "Read notes? No, not enough to hurt my music any." The servant soon learned that the very opposite was true. Jean-Marie Leclair did more than read notes. He could write them on paper, and he could make them up in his head wherever he would go.

He was pleased when he was introduced at court to her Royal Highness, the Princess of Orange. She was intelligent and loved music. She spoke German, French and English, as did Leclair. She was also adept at singing and the harpsichord. In fact, her teacher had been none other than Georg Friedrich Handel. Handel disdained teaching, and thought it was a mundane chore, but he said that he would make one exception, and that was for Anne, "the flower of princesses." The Princess of Orange remained a lifelong supporter of Handel's.

It was ironic that Anne and King Louis XV of France at one point had been considered potential marriage partners, but the idea was soon discarded when the French nobility insisted that Anne convert to Catholicism. Instead, she married William IV, Prince of Orange, who had a spinal deformity. She was afraid that she would remain a spinster for the rest of her life, especially since smallpox had ruined her looks when she was a child. Her father and brother were opposed to her marrying William but she retorted [something to the effect], "I'd rather marry him even if he were a baboon."

So the royal family in the Netherlands had its own troubles into which Jean-Marie Leclair stepped unknowingly, as long as he was paid for doing what he loved to do, without a Guignon to deal with.

The employment in Holland lasted from 1737 until 1742, a total of 5 years. During that time, Leclair met Locatelli again, one source says in Amsterdam, and took violin lessons from him. The source comments that Leclair convinced Locatelli to move the publication of the concerti and caprices of his Arte del Violino to Paris. Who knows? Could Leclair have been drumming up business for his almost ex-wife?

At any rate, the Locatelli influence is shown in Leclair's Fourth Book of violin sonatas, Opus 9 dating from 1737 to 1738, as sure compliment to a friend. The dedication, however, for the Fourth Book went to Princess Anne of Orange. It is not clear how many times she received him officially at court; it could have been when he first arrived at Leeuwarden, and perhaps again at a later date. But other than snippets of names and dates in various histories, there is little known about Leclair's mysterious life in Holland.

Apparently, in 1740, he conducted the private orchestra of Francois du Liz, a very wealthy man, living in The Hague. As often happens with mad speculators, du Liz went bankrupt, so Leclair ended up in Paris in June 1743. But in keeping with his earlier relocations between Turin and Paris, he again did not stay long.

He is next traced to Chambery in the mountains of southeastern France where becomes a mentor to Don Filipe of Spain who liked to reside there. Like Frederick the Great of Prussia, Don Filipe was an amateur musician who would get up at 4:00 a.m. to practice his cello or the treble viol. If you had the wealth, you could get private lessons from the likes of Jean-Marie Leclair. In 1745, Leclair dedicated a second set of concerti to the Spanish Prince.

"Then back to Paris," says a source.

One would wonder what his life would have been like had Jean-Marie stayed in Paris with his wife all along and been a father to little Louise? One could hear a faint echo of a complaint, also coming from his first wife who had wanted to stay in Lyons so many years before and not be bounced around between Turin and Paris. Jean-Marie Leclair was ever the rolling stone.

\* \* \* \* \*

# Chapter 22

In 1745, Jean-Marie Leclair was 48 years old. He was back in Paris. We wonder if he dropped in to see his wife and daughter at this time. The couple was still not officially divorced after an 11 year separation, probably more. There are no letters revealing how Leclair's wife felt about her itinerant husband, which was probably resentment, bitterness, maybe even hatred? Would there have been some negative transference to the little girl? How would the daughter have felt not having a father there, a father who felt his fame was more important than his family, than her? Jean-Marie Leclair was like a pirate on a fast running sailing ship, cutting through the high seas, not caring whom he swamped or what damage he left behind in his wake. But onward he had to go to conquer new shores!

In 1746, Leclair composed his first operatic work, "Scylla and Glaucus". Actually it was his one and only opera. He recently turned 50, and had high hopes for this new direction in his life, which did not quite pan out as he wanted. "Scylla and Glaucus" was staged at the Academie Royale de Musique on October 4. It was a lavish production and is noted as having been "politely" received.

The story came from Ovid's "Metamorphoses" where the beautiful Scylla falls in love with Glaucus, the sea god. But Circe, the witch, is jealous and turns Scylla into an ugly monster. One would wonder if Leclair transferred the jealousy and rivalry he experienced personally with Guignon during his service to the King into the characters of Circe and Scylla? Perhaps his own deep hurts in the King's Symphony fired up the words Jean-Marie used in the lyrics for his opera?

If you take aging into account, one could argue that Jean-Marie's composing ability got less and less over the last two decades of his life. This would mean from the age of 44 on, roughly the time period in which we are concerned here. It is reported that Leclair even burned some manuscripts which did not satisfy him. Apparently, Brahms was the same way.

Perhaps Leclair was like a wild boar rooting for truffles and finding clumps of clay instead. Perhaps a genius's clumps of clay are other people's diamonds. Maybe word got out to friends that Leclair needed reassurance, a friendly hand at the time, to say, "Good job".

In 1748, when Leclair was 51, his former student Antoine-Antonin, who also happened to be a French nobleman, a Duke, specifically "le Duc de Gramont", was just that hand, that Leclair so desperately needed. It would make a good Ph.D. thesis to trace the self-esteem and the lack of confidence which strangely plagues some men of genius. The Duke made Leclair principal violinist and director of his private orchestra at Puteaux. Again, like Francois du Liz, wealthy investor, or the Prince of Spain, wealthy royal patron, it helps to have money with which to buy your own private orchestra, as long as you remain solvent financially. Leclair had struck it rich several times with such wealthy men, but as many times, it seems, lost his job when they went bankrupt. The Duke of Gramont ended Leclair's employment as musical director in 1751 when he was forced to sell his Puteaux estate because of debts.

It is not clear whether Jean-Marie Leclair finally got an official divorce from Louise Roussel in 1758, or if he skipped the paperwork, and finally and permanently just moved out. Whatever the case, the disintegration of the marriage had been going on for years and it was a very tragic note in Jean-Marie Leclair's biography.

There could be a case made over the past two decades that Louise Roussel suffered from menopause, had no interest in sex, claimed it hurt, things which spiraled into other irritations in their lives. Enthusiasm in their jobs were tainted by needling and arguments around the supper table. Leclair imagined what life would be like again on his own. He yearned for independence as the 1750s drew to a close; he did not want to be tied to his wife's income.

They say, as you get older, you become more of what you always were, more stubborn if you were stubborn, more opinionated if you were opinionated. Leclair did not want to rely on the hospitality of friends. That is perhaps why he rejected the offer of hospitality made by his friend and former employer, the Duke of Gramont, when Leclair looked for another place to stay, away from his wife. 28 years of marriage just seemed to be thrown away. Leclair was 61 years old in 1758.

Perhaps similar to his wife's menopause, he, himself, was going through a male mid-life crisis. Perhaps, there was constant needling and a push on Louise's part for Leclair to succeed more as a composer and as a court favourite. Even though they might have had separate rooms in the upstairs of the engraving shop, she might have thrown comparisons in his face at the supper table, if they even ate together, "Look at Haydn, a younger man!" Leclair might have moved out and rented a small apartment further down the street from his wife to save his sanity. Louise apparently was also experiencing a financial downturn in her business around this time, perhaps as a result of the general family dysfunction.

By 1758, while Leclair moved all his belongings out of the upstairs of the engraving shop, Louise moved out too, and in with a stone and brick mason, named Monsieur Chavagnac. They had lodgings together in the Rue du Four-Saint-Germain. One would assume that living with a bricklayer, one could afford decent housing in Paris, a better situation than what Leclair chose for himself.

Leclair, for his part, chose to live in a hovel in the Rue de Careme-Prenant on the outskirts of northern Paris, in a notorious part of the city, called "Le Marais". A Ph.D. student could again investigate the psychological motivation here for a musical genius to deliberately live poorly in a demeaning way.

Leclair's patron, the Duke of Gramont, offered to take Leclair into his own home at this time, to house him on his property and perhaps feed him through the his generous hospitality, rather than see his principal violinist live in an unsavoury part of town. Our Ph.D. student could also investigate why Leclair left Louise or vice-versa in a study about genius psychosis. Maybe it all goes back to Monteverdi, the little dog, although now we are stretching it!

Leclair was no doubt stubborn and proud. Like a petulant child, he might have said, "I don't owe the world a thing; I can do it myself!" He preferred to live in a hovel for the last six years of his life out of pride, rather than live on a rich man's handout. Most likely if Leclair had accepted the Duke's kind offer, he might have been able to pull his bootstraps up, and recover his dignity, and not been murdered in 1764. Who knows?

When he first bought the little hovel in 1758 from a Monsieur Legras, Jean-Marie did not really check into what he was getting. They say, "Buyer beware!" Perhaps the location should have told him everything, a small house close to the Saint-Martin's canal. The canal district had a bad reputation for thieves, prostitutes and all manner of unsavoury people. He bought the house anyway, despite protestations from close friends, like the Duke of Gramont. This was his way of saying to Louise, "Look I own something of my own now; I don't need you." It may also have been a way to live the life of a miser or a bohemian, a deliberate choice, which said I don't need society or its demands to get ahead.

Jean-Marie Leclair sat alone one night in his chair in his little house on the Rue de Careme-Prenant with a blanket over his shoulders, and contemplated his life in the dark. He stoked the fire in the little fireplace, and shivered.

In the 18$^{th}$ century, people had to put up with draughty houses and fireplaces which were inefficient. A lot of heat escaped up the chimney and through ill-fitting windows. One could feel that especially in autumn and winter. Jean-Marie Leclair, despite his fame at one point in his life, and also some accumulated fortune, could not now afford the Franklin Stove, otherwise known as the "Pennsylvania fireplace" which was invented by Benjamin Franklin in 1740. It was basically a heating stove which didn't let all its heat escape up the chimney. Leclair would have to order one, pay for the import tax and shipping, and then, the installation in a house that wasn't worth it. This could be done if Leclair had enough money, but the expense was a very discouraging thought. So, Leclair shivered and drew his blanket tighter around himself.

He did not believe in God, but he feared Him. Leclair brushed his hand over his visage. Had he made a mistake in buying the house? Jean-Marie Leclair did not know anything about Cyrano de Bergerac, the play written much later in 1897, but he felt instinctively that his large nose meant he was destined for something great, and certainly better things than this. Even yet, it might not be too late! He shivered again, drew in his blanket tight around his shoulders, and stoked the fireplace. He had to talk with Monsieur Legras about fixing the leaky roof and the draughty windows better than he had the first time. He would have to pay the man extra money.

As one year dragged on to become six years in the little house, Leclair lost his health. He lost his suppleness which he had taken for granted as a young dancer years ago in Lyons. Once a beautiful dancer full of strength, he now felt his body had shrunk, and he had become a limping old man.

While Leclair's health of body and mind waned, Franz Joseph Haydn was on the rise, growing stronger and more famous. Born in 1732, Haydn became Vice-Kapellmeister of the Esterházy musical establishment in 1764. At the time, Haydn was 32 years old and Leclair was 67 [and shortly, dead].

The two men had different temperaments. Leclair was a rolling stone and Haydn was content to stay put. Haydn had a steady job and was employed with the Esterházys for nearly 30 years. Did Haydn sit in a coffeehouse in Eisenstadt, Austria, in 1764 and talk about Leclair's ignominious demise? Did the Esterhazys even care about Leclair's death? Did they ask Haydn what he thought about the tragedy, except to gossip about it? Maybe neither Haydn nor the Esterhazys knew about the death, or bothered to talk about it. Why should Franz Joseph Haydn be interested in a tottering old Frenchman who had had his time at fame and glory?

But let's look at the last six years of Leclair's life and the direction it could or could not have gone. Let's put Leclair in a granny suite, let's say, on the property of the Duke of Gramont, if Leclair took up the Duke's offer of hospitality. If the killer was indeed the nephew whom Leclair continuously rebuffed, then whether Leclair lived in the little hovel, or on the grounds of the Duke of Gramont, the end result would probably have been the same. Leclair would have been murdered! Somehow, the envious nephew would have found a way to get at his unco-operative and more talented uncle. If Leclair were living on the Duke's estate, the nephew would have stood a better chance of getting caught; however, mainly because the nephew would have been trespassing on a rich man's property. A dark little house in a shabby part of town stood little chance of having a witness or anybody caring. Especially if the house was located close to the canal.

So, in the early morning of October 23rd 1764, Jean-Marie Leclair was found dead!

Scholars agree that the nephew probably did it. They even tie the nephew and the ex-wife together in a conspiracy theory, saying that the nephew and the ex-wife conspired together to do Leclair in, one for revenge and the other for financial gain. There is even a far-fetched notion that the Duke, himself, might have done the deed, although credence in such a claim is thin. The

Duke of Gramont still had his nobleman's status and surely enough money, even if he had to sell Puteaux to pay various business or gambling debts. Why stoop so low from his status of nobility to kill a hired musician?

Indeed, it was a complicated case with only circumstantial, if no solid evidence, against the most likely of one or two suspects on the list. The killer was never accused or arrested, leaving behind inadvertently, a perfect crime?

*****

# Chapter 23

1764 was not a good year for composers. But then it's never a good year for composers when they die. There were Locatelli, Rameau and Leclair, a trio of big names of the Baroque era, who sadly passed away.

Pietro Antonio Locatelli died on March 30, 1764 in his house on the Prinsengracht in Holland. He had climbed the ladder of success, coming such a long way from Bergamo, his home town in the alpine Lombardy region of northern Italy. He was 68 when he died, a year older than his friend, Jean-Marie Leclair. Then Rameau died just over half a year later on September 12 of that year, and Leclair himself died, stabbed to death, on October 23rd or October 24th.

When Locatelli died in the spring of 1764, there was enough time for the news to travel to the ears of both Rameau and Leclair that Locatelli, the great violin virtuoso had died in Holland. We wonder what their reaction was when they first heard the news that this fellow musician, a virtuosic violinist and composer like themselves, had passed away? Certainly, Leclair would have been personally affected because Locatelli was a friend, with whom he had at least two friendly musical jousts in a concert series.

The first friendly competition came shortly after 1728, once Leclair had settled in Paris. Leclair made a side trip to Kassel where the two virtuosi publicly performed in a "battle of the violins". The idea was to publicize the difference between the French and the Italian styles of playing. A witness described Leclair's playing as angelic, graced with a beautiful tone, and not restricted to rhythmic rules. Locatelli, on the other hand, played like the devil, aggressively hitting the strings with a deliberate edgy sound. The audience loved it and the two musicians became life-long friends.

This relationship was so different than what Leclair had with Jean-Pierre Guignon, a member of King Louis XV's Royal Symphony. Guignon and Leclair competed for the first violin position in the orchestra, and could not stand each other's company. Perhaps it made some difference in that Locatelli and Leclair only met on occasion, and did not live in the same city. Whereas Leclair and Guignon lived in Paris, and played in the same concert series of the Concert Spirituel.

One other obvious factor is that the chemistry of personalities between the two men did not gel. They irritated each other and thought they were a better player than the other.

When Jean-Marie Leclair resigned from the King's orchestra in 1736, that left the field wide open for Guignon to slide over into the first violin chair in the King's court. Guignon must have been beaming with a smile as wide as the Cheshire cat's. Leclair in the meantime shook the dust off his feet in Paris and moved to Holland in 1737. Leclair was all of 39 years old at the time, maybe 40.

His job in Holland lasted 5 years from 1737-1442. He got reacquainted with Locatelli in Amsterdam. A biographical note says, that Leclair took violin lessons from Locatelli. One wonders how Leclair managed to subdue his ego enough to take violin lessons, as a pupil, from Locatelli. Somehow their personalities clicked agreeably.

It wasn't like Locatelli didn't have an ego of his own. A certain bearing and even exaggerated flashiness was expected from performers of his caliber in those days on stage. When the Italian maestro was in Germany, he played before Frederick William I. An anecdotal report describes the maestro's self-assurance, and indeed his vanity, in wearing glitzy, diamond-studded clothes.

There are other questions which come to mind in the collaboration between Leclair and Locatelli. Locatelli seemed to be protective of the secrets of his violin technique. He would give lessons to amateurs, but had a rule not to teach professionals. He feared that they would learn too many of his secrets, with the threat, perhaps, of becoming better than he? So, one wonders how Leclair convinced Locatelli to give him violin lessons, unless Locatelli made sure that what he taught his compeer was not everything about his violin technique.

People of wealth who professed to be amateur musicians flocked to Locatelli in Amsterdam to be taught by the great master. Locatelli grew rich. An amusing side-note is that in 1741, he opened up shop, selling violin strings out of his home, perhaps a seemingly lowly business transaction, but it made him money. Combined with his income from his performances and his violin instruction, he soon had the highest income of any musician in all of Amsterdam.

Perhaps part of Leclair's problem was that he didn't stay in one place long enough to put down roots, and he didn't have a shrewd business sense to save money for his old age.

A common bond between Leclair and Locatelli was that they both possessed curiosity about the world around them. Locatelli studied birds, church history, political matters, geography, art and even mathematics. Leclair was an educated man, reading Ovid, Virgil, Moliere and Milton.

Who knows what Jean-Pierre Guignon read, or cared about, except maybe getting the concert master's first chair in the King's Concert Spirituel and Royal Orchestra in 1736. Although that sounds like a cheap shot, one must give the man credit, as a great musician; otherwise he could not have held his own in the musical jousts between Leclair and Guignon in the 1734 concert series. M. Marc Pincherie wrote that there was no clear victory in the battle of the violins. "Their performing styles differed profoundly, Leclair's being more precise, more technically delicate, more cerebral, while Guigon's was more colourful, more fanciful."

The friction between Leclair and Guignon can be understood and forgivable though, in terms of just plain human nature. It's too bad that the one essential ingredient of personality between the two men was missing, i.e. liking each other.

Jean-Pierre Guignon [né Giovanni Pietro Ghignone] Leclair's archrival in the King's court outlived Leclair by another 10 years until January 30, 1774. He was still 15 years shy of the French Revolution. Thankfully, Guignon, the concert master for the King of France, died too early to see the guillotine at work, and that was all for the better!

Jean-Philippe Rameau died a little over half a year later on September 12, 1764 in Paris. This was just over a month before Jean-Marie Leclair met his untimely death at the point of a dagger. The murderer could have at least shown some consideration, and murdered Leclair at a later date, thereby putting some respectable space between the two deaths. Leclair, wherever he was in the heavenly realms, might have felt cheated about Rameau taking away some of his lime-light in the close announcements about their deaths.

It is interesting to ask, after all is said and done in one's life, what is the sum total of what they left behind? With some composers, it's the legacy of their manuscripts and what they taught their students. But what is also revealing, is the question of what these men left behind in terms of liquid assets and sellable goods.

First, their legacy. Rameau launched his career into opera with Hippolyte ET Aricie in 1733 when he was 50. Despite an initial stir of criticism, he became a leading composer of French opera, replacing Jean-Baptiste Lully.

In 1746, Leclair went in the same direction with his first operatic work, "Scylla and Glaucus" hoping to change the musical direction of his own life. His work was "politely" received and his operatic ambitions fizzled out with this first and only operatic work. He went back to composing what he knew best, concertos and sonatas.

Perhaps men of genius are naturally irritable. Rameau was known to be quick to anger and brusque, lacking social graces. In fact, he turned out to be a miser in his old age. He dressed in worn-out clothes, had a single pair of shoes, and played on a dilapidated old harpsichord. One source says that when people went through his rooms after his death, they found a bag of coins, containing 1,691 gold Louis d'or [gold coins].

Jean-Marie Leclair could have used that money to buy a better house in a better part of Paris than the hovel he chose to live in for the rest of his life.

When Locatelli died in March 1764, people in charge of his estate found very valuable items. Collected works of the great Italian maestro Corelli. Paintings by Dutch, Italian and French masters. A collection of instruments and much more which were auctioned off in August 1765, as part of the estate. Who got the money? Did Locatelli's heirs inherit, if he had any,  or were debtors paid off? Where is that Ph.D. research student when you need him or her to sort this all out?

It is amazing how many great men of fame blew away their fortune as they got older. Anton Paul Stadler, three years Mozart's senior, for whom Wolfgang Amadeus Mozart wrote the popular Clarinet Concerto in A, died at the age of 59 of emaciation, which means starvation. After being a Royal Imperial Court Musician from Vienna, one would ask, did the man not have enough money to feed himself at the end of his life? Unless the emaciation was caused by cancer?

Carl Stamitz, violinist and composer, lived through Mozart's lifetime, and had great success in his hometown of Mannheim, not only as a violinist but also as a viola player. He died in poverty in 1801, at the age of 56. There was an auction to pay off the debts he never could pay when he was alive.

Wolfgang Amadeus Mozart, a little boy when Leclair was alive, was buried in a common grave in 1791, though some people refuse to say "pauper's grave". He was only 35, and one can only guess at what the world lost in possible compositions from this musical genius. Where is Mozart's tombstone, so people can honour his gravesite? There is a legend that, in the attempt to find his grave, a gravedigger who apparently knew where the body was buried, snuck the skull out of the grave. Ironically, and despicably so, a similar thing happened to the body of Haydn.

How are the men who have been gifted with musical genius to be treasured during their life-times and honoured when they are gone? When they die of emaciation and in abject poverty, should angels not cry?

Jean-Marie Leclair was found dead in the early morning of October 24$^{th}$ 1764, in the doorway of his little hovel in Paris, stabbed to death! What were his worldly assets? Certainly not his house! The list would include his manuscripts, a broken fiddle, and a hidden bag of money under the mattress. The former landlord, Monsieur Legras, grabbed the loose coins in the bowl that rested on top of the little table by the doorway. That could have been Leclair's drinking money.

Louise Roussel gained access to the house through Monsieur Legras. She confiscated the manuscripts, Leclair's clothes, luckily found the bag of money under the mattress and snagged anything else of value she saw. She even took the broken violin and shattered violin bow, hoping that a repair shop could fix them enough to sell them. She had no idea what a Stradivarius was.

*****

# Chapter 24

When it came to the battle of the violins between Jean-Marie Leclair and Jean-Pierre Guignon, it was "a tie" according to one eyewitness in the 1734 concert series. Monsieur Marc Pincherie wrote, "Their performing styles differed profoundly, Leclair's being more precise, more technically delicate, more cerebral, while Guigon's was more colourful, more fanciful."

Probably for this they used a music stand and sheet music. So, how do you choose? Every artist plays in his or her own inimitable way. I'm sure there must have been someone in the audience in 1734 who might say that Jean-Marie Leclair was the clear winner. But then that is an opinion and a matter of taste.

There are so many variables which determine the characteristic of sound and its appeal to the ear. How did the performer feel that day? Grouchy, angry? What is the performer's personality? Buoyant, laid-back? What's the quality of the instrument? A Stradivarius, a $30 fiddle from the pawn shop? The tonality could even come from the dimensions of the player's fingers. How fat or how skinny are the fingers?

Maybe the music itself requires a biting sound, so the player has to follow the specific dynamics written in the piece. Vivaldi's Four Seasons, ranging from Spring's cheery phrasing to Winter's biting staccato. Maybe, you in the audience, don't even like the violin. Maybe your favourite instrument is the flugelhorn, the basset horn or the bassoon. Mozart even wrote a concerto for the bassoon. My second favourite instrument is the oboe, and then the piano.

But speaking about the violin and the types of violins: David Oistrakh started out with a 1702 Conte di Fontana Stradivarius, which he played for 10 years. He switched to a 1705 Marsick Stradivarius. Why? Again a matter of personal taste. Oistrakh produced a more biting clearer tone with his Marsick Strad. He could put muscles into his notes which carried the sound further out and with a sharper edge than the subdued softness of his 1702 Conte di Fontana Strad. Now, that did not mean he could not produce lyrical and soft sounds with his Marsick when he wanted to.

There is an excellent film written and directed by Bruno Monsaingeon on "The Art of the Violin", Part I and Part II. The film gives you visual and audio recording of the huge range of styles that great players of this and the last century had. They are all good and great players, and it's difficult to say, this one is better than the other one. Commentators include the likes of Ivry Gitlis, Ida Haendel, Hilary Hahn, Laurent Korcia, Yehudi Menuhin, Itzhak Perlman and Mstislav Rostropovitch. We see footage of George Enescu playing "Rumana" No. 3, and Jack Benny quipping with Isaac Stern on stage about the cost of a cheap violin.

Unfortunately, no one will ever be able to hear the real soundtrack of Jean-Marie Leclair, Guignon or Locatelli to compare their quality with modern players. Youtube is wonderful about making recorded video and audio available to the public of our modern virtuosi because someday our current great players, like our 18th century virtuosi, will pass away with the sands of time.

This novella is a written as a tribute to the man, Jean-Marie Leclair, who lived from 1697-1764.

Here is a list of my favourite violinists, picked subjectively and haphazardly out of Youtube. When I say that a person's playing is edgy or lyrical, it does not mean that the person could not choose to play in a lyrical style. It depends upon the dynamics required by the piece they are playing, and how the artist chooses to interpret that piece. Edgy or lyrical, the quality of playing is all good and lovely, and I'm glad that we have such musical talents in this world who are able to play at the virtuosic level. Who knows what gave them their gifts or what sacrifices they had to make to develop these gifts, so that they could pass the sound of their gift along to the world.

- 1891-1967 Mischa Elman, precision with emotion, plays Dvorak's "Humoresque", you can hear the little grace notes
- 1901-1987 Jascha Heifetz: sharp biting attacks, crisp and clear, once described as stone-faced with his music, Perlman describes him as a tornado of energy, Heifetz plays Paganini, Caprice No. 24
- 1903-1962 Fritz Kreisler, as usual he impeccable rubato depending upon rush of notes or sustenutos, plays "Schön Rosmarin"
- 1916-1999 Yehudi Menuhin, precision like a clock, Menuhin can be accused of standing there like a mechanical automaton, but this is his self-control, Mehuhin plays Paganini, Caprice No. 24
- 1932-1989 Al Cherney, fiddler who played on the Canadian "Tommy Hunter Show", great at double stops, biting style, played "Orange Blossom Special" in Grande Prairie, Alberta circa 1980 when I lived there. My orchestra played the first half, possibly conducted by Kerry Stratton, now a Classical 96.3 FM radio host. Mr. Cherney came in with his suit on a hanger and asked me, "Where's my dressing room?" I said, "I don't know, but the washroom is over there." He said, "Grande Prairie is a real hick town isn't it?" I said, "Yes."
- 1945-...Itzhak Perlman, heart wrenching, singing quality, touching the soul, Perlman plays "Raisins and Almonds"
- 1952-...Lenny Solomon, electric violin, known for jazz, biting edge, rhythmic and rocking style, plays "Going to Chicago". I first got introduced to Lenny Solomon's music when I was in my 20s, passed him by at the Mariposa Festival in Toronto. He was wearing a fancy cowboy shirt. I

bought his 1974 Myles and Lenny Album, and just loved his violin background music in the song, "Can You Give It All to Me". It would be great to have a time machine to bring Jean-Marie Leclair into the 21st century to square off with Lenny Solomon in a violin joust. Solomon would have to leave his electric violin home though.

- 1956 Nigel Kennedy, aggressive and edgy, great speed and volume contrasts, Kennedy plays Vivaldi's Winter
- 1967 Joshua Bell, emotional and soul rending, Bell plays Ladies in Lavender 2012
- 1976-...James Ehnes, haunting, able to build emotion to disturbing levels, Ehnes plays Sibelius Violin Concerto. James Ehnes is a Canadian, born in Brandon, Manitoba. When I was in fourth year university in 1971, Mark Hymers, Wally Scholtes and I decided to take part of the summer off to drive across Canada to British Columbia. I remember Brandon, Manitoba, particularly, because just outside of the little town, the read-end housing to my 1963 Pontiac Parisienne cracked, throwing hot gears all over the road. We coasted to the side of the highway and saw smoke coming out of the wheat field. There were miles and miles of wheat. "Hey, somebody started a fire," I yelled. It was us. We tap danced all over the ditch to get the fire out, then hitch-hiked into Brandon to see if we could find a garage. Yes, they could replace the rear-end housing. It would be a used one from the wrecker's and it would cost $120. I phoned my father, who didn't hesitate to telegram his wayfaring son the money to get us out of this jam. My mother, I'm sure, was listening in, and in her typical European way, was probably saying, "I see black." Needless to say, we got the car fixed by the next day, and drove out of Brandon, Manitoba, not realizing that this little town would be the birth place of one of the world's greatest violinists, James Ehnes, in 1976. Hitch-hiking was

a common practice in our university days. We picked up a hippie, named Milt, in British Columbia who showed us how to use his sling-shot to whip stones across the canyon of the Thompson River. To this day, I do not know why I remember his name. Then we picked up a young cowboy who told us he was going to become a famous writer. I can't remember his name. I hope he made it. We ended up taking the ferry to Nanaimo, Vancouver Island, drove across the island, and eventually strolled along the sands of Wreck Beach.

- 1979-...Hilary Hahn, precise with superb volume contrasts, exactitude of clear notes, Hahn plays Mendelssohn Violin Concerto E Minor Opus 64
- 1987-... Nicola Benedetti, full rich sound, singing quality, emotional, great contrasts, plays Erich Korngold's Violin Concerto

I must apologize for the list of unmentioned players, indeed great unmentioned players! There are so many, many virtuosi violinists, who have reached that high stratosphere of excellence! Arthur Grumiaux, Laurent Korcia, Hilary Hahn, Lara St. John, to name a few! I will make it up to them in the next life or maybe the next novel!

*****

# Chapter 25

My university friends have made me a better person, one who enjoys classical music because my family background with a father who was a forklift driver on construction would not necessarily create the environment that promoted the Art of the Violin. Mark Hymers introduced me to Gustav Mahler, and Waldemar Scholtes to choral music.

Another friend, Bill Oates, introduced me to Erik Satie. Bill lived in Rochdale College when he attended the University of Toronto in what was then a pretty tough program, MPC, Math, Physics and Chemistry. We went to Sam the Record Man, and browsed through all the LPs. I picked up an album of Rimsky-Korsakov's "Scheherazade", played by the London Symphony Orchestra, conducted by Leopold Stokowksi. I first fell in love with Rimsky-Korsakov's music when I heard the violin play "The Young Prince and Princess" in an old black and white movie that I was watching on television. I was in grade 8 at the time. Those were the days when I was hooked on Mantovani and also 101 Strings. There was one other record I purchased on sale at Sam the Record Man, and that was Schubert's Unfinished Symphony. I used to set up the portable record player downstairs in the basement, load up my barbells behind a curtain, and then lift weights to the rhythm of Schubert's Unfinished Symphony.

"What are you doing down there?" yelled my mom. "Oh, just listening to music." "Well turn it down!" Which I did, but I kept puffing away at the barbells in a steady rhythm. So, Schubert was good for something, even though he didn't finish the piece. After a workout with those barbells, I myself was finished!

There is sternness in Schubert's Unfinished Symphony which I also find in Beethoven's Fifth. Maybe their breakfast hadn't been cooked right or they needed another cup of coffee, so they were in a grouchy mood when they composed these pieces. Who knows? But there you go, an Unfinished Symphony and a Fifth, both of them rising in anger, then subsiding into a sense of peace, and then flaring up again to throw a challenging fist right into the very face of God.

Mind you, I also fell in line with my peers who also liked Simon and Garfunkel, The Brothers Four, Joan Baez, and Bob Dylan in those days. I like to think of myself as embracing an eclectic taste in music. Somehow by 1975 I had "The Best of Spike Jones and his City Slickers" in my record collection, and somehow through about 11 moves, that LP still survived. On the back of Spike's album are little pictures and ads for Perry Como, Al Hirt, Paul Anka, Elvis and Neil Sedaka. Oh yes, there's also an ad for Charley Pride and Henry Mancini Pure Gold...and at the very bottom, you get the call number for Disco-Soul and Polka Variety.

When I was in grade 9, Mr. Frederick Pohl was hired by St. Jerome's High School in Kitchener to teach music in 1962. The school administration had the ambitious idea of creating a high-school orchestra. We heard on the morning announcements that anyone wanting to learn a stringed instrument should come to the Annex across the street after school. I went and picked up my first violin. The school supplied the instruments for free. There was a whole group of us, two bass fiddles, two cellos, one viola and four violins, fresh and eager to become musicians.

Mr. Pohl stopped the rehearsal at one point. He pointed to me, and said, "You just did something clever." I thought I did something wrong and apologized. He said, "Don't be sorry for doing something clever with your fingers." To this day, I don't know what I did, but I appreciated the chance to learn the violin. Mr. Pohl didn't just open the doors for me to violin playing, but he introduced me to Claude Debussy, "Claire de Lune", and other names like Fauré and Ravel.

When I was in grade 11, I took violin lessons from Mr. Voldemars Lasmanis. I remember playing "The Happy Prince" because it was a lyrical and happy piece. I was about a grade 6 level at the time, and Mr. Lasmanis told me that The Transylvania Club in Kitchener needed a band to provide the music for their New Year's Eve dance. The band was directed by Professor Walter Scholtes. Professor Scholtes' son Waldemar or Wally played trumpet. He was about my age. Mr. Lasmanis and myself were to round out the string section. We each got an envelope with $30 in it at the end of the gig, and I thought, "Hey, there's money in show biz."

I will always have a soft spot in my heart for Mr. Lasmanis. I pedaled my bicycle to his place on Church Street during the winter one year. I was 3 kilometres away from his house, so I had to pedal my Raleigh bicycle from Pandora Ave, down King Street, then up the steep hill on Eby Street, and finally to Mr. Lasmanis' house. Eby Street was a 30 degree steep hill which was a tough climb on my bicycle, especially in winter. It felt like a 90 degree climb by the time I got half way up the hill. There was snow along the ditch beside the sidewalk.

Half-way up the hill, my violin case popped open. Out fell the towel, and out fell my violin, which slid down the hill like a toboggan. A tree stopped it most unkindly. When I retrieved my violin, the neck was broken. I bundled it up into the case and trudged to the top of the hill, and pedaled the rest of the way to Mr. Lasmanis' house for my lesson. I was in tears.

He said, "Well, there will be no Happy Prince this evening." He disappeared to a back room and came out with a bottle of Elmer's Wood Glue. Mr. Lasmanis gently squeezed glue into the crack by the neck, and fitted it tightly in place, not with a rope, but with an electric cord, a brown one, I remember. He said, "Come back next week." There was no charge for that night's lesson. That same violin, a $30 instrument, saw me through the next 9 years.

In 1966, I was in grade 12. The conductor of St. Jerome's High School Orchestra wanted to start a smaller dance band which he picked from the orchestra, musicians who would be willing to play for special events at various Hotels and Inns around the Kitchener-Waterloo area. Mr. Mike Bergauer picked 13 of us, and called the group "Opus I". We wore black pants, and glitzy green shirts with shiny buttons, and frilly cuffs. I felt silly in the outfit, but hey, we each got $30 after each gig. That was a pretty good return at a time when my violin lessons from Mr. Pohl and then Mr. Lasmanis cost me $5 for one hour. My father was making $2.50 per hour on construction, though he wasn't the one paying for my lessons.

I remember my first pay cheque in grade nine, my first summer on construction working with my dad, hauling in $66 that week, from a special student rate of $1.25 per hour. I think I had to work Saturday. Essentially, I paid for my own lessons.

Later at the University of Waterloo I reached a grade 8 level of playing. I was good enough to be in the orchestra which was put together by Alfred Kunz. But I wasn't good enough when it came to the part which required a quick spiccato. I couldn't keep up so I just shook my bow furiously. As a result, I would have to say, No, if ever the Toronto Symphony made me an offer, and stick to what I know, playing in amateur orchestras where my fake spiccato is tolerated. Seriously, wherever I've lived, I've always joined a community orchestra and have, I felt, added something positive to the community.

Thinking back on the Leclair assassination, I have never felt envy or hatred toward another player in my orchestra where I wish them harm, like Guillaume-François Vial did with his uncle, Jean-Marie Leclair. I'm just glad I have a healthy hobby. Perhaps, fierce competition rears its ugly head when people actually get close to the top, and have an amazing talent and achieve a "super skill". Most likely Vial was quite a good player but not an exceptional phenomenon, like his uncle. Maybe for that reason, somebody like Locatelli would give lessons only to amateurs and not violinists who were already accomplished. The instinct is primitive, territorial, like a dog guarding his turf.

*****

# Chapter 26

The Lieutenant of Police, Antoine-Gabriel de Sartine, was smoking his pipe. Along with strong Turkish coffee, he enjoyed his tobacco. France had been a smoking nation for over two hundred years. It was a Frenchman, Jean Nicot, who introduced the habit to France in 1560 from Spain. The word, nicotine, is derived from his name. With the stress of his job, de Sartine found his little vices of sipping coffee and smoking tobacco relaxing, a way to cope, and a way to think. Coffee and tobacco put the world into perspective.

Puffing a soft white cloud into the air, de Sartine called his sergeants into his office. "I've found a new clue!" Gentilhomme was ready to take his notepad out. "Not now," said de Sartine, "let me think first."

He explained how he rented a carriage over the past few days, out of the department's budget, to interview several people for whom Jean-Marie Leclair had previously been employed. The "Duc de Gramont" was one of them. "There was no other way to do this, but through the department's expense," he confessed. "Don't write that down yet, Gentilhomme!" he commanded.

A big white puff of smoke came out of his mouth. He paused and tossed back his head. "Now," he nodded to his note taker, "you may write."

"Apparently, Monsieur Leclair was very fond of a certain pocket watch. He showed it to the Duke of Gramont several times and boasted that Louis XV had given the watch to him personally. It was gold plated and had the profile of the King on the inside, as well as the coat of arms. If we find the man with the watch...guess what, Gentilhomme?"

"No, what, Lieutenant?" asked his sergeant.
Lebrusque stepped forward, having no time for Gentilhomme's dull wit, "Why sir, then we have our killer!"

This new clue fired up the investigation. "Thank God for carriages," thought de Sartine, "I'm glad I did not have to walk or go on horse-back. I have enough trouble with my hemorrhoids." Smoking took his mind off the itchiness.

The Lieutenant felt that the list of suspects could be reduced. The gardener was too much of an oaf and did not fit the profile of killer, perhaps petty crimes, but not cold-blooded murder.

The Leclair brothers could also be eliminated because, first of all each of them had success of some sort of their own, and second of all, they all seemed fond of each other as a family.

This left a few possibilities. The 40 year old nephew, Guillaume-François Vial, who was big and strong, an envious violin player who could not climb to the same heights of success as his uncle, and of course, the ex-wife, Louise Roussel, who apparently was having financial difficulties keeping her engraving business afloat.

The other two possibilities existed as well. A "rôdeur", or prowler, and lastly a mistress or prostitute. De Sartine doubted that a prowler had done the deed. The coins were left in the bowl inside the house. And why would a prowler destroy the violin? Logic dictated that a neighbourhood sneak would have stolen the violin and sold it on the black market. If a prowler had stolen and sold the violin in the black market, then that sort of crime would leave a path of evidence, something which was in the capacity of the police to track down.

The prostitute? No, She would want instant cash, and would not smash the violin. She would take the coins in the bowl instead. A mistress? Now, that is a possibility for rage and passion. The mistress must not be dismissed.

The nephew, the ex-wife, the mistress.

These were things still on the list. De Sartine said to Gentilhomme, "Make a note of that." Gentilhomme said, "Yes, sir."

Other than that, the Lieutenant was hoping to find some bloody clothes perhaps in a side street, and question whose they might be, or better yet, from some drunken wastrel in the tavern, get a confession. He could not see this happening.

The Lieutenant of Police decided. "Gentlemen, we must find the prostitute and the mistress, so we can strike them off the list."

Gentilhomme asked, "But how do we do that?"

"Use our feet, man. Use our feet!"

They canvassed various streets around the Rue Careme-Prenant.

The streets were narrow and filthy. Shuttered windows pealing and unpainted for years. Clothes lines hanging outside from upper floors. Broken windows blocked by wood. "Les clochards" or unemployed bums sitting on stoops, some of them smoking pipes. Or drinking wine out of the bottle. Where did they get the money to afford these things? Occasionally a man would get up and relieve himself against a building or pee in the street filled with daily garbage, waiting for the rain to flush things away.

The Lieutenant assigned Gentilhomme and Lebrusque opposite sides of the main street to knock on doors and ask if they knew a Monsieur Leclair who played the violin. He, himself, took the side streets within a one block radius since he was faster at the job.

They commenced their job late morning since nobody in this area seemed to get up early for work. After an hour, Gentilhomme hit pay-dirt.

"Yes," said a sleepy blonde, wiping her eyes and yawning. "He even played his violin for me once, after I serviced him. Didn't like his music, but I knew he was very good."

Gentilhomme said, "I'll be right back with my Lieutenant."

She said, "Is there anything in it for me?" Gentilhomme had to promise her a 10 livre note. She was smart enough to know that paper money had no value, so she held out for a "demi-Louis d'or ",  a gold coin worth about 12 livres.

Both Lebrusque and especially de Sartine were impressed with her shrewdness. "Bonjour," she said, "my name is Cloe Bonbon, charmed I'm sure!" She confided that word had gotten around the neighbourhood that the Monsieur had been killed. "Too bad, he was a nice gentleman, can't say I liked that Baroque stuff, but he paid me regularly after we done."
The policemen thanked her after giving her the "demi-Louis d'or ".

"Now, Lieutenant," she said, sidling up to him with her ample breasts. "For another demi-Louis d'or, the four of us could go upstairs. I've had a 'ménage à trois', but never a 'ménage à quatre'. You could brag to all your friends."

"Mademoiselle Bonbon," declared the Lieutenant, "I'm working. You are attractive and tempting. I want you to know that, but I never mix business with pleasure."

"Shame," she said, "when I'm working, I mix pleasure with pleasure." She laughed. Then she walked around the three officers and touched each one affectionately on the cheek. The Lieutenant she called, Monsieur L'Alpiniste. Gentilhomme she called, 'Mon petit chou'. Lebrusque she called 'mon grand lion sans coeur'.

When the three officers got out the door, Lebrusque said quickly, "She sure has our number."
Gentilhomme was more worried about the money they had spent here just on information.
"That's something else out of the police budget," comforted the Lieutenant. "Don't worry about it. I will square it with the chief."

"What do you think Lieutenant?" asked Gentilhomme. "Could she have done it?"

"What do you think, Lebrusque?" asked de Sartine, bouncing the question over to him.

"No," he said, "if she had done it, it would have been like the cottager and his wife who killed the goose that laid the golden egg."

Gentilhomme didn't get it. Lebrusque explained, "She got her living out of Leclair. Why kill him?"

"I was mistaken," thought de Sartine. "about both men. Maybe both of them will go far in the bureaucracy. Gentilhomme for being the 'Yes man' and Lebrusque for having brains."

He smiled to himself. "Now all we have to do is find the mistress. I know there is one! Leclair did not suspect the prostitute, Mademoiselle Bonbon. But a mistress? That could be a possibility. Leclair had no wife. He needed a lover with whom he could share his feelings, fears, confidences and his heart."

*****

# Chapter 27

They canvassed the streets again the next day. Nothing turned up.

"We must refocus our attention," thought the Lieutenant. "Look outside these dirty, dingy streets. What other approach?" He explained to his officers that the prostitute was a dead end. At least, it struck another suspect off the list. The next possibility was to find the mistress and hopefully with an interview there, strike her off the list too. The pathway to finding her was clear, at least to him and Lebrusque, not so much to Gentilhomme. "Make a new list," he said to Gentilhomme. "Who were Leclair's friends? His acquaintances? That goes for both Leclair and his ex-wife. We have more canvassing to go, preferably in a better part of town."

They left the seedy streets in the north end of Le Marais, and headed toward the lodgings of a Monsieur Chavagnac, the stone mason in the Rue du Four-Saint-Germain. Certainly a nicer, more upscale neighbourhood, than the Rue de Careme-Prenant, where they had gone door to door earlier in the day and all day yesterday.

When they knocked at the Chavagnac door, a huge burly man opened it, and simply stared at them with unfriendly eyes. He simply stood there, arms crossed at his chest.
"Monsieur Chavagnac?" asked the Lieutenant.

"Yes." Ah, finally some response out of the tree trunk. "We would like to speak with Louise Roussel. He shouted backwards, "Louise, the police are here." They did not get invited in.
Finally, Louise squeezed in beside the burly giant, and commented, "Ah, the boys in blue. Back again?" The Lieutenant was sure she must have been pretty at some point, perhaps the blue eyes and the dimples. Her face was wrinkled and the Lieutenant couldn't help but be reminded of an old crow.

The officers explained from the door that they needed to speak with any other female friends or associates her former husband might have had who could shed light on their investigation. Louise knew what the officers were after, "Ah, a mistress perhaps? Another suspect to add to your list?"

Lieutenant de Sartine was impressed by her quick mind. His eyebrows rose up a bit with new respect for the former Mme 'Leclair'. The Lieutenant held his own council, "She's a quick one. But maybe there is something she may be willing to divulge, provided she isn't in on Leclair's murder herself. And in that case, she may be sending us on a wild goose chase."

Surprisingly, Louise Roussel was co-operative. She told the police to go back to her old neighbourhood where her engraving shop was, and knock on the door several houses down, the one with the green door. "Ask for a Virginie Leblanc. Maybe the whore can tell you something." Then she nodded to Chavagnac, and he squeezed the door shut in the police officers' faces before they could react. It did not make sense trying to knock again. They had gotten a name from the old prune.

If Virginie Leblanc was the mistress, Lieutenant de Sartine found the name ironically symbolic. Virginie meant a fresh water spring and Leblanc meant white, perhaps like the "sins that were washed as white as snow". She had to be the mistress.

"Let's go men," encouraged de Sartine. "We have just enough time to wrap up another fine piece of police work today before we go back to the Maréchaussée." Lieutenant de Sartine hailed another carriage for the three of them at the department's expense. The springs of the carriage bounced up and down, and squeaked, as the three men got in and jostled for position.

They were headed for the neighbourhood of the old engraving shop on the Rue Saint-Jacques where they hoped they could find and talk to Virginie Leblanc. The police were making progress with the high hope of wrapping this mystery up with a neat bow and tie. The Superintendent would be pleased.

Lieutenant de Sartine enjoyed surprises. He wondered what was behind the green door as he knocked. A petit lady, about 40, opened the door, and asked, "Can I help you?" She certainly was more attractive than Louise Roussel.

"Are you Virginie Leblanc?" asked the Lieutenant. She nodded.

"It's about Jean-Marie Leclair. He used to live across the street upstairs in the engraving shop. Did you know he was killed?"

"Yes, I heard. Another neighbour told me." It never ceased to amaze the Lieutenant how fast bad news traveled by word of mouth. Maybe it was the grapevine and gossip started by the gardener?

"We'd like to come in and chat," said the Lieutenant. With all courtesy aside, after a preliminary tea, they talked. Gentilhomme, as usual, took notes and sat to the side.

"Yes, I was his mistress," she openly admitted. She was widowed; her husband having been a carpenter, and a successful one at that, left her a small fortune. She used that to start her own business, a pottery shop, because she had a natural affinity and love, like her husband had, of making things with her own hands. She had a busy and loyal clientele from the nobility in Paris who raved about the glazes, shapes and designs in her plates, bowls, cups and saucers. She even started initialing them.

"So it's become a lucrative trade," said the Lieutenant.

"Trade, no! It is an art; I am an 'artiste'!" she objected with a spark in her eyes.

"Yes, yes," said the Lieutenant, "I see and appreciate the difference."

She informed the three officers that Jean-Marie Leclair had an eye for pretty women, and so, dropped over some years ago when he was still living with his wife, "just to look at the pottery, you know, at first. Soon it was other things."

"Mind you my husband was dead, and then when Jean-Marie's little dog died, the relationship between him and his wife died too. Things, you might say, 'picked up' between us, however. By then, Jean-Marie had already moved out of Louise's engraving shop and found his own apartment. Our relationship was not only as lovers but as confidantes. Jean-Marie became my friend, and gentlemen of the police, I'd like to consider myself more than his mistress."

She confessed she knew Jean-Marie's nature. He could not stay put in one city for very long, and like most men, he was, for want of a better word, she said "chien", a dog. The three officers nodded with submissive understanding, and some sympathy.

"I accepted all that in Jean-Marie," she said, "but I did not kill him, if that is what you are here to find out."

Lieutenant de Sartine trusted his instinct. "No, I don't think you killed him. We are sorry for your loss."

"Thank you, I have lost three things in Jean-Marie. A friend, a confidante and a lover."

After the three officers were led outside the green door onto the street again, they hailed another carriage. Amid the jostling and bouncing of their ride, they assessed the interview with the mistress. Gentilhomme could barely keep his pencil from bouncing up and down on the notepad. But he managed.

The Lieutenant commented, "So the mistress is eliminated too from the suspect list. She has enough money on her own. It's not like Leclair was her 'golden goose' and a free meal ticket to an easy life." He asked, "How many viable suspects does that leave us, Gentilhomme?"

Gentilhomme was ready, "The nephew who was ambidextrous, and the ex-wife!" He wrote that down with an exclamation mark in his notepad.

"Let's do some more digging," said the Lieutenant. "We did a good day's work, and tomorrow is another day."

*****

# Chapter 28

Guillaume-François Vial, son of Leclair's younger sister, Françoise, was the most likely suspect. He was big and strong, and had a nasty disposition toward others. He had been pestering his uncle for years for a letter of recommendation to the King's court that he was good enough to be a member of the Chapelle and the Chambre du Roy. Leclair thought his nephew did not have that skilful a talent, and merely thought more of himself than he was; therefore, he had the means and the motive. When Vial bragged that he was ambidextrous, that revelation pretty well clinched it in de Sartine's mind about Vial being the murderer. The way the wounds were inflicted in Jean-Marie Leclair's neck and back, their slant, indicated that the direction of the blow came from the back from a left-handed man. But this was all likelihood and not proof. If there were only some way to link whatever things Vial touched to the crime scene itself?

But then, Vial probably had visited his uncle on several occasions at the little house, probably begging for some letter of recommendation to a duke or duchess, and any signs of him left there was no proof that he was the one who had wielded the blow of the dagger. Strong suspicions were not enough, as they say, to take to the bank.

He didn't know how many times. It must have been numerous. Lieutenant of Police, Antoine-Gabriel de Sartine, complained there was no solid evidence. If only they had the murder weapon itself, a dagger found hidden in a drawer at the nephew's place, or if they found that gold pocket watch that reputedly had been presented to Leclair by Louis XV himself. If only the big brute had a guilty conscience and confessed. Then it would be slam bang, a case solved with a neat bow tie to present to the Superintendent, and promotions would be waiting in the wings for everybody. Maybe Sgt. Gentilhomme might glory in becoming the chief note-taker for the King. The Lieutenant laughed at the idea, and then thought again how frustrated the police were in the case. No solid proof, no nothing.

The nephew actually did suffer deep pangs of conscience, unknown to anybody. He had insomnia. He took a long walk at about 3:00 or 4:00 in the morning along the Seine River near the Notre Dame Cathedral. The chill and the blackness of the night made his dark thoughts worse.

Yes, he had killed his uncle, stabbed him from behind, three times to make sure. He was so angry he could have strangled his uncle as well. Isn't a blood relative supposed to promote their own? "He said one time, I was mediocre at best, why should he give me a glowing report?" Vial's blood boiled over at the thought. "Uncle Jean-Marie laughed in my face." "But uncle, I am an excellent violinist, a virtuoso, in fact!" "Then show me!" "I faltered on the arpeggios and scratched on my sustenutos." "My boy," he said, "if you practiced more often like I did, then maybe you would get somewhere. Determination and devotion and hours and hours of practice...but then there is also that little thing called, God-given talent." "I'm sure if I got a promotion, was in the right spot, sitting right beside you, Uncle, in the orchestra, the talent would come." "My boy, it does not work that way. You either have it or you don't, and you don't!" "How that hurt; I could have killed him!"

By this time, Guillaume-François Vial had sauntered onto the Pont Neuf Bridge, getting there without a real sense of where he was going.  Soon morning would break, but for now, everything was still dark to fit Vial's dark and depressed mood. The Seine River floated leisurely by underneath the bridge not caring about the little humans who lived around its banks. The bridge had been started in 1578 and took a quarter of a century to build. It was a beautiful monument, a stone guardian that spanned over Paris' giant water way. How many suicides had the Pont Neuf seen? Vial wondered if he should add himself to that number. He thought seriously about this, as he leaned with his hands clasped over the railing of the bridge.

He wondered what it would take to swim across the Seine? Perhaps he wouldn't make it and drown half-way across. Le Chevalier de Saint-Georges, "the black Mozart", succeeded in a night swim across the Seine River years later prior to the chaos of the French Revolution. Champion fencer and master musician, he was the toast of French society and socialized with Marie Antoinette in the 1780s, not only because of his prodigious talents, but also because he was black and the son of an African slave. During the Revolution, Saint-Georges served as a colonel of the Légion St.-Georges, the first all-black regiment in Europe. The music he composed coincidentally sounded very much like Mozart.

Ironically, Saint-Georges played violin in the "Concert Spirituel" in the early 1770s, cutting a parallel swath like Jean-Marie Leclair some 40 years before. The muscular "mulatto" was appreciated for his flamboyant violin technique, "enrapturing especially the feminine members of the audience."

But Vial did not know any of this as he brooded darkly above the Seine River from the solid safety of the bridge. He wondered how the ripples of the water intersected each other like the lives of people above. Vial gave up the idea of jumping into the river from the bridge, as well as the more ridiculous idea of swimming across the Seine from shore, because he did not have it in him.

Guillaume-François Vial took the dagger deeply tucked into his coat pocket. Looked at it once and heaved it, with his left-hand, as far as he could from the Pont Neuf into the middle of the river. He cried because there was some pinch of regret which now cooled the heat of his old anger toward his uncle. He shook off the soft feeling, and said to himself convincingly, "I'm glad I killed the old bastard anyway."

He then took out the gold pocket watch from the other pocket, opened the case to peer at the image of Louis XV, which he could barely make out by the light of the silvery moon. He felt the engraving more than saw it. He could see the time because of the white face of the watch which made the dials stand out. The time was nearly 5:00 in the morning. He said in a tone, imitating his uncle's voice, "I see by the King's watch, that it is time to get rid of this evidence." He flung the gold pocket watch into the Seine River as hard as he could. It glittered in the moonlight as it flew in a high arc through the air, fell and then splashed lightly and submerged into the murky depths of the river.

Who was it who said, you cannot step into the same river twice? Yes, Heraclitus, five centuries before Christ, a saying the simple truth about the universe. The dagger was in the hand of the killer on the night of October 23rd ; that same hand played in a church service on the night of October 24th and moved on now, to throw the evidence into the Seine River.

But Guillaume-François Vial had no interest in the bigger picture of life or the universe. He was focused on his own petty acts of the moment, and how to get rid of the dagger, which would link him to the killing. He got the idea to chuck the dagger and pocket watch luckily before the police thought of looking for those items either on his person or at his lodging.

"Now that this is done," said Vial to himself, "I can go home and sleep."

"No pangs of conscience and no regrets," he vowed.

*****

# Chapter 29

"If only we had the dagger and the pocket watch," thought Lieutenant de Sartine. "It would serve justice if we could catch the nephew with those items in his house. We'd have him red-handed."

Then a thought occurred to him. "What if he's thrown them into the Seine River?" He asked Sgt. Lebrusque to be discreet and to follow the nephew, just in case he took a walk toward the river. Lebrusque and Gentilhomme could take turns in a stakeout at the apartment. "Wherever he goes, you go, understand? But do it at a distance, and try not to be too obvious."

The only problem was, the police came up with their idea too late. Vial had already disposed of the dagger and the pocket watch several nights earlier. He was not greedy enough to keep his uncle's gold plated watch. He thought of it as a trophy at first, but then thought better of it, as a silly idea. In fact, he grew to hate the sight of the watch. He also knew it was a stupid idea to keep the dagger in his apartment.

De Sartine, meanwhile, was hoping that Vial was one of those killers who kept a trophy of his kill, but apparently he wasn't.

The Lieutenant tried to put himself into the mind of the killer. "You'd think the gold pocket watch was too tempting to just throw away, but then if the watch reminded him too much of his late uncle, then where would he dispose of it?"

"If I were the killer," said the Lieutenant to himself, "I'd throw both items into the river. Yes, that is what I would do. And if Vial was successful in doing that, then Vial is a fish that unfortunately got away. The Superintendent won't be pleased."

After several days, both Gentilhomme and Lebrusque reported that Vial wasn't going near the river, but that he frequented the tavern instead , La Dame Chantante, like usual. He played billiards there, drank his wine and then went home, apparently to bed. He brought no prostitute home with him and apparently had no mistress. "Maybe he's not well liked," quipped Gentilhomme. "Or else, he smells," commented Lebrusque. They had no good words to say about Gujillaume-Francois Vial.

The Lieutenant leaned back in his chair, and puffed some more on his pipe, "If he went to the river before we came up with our brilliant idea to follow him, then he was one step ahead of us. If the dagger and pocket watch are already at the bottom of the river, we don't stand a chance of finding them." He consoled his sergeants, "and that gentlemen, is something beyond our control. How about if we knock off for the night?"

Thus, timing and luck conspired to give the killer a break, out of jail and out of the hands of justice. The Lieutenant had said at the beginning of the investigation, "We may never know who the killer is." Now at the end, they did know who the killer was, but they could do nothing about it, nor put it in the official record.

Unknown to the three police officers, they almost caught a break three years later in 1767. Guillaume-François Vial requested that Louise Roussel set up a "business meeting" with him at the engraving shop. Vial wanted a booklet he had written to be published. It wasn't much, 6 pages, entitled, "L'arbre généalogique de l'harmonie". The title of the pamphlet was longer than the actual tract. Compared to the beauty, originality and importance, of musical compositions and works of art, which passed through the shop over the years, Vial's little pamphlet was shallow, small and of no real importance. He just wanted it published because he wanted to be published, so he could claim he was an actual published author.

A long title for 6 pages! Ludicrous! Louise laughed at him. "If you do not publish it," he threatened, I will go to the police and explain how you paid me to murder my uncle, your ex-husband." Louise gave in; she bought his continued silence by publishing the little tract, "L'arbre généalogique de l'harmonie".   The long-winded title made him sound so important and "erudite". But often with people who have a higher opinion of themselves than they actually are, long-winded speeches and phrases are padding to cover up that there is really nothing underneath their "erudite" exterior.

Louise was 64 years of age at the time of her husband's death. Vial was 40 years old. Louise was old enough to worry about money in her old age; who would provide? Vial was old enough to hate his uncle for not promoting his career.

Louis Roussel was proud of her engraving business which she inherited from her father. It was a rare thing for a woman in the 18$^{th}$ century to own her own business and to run it by herself. However, when her ex-husband died in 1764, she found debts which were catching up with her. His death was like a God-send, giving her access to his remaining assets in manuscripts, some coins, clothes and even the broken violin, she could sell. She had a new infusion of cash in her engraving business.

She swooped in on the old house; collected his belongings, and auctioned them off. She reissued his compositions, and then took a couple of as yet unpublished manuscripts to her shop, so she could publish and print them. She salvaged his unpublished manuscripts, not as a good deed to save his works for posterity, but because there was money to be had in this to save her shop.

The nephew did not show up for the funeral on October 25$^{th}$ at the Eglise Saint-Laurent. Louise made sure she was there; however, as well as at a later memorial service, held at the Eglise de Feuillants in the Rue Saint-Honoré on December 2$^{nd}$ 1765. The "Concert Spirituel" saw to it that both its choir and orchestra performed Mondonville's "De Profundis" during that memorial service. It was truly a moving ceremony in remembrance of a great violinist and composer.

The three police officers thought they might as well show up at the 1765 Concert Spirituel's commemoration, in hopes of cornering the nephew, and perhaps having another inadvertent chat with him. But since he did not show up, they had to sit and enjoy the music.

Louise Roussel died in 1774. Guillaume-François Vial continued to live a life of insignificance, with no obvious documentation about the date of his death. Neither one of them was ever charged or arrested for the murder of Jean-Marie Leclair. The case remained unsolved, despite strong suspicions.

Jean-Marie Leclair received belated accolades for his mastery of music. He has been called "the French Bach" and "the French Corelli". It is said that he did not like extra flourishes in his music, just for the sake of ornamentation. He preferred a direct simple approach in his compositions. The man was knowledgeable both in the solo instrument for which he composed, as well as the well-balanced sense of harmony in a symphony. He loathed fawning and flattery. Jean-Marie Leclair is recognized as the founder of the French school of violin. He left quite a legacy, and possibly could have added more had he not been murdered so cowardly, as to be stabbed from behind in late October 1764.

Musicians are generally acknowledged to be nice people because, well, because they are given a special gift by God. Maybe it's a warning that there is a Dr. Jekyll and Mr. Hyde in all of us because the nephew, a violinist, killed his uncle, a better violinist.

There is a profound piece of irony found in Leopold Mozart's letter to his son, a piece of advice he wanted to impart to his young son, who was 22 at the time. This letter was penned 14 years after Jean-Marie Leclair met his untimely death. Father Leopold recalls that, in his own youth, "I avoided all contact with others and in particular preferred not to become over familiar with people of our own profession." In other words, he tells his son to stay away from musicians! Though Leopold Mozart was serious, to us the thought of such advice from a musician father to his musician son, is strikingly amusing.

While Leclair lay dead in his grave, the world continued on with its own concerns and its own inevitable direction. Throughout the

18<sup>th</sup> century the French government was not able to control its mounting debts. It was the common folk, the average taxpayers, who were obliged to pay for "a war badly begun [the War of the Austrian Succession 1741-1748] and badly supported, the greed of a prime minister, of a mistress, of foolish expenditures, and the prodigality of the King."

This all ruined the finances of France, with the last straw coming when Louis XVI dismissed his finance minister, the Swiss-born, Jacques Necker. Paris was in a direct path toward the French Revolution in 1789.

_____

**I'D APPRECIATE IT IF YOU WROTE A BOOK REVIEW ON GOODREADS OR AMAZON, IF YOU HAVE THE TIME**
– John Hartig Author

\*\*\*\*\*

# Postface

Unfortunately, what I dug up about this great violinist has mainly been a string of dates, locations and what he did there at that time. A skeletal structure of the barest documentation. Certainly not enough to fill a detailed biography of one of the greatest violinists of the 18th century France! Jean-Marie Leclair established the French school of violin. He was dubbed "the French Corelli" and "the French Bach".

As an author, I asked what can one do with only a skeletal string of dates and locations. As a writer, I decided that I needed to fill in that skeletal framework with enough fancy and dialogue to generate a novel, or at least a "novelette", out of it. I think I've succeeded and I hope you enjoy this story of fact mixed with fiction.

Jean-Marie Leclair was one of 8 children, the oldest born in 1697. His parents owned a haberdashery business. His father played cello as a hobby; the mother made gowns for ladies of the nobility. Jean-Marie made his living at first as a ballet dancer, and then concentrated on his talent as violinist and composer. When he took advanced studies with accomplished violin player, Giovanni Battista Somis, he was advised to shove his ballet dancing into the background and make the violin his primary occupation. That advice served him well because Jean-Marie Leclair gained a reputation as a great musician.

Later in life, he deliberately chose to live in a seedy part of Paris. We know that he was stabbed to death outside his home at the age of 67, cruelly murdered, and the crime was never solved.

This novella is mostly made-up. I'm sure historians can find inaccuracies in the factual parts of my work. However, this small novel is meant to entertain and not to be accurate as a full-proof factual biography. I must admit that my research and the ensuing imagined part of Jean-Marie's secret life has been tremendous fun, mixing fact with fiction. It has also been quite instructive digging up facts about the lifestyles, the clothes, the homes, the mores and even the foods of the 18th century in France.

*****

# Resources and References
## JEAN-MARIE LECLAIR 1697-1764

BIOGRAPHY AND MURDER

Jean-Marie Leclair – Wikipedia
https://en.wikipedia.org/wiki/Jean-Marie_Leclair

Jean – Marie Leclair (1697 – 1764) - early-music.com
http://www.early-music.com/what-is-early-music/jean-marie-leclair-1697-1764/

Jean-Marie Leclair Biography
https://play.primephonic.com/artist/jean-marie-leclair-1697

Who murdered Jean-Marie Leclair- - Orchestra of the Age of Enlightenment
http://www.oae.co.uk/murdered-jean-marie-leclair/

What Killed the Great and Not So Great Composers? Joseph W. Lewis, Jr., M.D., Google Books
https://books.google.ca/books?id=Jf5LiICDWl8C

Une mort trop petite pour eux (2-10) - Actualités - Ôlyrix
https://www.olyrix.com/articles/olyrix/156/une-mort-trop-petite-pour-eux-610

Rebels and Rivalries - SFEMS
http://sfems.org/?p=8085

Murder in the Rue Careme-Prenant
http://www.interlude.hk/front/jean-marie-leclair/

Finale Marked Presto- The Killing of Leclair on JSTOR
https://www.jstor.org/stable/948121?seq=1#page_scan_tab_con
tents

A Baroque Music History Murder Mystery - Music History Matters
https://musichistorymatters.org/juicy-baroque-murder-mystery/

Jean-Marie Leclair pdf
https://www.wrightmusic.net/pdfs/jean-marie-leclair.pdf

Jean-Marie Leclair - Biography & History - AllMusic
https://www.allmusic.com/artist/jean-marie-leclair-
mn0001439658/biography

Jean-Marie Leclair (1697-1764)
https://www.musicologie.org/Biographies/l/leclair_jean_marie.ht
ml

Jean-Marie Leclair (1697-1764) - Find a Grave Memorial
https://www.findagrave.com/memorial/21793061/jean-marie-
leclair

Jean-Marie Leclair- Seduction and Rococo Art - Playing the Palace
https://www.artsjournal.com/palace/2013/06/jean-marie-leclair-
seduction-and-rococo-art.html

Jean-Marie Leclair, a Narrative of His Life and Death - YouTube
https://www.youtube.com/watch?v=HLaLBQ5xegs

The Leclair Caper – Simanaitis Says
https://simanaitissays.com/2018/02/01/the-leclair-caper/

L'assassinat de Jean-Marie Leclair- Une des plus grandes énigmes
criminelles du XVIIIe siècle eBook- Gérard Gefen, Philippe

Beaussant, Roger Le Taillanter- Amazon.fr- Amazon Media EU S.à r.l-
https://www.amazon.fr/Lassassinat-Jean-Marie-Leclair-grandes-criminelles-ebook/dp/B077NHG3HN

Jean-Pierre Guignon, *né* Giovanni Pietro Ghignone (10 February 1702 – 30 January 1774) was an 18th-century Franco-Italian composer and violinist
https://en.wikipedia.org/wiki/Jean-Pierre_Guignon/


## THEIR MUSIC

Women & Music  - A History  -Google Books
https://books.google.ca/books?id=XBXggAcjnEoC

The Birth of French Opera
https://en.wikipedia.org/wiki/French_opera#The_birth_of_French_opera:_Lully

Dances of the Baroque Era
https://socialdance.stanford.edu/Syllabi/baroque.htm


## 18TH CENTURY PARIS

A Concise History of FRANCE, Second Edition, Roger Price, Cambridge University Press, 2005  pp. 87-89

Louis The Beloved: The Life of Louis XV, Olivier Bernier, Doubleday 1984.

Queen of Fashion: Marie Antoinette, Caroline Weber, Henry Holt & Co. 2006.

Paris in the 18th century
https://en.wikipedia.org/wiki/Paris_in_the_18th_century#Food_and_drink

Paris in the 18th century
https://en.wikipedia.org/wiki/Paris_in_the_18th_century#Workers,_servants_and_the_poor

The Paris Police
https://en.wikipedia.org/wiki/Paris_in_the_18th_century

The 18th century social sciences McMaster pdf
https://socialsciences.mcmaster.ca/econ/ugcm/3ll3/see/18thCentury.pdf


NEWS AND COFFEE

HISTORY OF THE EARLY PARISIAN COFFEE HOUSES
http://www.web-books.com/Classics/ON/B0/B701/16MB701.html

English coffeehouses in the 17th and 18th centuries - Wikipedia
https://en.wikipedia.org/wiki/English_coffeehouses_in_the_17th_and_18th_centuries

18th century coffee houses.docx
http://www.web-books.com/Classics/ON/B0/B701/16MB701.html

17th century - How did people receive news before the advent of the newspaper- - History Stack Exchange https://history.stackexchange.com/questions/1976/how-did-people-receive-news-before-the-advent-of-the-newspaper

A Brief History of the First French Encyclopedia - Mental Floss
http://mentalfloss.com/article/502589/brief-history-first-french-encyclopedia


## HOW THEY LIVED

Hygiene In The 18th Century – YouTube
https://www.youtube.com/watch?v=BoT3C-ae8io

A brief history of body odor
https://theweek.com/articles/614722/brief-history-body-odor

Madame Isis' Toilette- Keeping clean in the 18th century
http://madameisistoilette.blogspot.com/2014/09/keeping-clean-in-18th-century.html

10 Revolting Facts About the 18th Century - List verse
https://listverse.com/2012/10/22/10-revolting-facts-about-the-18th-century/


A quick history of domestic lighting - Lucy Worsley
http://www.lucyworsley.com/a-quick-history-of-domestic-lighting/

keeping warm in the 18th century - Jane Austen's World
https://janeaustensworld.wordpress.com/tag/keeping-warm-in-the-18th-century/

Heating the 18th century house

https://www.jstor.org/stable/988150?seq=1#page_scan_tab_contents

18th Century Marriage Customs
http://www.wondersandmarvels.com/2014/07/18th-century-marriage-customs.html
Late 1800s Wedding
https://www.geriwalton.com/marriage-etiquette-france-late-1800s/

The Composers' Houses
by Gerard Geffen in French,
no trans. , could not get a copy


CONTEMPORARIES

Jean-Pierre Guignon - Wikipedia
https://en.wikipedia.org/wiki/Jean-Pierre_Guignon

Joseph Haydn - Wikipedia
https://en.wikipedia.org/wiki/Joseph_Haydn

Symphony No. 22 (Haydn) - Wikipedia
https://en.wikipedia.org/wiki/Symphony_No._22_(Haydn)

The Mozarts in London – Music Blog
https://blogs.bl.uk/music/2018/05/mozartinlondon.html

Leopold Mozart's Advice to His Son Wolfgang Amadeus - The Intermediate Period
https://theintermediateperiod.wordpress.com/2015/09/20/leopold-mozarts-advice-to-his-son-wolfgang-amadeus/

European Mozart ways - European Mozart ways
 https://www.mozartways.com/content.php?m=2

Visit from the child Mozart, 1763-1764 – Palace of Versailles
http://en.chateauversailles.fr/discover/history/key-dates/visit-child-mozart-1763-1764

Jean-Baptiste Lully
Music, style and influence
https://en.wikipedia.org/wiki/Jean-Baptiste_Lully_-Ballets_de_cour

_____


**I'D APPRECIATE IT IF YOU COULD DO A BOOK REVIEW EITHER ON GOODREADS OR AMAZON, IF YOU HAVE THE TIME**
– John Hartig Author

\*\*\*\*\*

# Acknowledgements

When I first started out as a novelist, I forgot to mention Acknowledgements. Now, I realize that is it important to publicly thank people because people need to feel appreciated.

I'd like to thank my St. Jerome's High-School teachers, in Kitchener, Ontario, for giving me a good classical education. First of all, my English teacher, Mr. William Klos, who ignited a love of literature in me and who read poetry and excerpts with feeling. Also, Mr. Ronald Haston, who made history come alive, especially with his narratives and spirited introductions to every history class.

Thanks goes to Michael Kositsky for excellent redirections in my first novel, and for his careful work in proofreading. Michael is a composer in a variety of musical genres. His wife, Lynne, is also a Shakespearean scholar and author. It was their moving down the street from me some years ago which prompted me to see if I could write a novel myself.

I'd like to thank Klaas Smit who corrected me on a point of history and told me about how European people, in the old days, actually slept in "bedroom closets" in order to keep warm.

Thanks also to Lubomir Cekota who is not shy about giving his opinions about history and pointing out inconsistencies. Dates and the facts have to be right. I used interesting anecdotes from Lu's teaching career for parts of this novel.

Veronika Reiser, at the Rittenhouse Public Library, in Vineland dug up some excellent resources for me about France and how people lived in the 18th century. That was for the Jean-Marie Leclair murder mystery of 1764.

Helen Basson, former wardrobe mistress at the Stratford Shakespearean Festival, shared knowledge about how unsanitary it was to walk on the seedy streets of cities in the 18<sup>th</sup> century for ladies wanting to protect the fringes of their long dresses.

Thanks to my wife, Marjorie, who prefers to remain anyonymous and who let me sneak off at midnight, close the bedroom door, and fire up the computer with a cup of tea by my side, so I can type. Insomnia has its good points.

\*\*\*\*\*

# *Battle of the Violins*

## Time Travel with James T. Kirk

Jean-Marie Leclair 1697 – 1764
Jean-Pierre Guignon 1702-1774
Pietro Antonio Locatelli 1695-1764
Fritz Kreisler 1875-1962
Lenny Solomon 1952-...
Nicola Benedetti 1987-...

**Copyright © Author: John Hartig**

**First Edition 2019**

# Synopsis

Jean-Marie Leclair

It all started with Jean-Marie Leclair, a great French violinist and composer. Well, at least, the battle of the violins idea started with him. The time travel came later.

Jean-Marie made a trip to Kassel, Germany, in 1728 where he met Pietro Antonio Locatelli, another great violinist and composer. They seemed to get along, and decided to have a friendly violin joust in a public performance. The crowd just loved it.

A few years later, in 1734, Jean-Marie got back to Paris where he played in the orchestra funded by King Louis XV of France, in what was called the "Concert Spirituel". Jean-Marie liked being first chair, or top dog, in the orchestra, except he had competition from Jean-Pierre Guignon, who thought he was good enough to be first chair violin. The King thought it was a good idea to have friendly violin jousts in public, where the two squared off, except the competition was anything but friendly. Jean-Marie packed up his violin, quit the orchestra and moved to the Netherlands. So, that is the background story behind the Battle of the Violins.

Fast forward to the year 2328. Admiral Fritz Kreisler, you guessed it, great, great great grandson of the Viennese Fritz Kreisler, always asked the question, who was best in the violin world? The Admiral could afford to ask such questions because he was after all, an Admiral in Star Fleet, and what's more he could pull strings, as it were, with certain departments like the UWAC, Unted Worlds Arts Council.

"Captain Kirk," he asked, in a teleconference, "you are familiar with the light-speed breakaway factor?"

"Oh," said Kirk, "you mean the slingshot effect, using the gravitational field of our sun, to go back or forwards in time?"

"Precisely," said the Admiral, "I'd like you to retrieve a few violinists, 6 of them to be precise, bring them back here to our future, so we can have a fiddle contest to see who is best."

James Tiberius Kirk thought the exercise was rather whimsical, not to say, a huge waste of Star Fleet energy...and Time. But he bit his tongue. Kirk merely said, "Yes, Sir."

The Captain glanced at the list of the 6 virtuosi he was supposed to "retrieve" from the past. "Oh, if I may , Sir," he asked the Admiral, "I notice Paganini isn't on the list."

"Well, yes. He's a hot topic. He was supposed to have made a pact with the devil which accounted for his superhuman ability on the violin. He also had some sort of wrist disease which gave him unusual flexibility on the fingerboard. Because of these extenuating circumstances, especially the pact with the devil, we felt it was best to exclude the man." The Admiral added as a humorous after-thought, "Besides Paganini would probably have won hands down in a pact with the devil."

Kirk saluted, and merely said again, "Yes, Sir."

# Preface

Since time travel expended so much energy, Captain Kirk had a notion to borrow Mister Herbert George Wells' Time Machine, which could do the job more efficiently; than having the big bulk of the NCC Enterprise 1701 bulldoze its way through the time-continuum. "We'll just borrow Mr. Wells' smaller machine for a little while," said Captain James T. Kirk. Scotty readily agreed to the idea to use the Enterprise as little as possible for time travel, always eager to protect his beloved engines from undue stress or abuse.

So NCC Enterprise 1701 set off on a new mission, one in time travel. The Captain had six envelopes each of which held a Golden Ticket, an invitation to the Battle of the Violins to be held at the Hollywood Bowl in the year 2328. The Ticket was holographic and could talk, a convincing stratagem to persuade someone from the 18th century to come along into the future.

"We've got our task cut out for us," said Kirk. Mr. Spock, Chief Engineer Montgomery Scott and even Chief Medical Officer, Leonard McCoy couldn't agree more. They were thinking about the Temporal Prime Directive and also a possible Time Paradox.

"Don't worry about it," said the Captain, "it should be safe, within reasonable parameters." He sipped his black coffee just for reassurance.

*****

# Golden Tickets
# To Time Travel

## The First Trio

"I'm giving it all she's got, captain. If I push it any harder, captain, the whole thing will blow." That was a dire warning from Chief engineer Montgomery Scott, "Scotty", as the USS Enterprise (NCC-1701-A) flung itself into a slingshot effect around the sun, counter clockwise. This was in an effort to go back in time to bring the starship into the year 1901, six years after the famous British writer, Herbert George Wells, published *The Time Machine*.

Captain James Tiberius Kirk was now at liberty to reveal his secret orders to his First Officer, Mister Spok, to Chief Engineer Scott and to the rest of the crew. "Gentlemen," he said, gripping the arms of his Command Chair, "welcome to 1901 and the 20th century, Earth time."

He continued, "As you know, time travel has been banned by the Temporal Prime Directive because of the risk of creating a Temporal Paradox. However, in this case, we are safe enough." Captain Kirk opened the secret envelope. In it were his orders from UWAC, the United Worlds Arts Council. There were also 6 golden tickets, apparently invitations of some sort to an artistic joust, a Battle of the Violins.

"Ridiculous," uttered Scotty. "We risked time travel for this? Some artsy thing?"

Captain Kirk, nodded, and took a sip of his steaming black coffee.

"Indeed, we did. I got the orders directly from Admiral Fritz Kreisler. He is the grandson, of the famous violinist, Fritz Kreisler, 16 generations removed. He has the idea that his ancestor was the best violinist there ever was. In that vein, we received orders to bring back his ancestor, in person, along with a few other wayfaring violinists strung along the time-continuum, so that we may have, what the admiral called, a jamboree of violins."

"And the admiral risked the Temporal Prime Directive, a Temporal Paradox, and our lives to have this happen?"

"Rank has its privilege," said Kirk. "It should be interesting. If I'm right I already know the outcome."

"And what is that?" asked McCoy, "if I'm so bold as to ask your prognostication about something that hasn't happened yet."

"We shall see," said Kirk, "we shall see."

The slingshot effect had been used sparingly in the Enterprise's long history, but most notably in the year 2286, when the ship traveled back in time to the 1960s, in order to rescue a pair of humpback whales to satisfy a probe which threatened 23rd century Earth, looking for the extinct whale species.

"But now, Captain," complained Montgomery Scott. "To satisfy the whim of an Admiral about his musical ancestor?"

"Like I said," declared Kirk, "rank has its privilege."

He showed the crew the 6 Golden Tickets. "These are personal invitations that are indestructible. We must give them to these named violinists: Jean-Marie Leclair, Jean-Pierre Guignon, Pietro Antonio Locatelli, Fritz Kreisler [Junior, Junior, if you will], Lenny Solomon, and thank goodness, a woman, named Nicola Benedetti."

"But I'm sure there were so many other worthy violinists in musical history," observed Doctor McCoy. What made Admiral Kreisler pick these? I recall listening to Joshua Bell, and Itzhak Perlman, and enjoyed them immensely."

"The Admiral assured me, it was all a matter of taste and haphazard choice, picking out 6 champion violinists," admitted Kirk.

"But Captain," objected Scotty, "these players are all from a different time period. We would have to jump time, several times over, to kidnap each of the players, and bring them where and when to do this, this outrageous jamboree?"

"I wouldn't use the term, kidnap, Mr. Scott," corrected Kirk, "we will present each player with a Golden Ticket, which is their invitation to a violin joust, or virtuosi show-off, if you will. It's also convenient, since our competitors all have different native languages, which the Golden Ticket is able to speak in their native language."

"I like that," said Scotty, "a universal translator that talks as well as translates."

"But what about the drain on our engines with all this jumping about in time?" asked Scotty with deep concern.

"Astute observation," said Kirk, "I know you are concerned about the strain on your 'bairns', But don't worry, we have new dilithium crystals installed, and besides, we also have an ace up our sleeve."

"Well, Jim?" asked the fine doctor, "I'm no lawyer and certainly no physicist. But what do you suggest we do for this multiple infraction of the Temporal Prime Directive?"

Captain Kirk took another swallow of his black coffee, somewhat tepid by now. "Heat this up for me, Ensign," he said. The ensuing explanation astounded even Mister Spock. "Fascinating," he said.

In order not to tax the dilithium crystals too much by bouncing back and forth in time several times, and then leaping back into the future where the Battle of the Violins was to be staged, the crew was assigned to find Mister Herbert George Wells at his large family house, known as the Spade House, located in Sandgate, England, in 1901.

"Through secret documents on the author, and dabbler in science, we have established that the man had a working model of a time machine in his basement. It is this machine which will be used to slip myself, Mr. Spock and Doctor McCoy back and forth in time several times over to hand our competitors their personal Golden Ticket for the grand event. We understand that Mr. Wells built this particular time machine to be a six seater. There is enough room to take us and three of our virtuosic guests, in two separate trips, back to the Enterprise and then to our rendezvous at the

Hollywood Bowl where the competition will be held in January 2328."

Commander Montgomery Scott did not like the sound of this at all.

"Ach, a pleasant contest with violins, is a fine thing, I'm sure, captain. But to abuse Science like this for the sake of the Arts, now there I get hot under the collar!"

McCoy was disgruntled as well, "Now I know what they mean when they say, Artsy!"

Mister Spock merely raised his eyebrow.

The away team would be the Captain, Mr. Spock and Dr. McCoy. Scotty murdered his French even with the universal translator. The machine spoke French with a Scottish brogue. Scotty's linguistic struggle was solved anyway, when Kirk said, "You will remain on board, Scotty, to beam us up safely when we need it."

"Ay, Ay," said Scotty, 'as ye wish!"

The away-team outfitted themselves with appropriate early 20th dress, each wearing a suitable Homburg, and Spock with a special "Docker" which he pulled down over his pointy ears.

In no time, the trio found themselves knocking at the front door of the Spade House. H.G. Wells himself answered the door.

"We are travelers," said Kirk.

"I'm sure. You look like Americans."

"Yes, we have a matter to discuss with you. We admired the work you did in your 1895 novel, The Time Machine."

"Well, come in. I always like to listen to words of adulation. Makes me feel like my hours writing late at night were almost worth the effort."

Jane, his second wife, served them crumpets and tea.

Then Kirk revealed the real reason they were there. "We are indeed travelers," admitted Kirk, "we come from the 23$^{rd}$ century, not just America. Mr. Spock is a Vulcan coming from the planet of Vulcan." Mr. Spock took off his hat. H.G. Wells was not surprised. "Yes, indeed, you are travelers. I called my hero that in my novel about time travel, 'The Traveler'."

"We would like to use your new time machine," revealed Kirk. Mr. Wells was most willing to oblige. "If you follow me, gentlemen." He led them to the basement. The sight was something which even astonished Mr. Spock. "Fascinating," he said looking at the machine. The same large dish that would start spinning once the machine was activated, the levers which glowed and controlled the speed through time. "We need the machine for two months perhaps," said Kirk, "and it will be brought back to you, intact, I assure you."

"You still haven't proved to me that you are in fact travelers of time," observed Mr. Wells.

"That will be made apparent," reassured Kirk, "once your machine disappears right in front of you from your basement." The machine shimmered, and poof was gone in the blink of an eye, reappearing on the shuttlecraft deck of the NCC-1701 Enterprise.

"Now we must go too," said Kirk. The trio didn't use the front door. Captain Kirk spoke into his communicator, and told Mr. Scott, "Beam us up Scotty!"

They shimmered out of existence from the basement to appear on the command deck of the starship Enterprise. Kirk took the captain's chair. "It's always reassuring when we return from an away mission," said Kirk to Spock standing beside him, "it's like coming back home to a mother's womb. I feel safe inside our ship." Spock could only raise one eyebrow. Lights blinked reassuringly on the dashboard at Sulu's work station.

Captain Kirk ordered coffee, black. "How are we doing Mr. Sulu?" asked Kirk. "Course laid in," answered Sulu, "we are out of sight and out of mind hidden on the dark side of the moon." Kirk nodded with satisfaction as he sipped his coffee.

Meanwhile, back in England, at the Spade House, Jane asked her husband, "Where are our guests?"

"Oh they had to rush off, you know. They are Americans!"

And on the Enterprise, Kirk was already planning his approach to the next order of business, presenting Jean-Marie Leclair and Jean-Pierre Guignon with their Golden Tickets to the Battle of the Violins. They had the opportunity to refuse the tickets, of course, but knowing human nature, Kirk surmised that each one of the chosen invitees would accept, not only to show off their talent, but even if they failed, to seize a once in a lifetime adventure.

Through their computer, the Enterprise found a perfect cave, just outside of Paris, in which they could position Wells' time machine. From there, in the perfect spot, Kirk, McCoy and Mister Spock could move the machine through time to the year 1738. From that very cave, which had been in existence for millennia, they could walk to Paris and find the two men whom they sought. All three of them were dressed in the appropriate attire for the 18<sup>th</sup> century, although the three cornered hat for Spock was a bit of a problem with the ears. Dr. McCoy used a synthetic rubber, simply to reshape the pointiness and make the ears bigger. Kirk thought he looked like a Vulcan "Dumbo". McCoy urged, "Say Spock with big ears like that, it would help if you actually acted dumb. Makes it more convincing."

Spock raised his eyebrow at that, but conceded with a nod. He knew enough not to talk if he was going to act dumb. "Fascinating," he thought.

They found Leclair and Guignon practising in separate rooms at the "Concert Spirituel", which was Paris' first venue for a public music series.

"We are angels from the future," said Kirk opening Leclair's door. "Did Guignon send you to sabotage my practice?" asked Leclair. Kirk used his hidden communicator. "Kirk here. Mr. Sulu make Monsieur Leclair's violin disappear." Leclair heard the room say, "Ay, Captain." The violin disappeared, shimmered out of sight. "Are you sure you are not working with Guignon?" asked Leclair. The violin instantly reappeared again.

"We have a challenge for you," offered Kirk, handing Leclair the Golden Ticket. It stated in French that Leclair was invited to a Battle of the Violins, to be held in a Heavenly Abode.

Leclair said, "I knew it. I was always worthy of such a challenge."

Pretty well, the same thing happened with Guignon. The two men descended upon the secret cave from opposite directions. "What's he doing here?" they both asked at the same time. Kirk explained that they already had been involved in a public violin joust in the Concert Spirituel. This was merely an extension of a violin duel of the best. They both had packed their violins in their cases, and now, they themselves were packed into the time machine. Kirk hoped they were not backseat drivers. Thankfully, they kept their mouths shut as the machine sped back to 1901, from which they would launch into the far future of 2328, and the "Play Off" of six of the greatest violinists the world has ever known.

Jean-Marie Leclair, Jean-Pierre Guignon, Pietro Antonio Locatelli, Fritz Kreisler, Lenny Solomon and Nicola Benedetti.

"We still have to fetch Locatelli," said Kirk. "Since he moved to Holland, and we have hidden our time machine just outside of Paris, we have to move the thing again, to a discrete spot just outside of Amsterdam.."

"I suppose we'll have to use the universal translator again," said Spock, "since none of you, Captain,  or Dr. McCoy speak either French or Dutch."

"And I would do no good down there with ye folk," said Scotty interrupting through the communicator, using his heaviest Scottish brogue, "I'm best at me controls up here to beam ye up or down, as ye please."

Kirk directed his attention to the other two Starfleet officers, eying Spock with his big ears and dumb look on his face, and McCoy with his his typical air of disgruntlement. "At least it's the same time period," said Kirk, "so let's find Locatelli and give him his Golden Ticket, and then get back up to the Enterprise."

The trio stood outside of Locatelli's door, impressed with how well the violinist was doing as a guest composer in the Netherlands.

"Did you come to buy violin strings?" asked Locatelli.

"We are angels from another time," explained Kirk, using the line as something a mind of the 18th century could understand."We have an invitation for you," Kirk said, as he handed Locatelli the Golden Ticket. It spoke Italian to him, then Dutch, kindly inviting Locatelli to participate in a violin joust in the future.

"Well," said Locatelli, "if my friend, Leclair has already accepted, so will I." It was settled then, another traveler and his violin to transport to the Enterprise which hovered undetected on the other side of the moon in the year 1901.

"Where are we going?" asked Locatelli, still assuming that these messengers from the future were actually angels from God. "All will be revealed to you in due time," assured Kirk.

The crew of the Enterprise had secured half of their objective with Leclair, Guignon and Locatelli safely secured in comfortable quarters on board the Enterprise. They each were given a female guide so they would not feel threatened, and they fancied the idea getting a tour of the ship by a woman in a short skirt. "So this is a vessel of the air?" asked Locatelli. He was most interested in scientific things of an ornithological, theological, and mathematical nature.

# The Second Trio

"Well, gentlemen," said Kirk, "let's transport Mr. Wells' time machine back on board and go and find Mister Fritz Kreisler." According to research, the best time to present Mr. Kreisler with the Golden Ticket was in 1938 in France before the outbreak of World War II.

"At least," said Kirk with a conciliatory tone, "we don't have to move our time machine far in order to intersect it with Mr. Kreisler in France."

Captain Kirk could not use the line about an angelic visit, because Flash Gordon and space travel comics were all a rave at this time, among young people even in Paris.

So once Kirk found Kreisler, he was honest. "We are time travelers from outer space."

"Funny," said Fritz Kreisler, "you look more like Americans."

Kirk had Sulu do the same transporter trick with Kreisler's favourite violin, the Giuseppe Guarneri, and then return it to the violinist intact. Kirk presented Kreisler with the talking Golden Ticket which convinced Kreisler of a great adventure ahead. He gladly accepted the challenge to the Battle of the Violins. He wondered how good the other players were, since he himself had won the "Premier Grand Prix de Rome" gold medal at the age of 12 in Paris.

Fritz Kreisler had fought for Austria in the First World War and was injured, and although honourably discharged, this put a new perspective on his own value as an artist and as a human being who hated war.

Captain Kirk broke the Prime Directive in regard to Fritz Kreisler's personal situation telling him to move to America because Germany would round up Jews and annihilate as many as they could in a Holocaust. Kreisler, being Jewish, was horrified at the thought. Being Viennese, he also did not like the idea of Austria being annexed by Hitler in an "Anschluss" in March 1938 which would march all of Europe into another World War. Kreisler therefore, promised his wife, they would settle in New York City and become naturalized citizens, to get out of Europe just in the nick of time.

Kirk did not tell Kreisler that he would be in a car accident three years later, in 1941 in New York, hit by a truck while crossing a busy street. Kreisler suffered a skull fracture and was in a coma for over a week.

"Well," said Kirk privately to Dr. McCoy, "at least we have our man at his peak, before the accident."

So, with the time machine stowed safely back on board in the space dock, Kirk, Spock, and McCoy focused their attention on Britain next to fetch Nicola Benedetti. After that it would be North America and Lenny Solomon.

"We will have to place our time machine," said Kirk, "in some secret spot inside Britain to pick up Ms. Benedetti, and then teleport the machine to North America to pick up Mr. Lenny Solomon."

Kirk went on, "I love our clandestine act in hiding on the dark side of the moon. I could almost write lyrics to the thought. At least we remain undetected from our base in the moon's dark side, in the year 1901. We won't even have to move the Enterprise when we give the Golden Ticket to Ms Benedetti and Mr. Solomon. We'll just teleport Wells' time shuttle, and ourselves as need be."

"So," said Kirk, "instead of us, let us have Mr. Wells' smaller craft do all the work in running through time like a busy bee."

The time machine shimmered into existence again somewhere in Britain near Nicola Benedetti' house. It was appropriately out of sight. The British violinist was born of an Italian/Scottish heritage. She began violin at the age of five.

"She must really be good then," commented McCoy. "Well," added Scotty butting in again through his communicator, "her being half-Scottish, she's sure to be a crackerjack at winnin' this competition."

"It remains to be seen," said Captain Kirk, "it remains to be seen."

Captain Kirk mulled over when the best time was in which to bring young Miss Benedetti on board the starship. McCoy had researched her and found she had recently broken up with her cellist boyfriend, who she'd been dating for 9 years. Now at 31, Benedetti was headed not only laterally away from her former boyfriend, but also accelerating upwards to a new level of playing and international fame and recognition.

In McCoy's mind he could see the youngster being happier with her boyfriend before the breakup and perhaps she would in a mood to play better. On the other hand, a deep hurt, like a breakup, could make her a more profound player and know how to touch the heartstrings of an audience.

"Let's get her after the breakup," advised McCoy, "she'll get over her hurt and play even better."

The away team focused on the year 2019 to whisk Nicola Benedetti away to the NCC Enterprise. The Star Trek trio descended upon her parents' house. She had a flat of her own, but was now visiting her parents for the weekend, and decided to practise a wee bit before breaking for lunch with her mom and dad. But it was Dr. McCoy's firm knock on the door, that put an end to the lovely phrasings in the practice. Benedetti, herself, opened the door, a pretty young woman.

Captain Kirk said they represented an international group who were organizing a Battle of the Violins and were inviting all contenders to compete at the Hollywood Bowl in Los Angeles. He simply did not say what year this competition would take place. He handed her her talking Golden Ticket, which recited the invitation to a Battle of the Violins, doing so in English with a Scot's accent and also in Italian, again with a Scottish brogue. She grabbed the ticket, said "I accept," and invited the trio in for tea. Mom and dad were home. "Oh," they said, "Americans."

It was no secret how Benedetti, a young woman, was so awed by this invitation from a Golden Ticket that talks. "Um, Mr. Scott, four to beam up. We have Ms. Benedetti."

After shimmering aboard the Enterprise, the young violinist was star struck with everything, though she was miffed that her cell-phone didn't work up here. She didn't know it was blocked. At least, she got a male tour guide, a suggestion made by the captain, though not quite willingly. He had confided in Dr. McCoy, in all fairness, that he did have scruples now that he had an "understanding" with a certain Ensign Hartley, a curvaceous blond who caught Kirk's eye several missions ago. He didn't quite want to let go of the Ensign for a pretty violin player, no matter how good she was."

"Bones," said Kirk to the good doctor, "we have to make sacrifices for the greater good." He passed images of Ensign Hartley through his head. She was not only sexy but also lovely.

Nicola Benedetti had gladly taken the Golden Ticket, and welcomed the sweet company of the young tour guide who would show her around the non-restricted zones of the spaceship. To her, Captain Kirk seemed too superior and too full of himself to take on such a mundane task himself to show her around.

The captain was planning the geographical relocation of Wells' time machine, a physical necessity since it would only move through Time and not through Space or Place. Scotty found the perfect spot in one of the green ravines which covers 17% of Toronto's land mass. Toronto is, after all, a city within a large park. Scotty had to make sure that the spot he picked would not be rezoned by the city so that developers could build their high rises between 1901 and 2019. Scotty found another cave within a ravine.

So, in the year 2019, Kirk, Spock and McCoy went knocking at the detached Georgian, white brick, three-storey home of Lenny and Wendy Solomon in Toronto. Wendy was an accomplished cellist who performs in the musical group, Bowfire. This had been their home for a decade now.

"We have an invitation for you to a fiddler's contest," said Kirk over the intercom. Lenny was intrigued. When he buzzed them in, he asked, "Americans? This had better not be a sales gimmick!"

"I assure you," replied Kirk handing him the talking Golden Ticket, "although this ticket talking, makes it seem rather like a gimmick doesn't it?"

"We represent UWAC, the United Worlds Arts Council."

"Never heard of it. Is that like the United Nations?"

"More than that," said Kirk, "more like an interplanetary Arts Council."

Lenny said, "It's about time!"

His wife, Wendy, was not convinced. "Prove it," she said.

Kirk held up his communicator. "Scotty," we need a little proof here."

Before you could say, Bowfire, Lenny's electric violin shimmered out of existence. "Hey where did it go? This could constitute theft, you know."

"Not to worry," reassured Kirk, "it will be back in its cradle in no time." Which it was as it shimmered back into existence safe and sound.

"Am I mistaken or has that violin got holes in it?" asked Kirk.

"Well, yes, it's an electric violin. I have reverb and wawa sound controls on it." Kirk said, "I'm sorry, Lenny, if you are to play in our Battle of the Violins, you have to go traditional. A regular violin with no electronics. Do you have one of those?"

"Why yes, the one I used for our Myles and Lenny Album from 1974."

"We're all set then," said Kirk, " you accept the challenge."

"More than glad to," answered Solomon, "I suppose the gig is out of town?"

"Yes," said Kirk, "the Hollywood Bowl in Los Angeles."

"Oh," said Solomon, "if it was good enough for Jascha Heifetz, it's good enough for me." Solomon did not know that the contest would take place in the year 2328.

Kirk explained that it wasn't that wives were not welcome; it was a matter of physics, the expenditure of energy if extra passengers were carried along into the future.

"The future?" asked Solomon.

"Well yes," affirmed Kirk, "we will host the Battle of the Violins at the Hollywood Bowl in 301 years from now."

"I guess," said Wendy, "it's going to be an overnight thing, then." She got up to pack his clothes and pajamas. The pajamas had little cartoons of cowboys on it on rocking horses.

Before anybody could say, "light-speed breakaway factor", the Enterprise had its latest passenger on board, Wells' time machine safely tucked into the cargo bay, and all the away team back on board.

"Let's head for the sun," commanded Captain Kirk from his chair, "and let's get out of 1901. I feel claustrophobic here in this era, especially hiding behind the dark side of the moon." He explained to his 6 guests that they were about to slingshot passed the sun, using its gravitational field, to hurl back into the future.

"You will be guests of Admiral Fritz Kreisler," noted the captain, "he has made arrangements for a gala dinner once you are settled into your new quarters."

"Kreisler?" asked Nicola Benedetti, "I thought he died ages ago. A great Viennese composer. Beautiful stuff, Liebesleid, Liebesfreud, and Schön Rosmarin."

Kirk reassured her that for this contest, the man would be alive and well, still at his peak and able to perform his beautiful songs. Benedetti smiled with pleasure. She always liked Kreisler's music growing up as a child.

The six musicians were marched into Admiral Fritz Kreisler's office.  "I present to you, Admiral Fritz Kreisler," said Kirk. "Admiral, our contestants." He swept his arm out by way of introduction. Then Kirk introduced each of the virtuosi separately doing, as usual, a respectable job.

Fritz Kreisler walked up the admiral. "So are you my great grand pappy?" "Why more than that," replied the Admiral, "I'll just call you, junior, junior, to keep it simple, and not confuse the issue that we are 16 times removed, but then that's long to say. So you call me Admiral, and I'll call you Fritz Junior, Junior." They looked almost identical.

"Let me explain the rules of the contest to you folks," said the Admiral. "Since I have a vested interest in this, as you can see by the man standing there in front of me, with the lush Viennese mustache, you will be judged by none other than the 9 Justices sitting on the Supreme Court of the United States." Since none of the violinists was American, they all felt that the judging would be, or rather should be fair.

"The array of music will be the same pieces from different eras, the Baroque [1600-1750], the Classical [1750-1820], the Romantic [1810-1910], Contemporary [1910-2010] and finally one choice of your own. You will each be assigned a practice room with a music stand and the required pieces of music. You will have one week to prepare."

"To reiterate, the pieces chosen from these different periods will be the same for each of you, to give us a more accurate judgment about what each of you is capable of. During the contest, you may use a music stand, have the sheets of music in front of you, and of course, each of you will have a microphone in front of you. That includes you, Mr. Solomon. No electric violin, however!'"

Admiral Kreisler explained that making each of the contestants play the same pieces would ensure that there was a control factor in the contest. The judges would determine how well or badly the pieces were played on a scale of 10. Decimal points would be allowed. The maximum total possible was 50 points.

"Well," said the admiral, "During the contest you are welcome to use any sheets of music you wish. I shall look forward to seeing you at tonight's dinner which has been prepared in your honour. We are having roast duck, ham, and roast beef. I understand that some of you may be Jewish, so the ham has been prepared as a separate dish. There is no cross-contamination, and for those of you who are gluten free, we have that too. Our beverage will be anything from coffee, tea and an assortment of white and red wines, as well of those of you have a refined taste, we have several choices of champagne." The admiral had them all escorted out as he lit up a pipe, puffed away meditatively and smiled. "This will be fun."

# The Hollywood Bowl

The week of practice was up. The pieces of music chosen by Fritz Kreisler Junior, Junior were as follows:

**The Baroque Period** [1600-1750], A. Corelli - Sonata per Violino Op.5 - No.9 in A Major, everyone played this piece equally nicely, measured tempo, lovely trills,  no problem for Leclair, Guignon, Locatelli, right up to Benedetti.

**The Classical** [1750-1820],  Beethoven.Violin.Sonata.No.9.Op.47, Leclair, Guignon and even Locatelli got lost in the aggressive and quick notes of this Beethoven piece; Kreisler, Solomon and Benedetti had no problem in the jumping bow and the quick spiccato, there was a lullaby section which the Baroque era players felt more at ease with; then problems again with the quick changes of tempo and aggression in Beethoven.

**The Romantic** [1810-1910], Max Bruch, Violin Concerto 1, in G minor, Opus 26, premiered in Bremen, Germany, in 1868. Leclair, Guignon, and Locatelli were a bit shaky on the sustenutos at the start of the piece, and then in the aggressive spot, a third through, they missed a few notes. Kreisler even missed a few notes in the fast parts. Benedetti and Solomon breezed right through.

**Contemporary** [1910-2010] David Foster, The Prayer, expressively played by all contenders.

and finally, **the player's own choice.** Thank goodness the players had one choice where they could let their individuality shine.

These are the pieces they chose, and how they interpreted their choices:

- Jean-Marie Leclair played his own violin sonata in D major, lovely, singing quality, excellent double stops.
- J. P. Guignon chose his Sonata op. 4 No. 2 in D major, measured phrases, trills nicely placed.
- Pietro Antonio Locatelli Violin Concerto No. 1 in D major, played in measured stately style, peaceful rendition with lovely trills in the high register, then controlled jumps, somewhat of a Handelian influence, nicely performed by Locatelli of his own concerto.
- Fritz Kreisler played Kreisler, as only he could, Schön Rosmarin, very stately, nice run on the spiccato, grace notes pretty, excellent pauses,
- Lenny Solomon plays in The Rex Jazz & Blues Bar in Toronto, cool job, the Baroque players ordered wine, Kreisler, Solomon and Benedetti had tea, and the Baroque players stared in amazement at the tempo and the jazz timing. "You should hear Going to Chicago, when I rev my electric violin up to speed!" said Solomon to the group.
- Nicola Benedetti gave it her all, in Erich Wolfgang Korngold's Violin Concerto in D major, Op.35, very dreamy. The UWAC funded the orchestra which accompanied Benedetti in this emotional piece of music. Jumping bows were controlled, very lovely performance.

The panel of judges had their seats at the very front. The Hollywood Bowl was opened to the public, first come first serve, a free concert, filled to capacity with 17,500 eager listeners.

The contestants generally did quite well in their performances. If one sat close enough, one could see the beads of sweat on the foreheads of each of the players. They were given white silk handkerchiefs in case they needed them. Bottles of water and Gatorade sat on a small table off stage.

The judgment came in from the Supreme Court. It was unanimous, "a tie", all the way around. Captain Kirk sat back smugly and said, "I could have told you that from the beginning." The lead Justice explained, "We voted a unanimous tie because something like this cannot really be judged. To say one era in music is better than another is a false concept. We have to give each era its own intrinsic value. Perhaps, modern players can play faster or fancier, but the value of the era that has gone before must be judged on its own merits, and honoured as well."

The Chief Justice suggested that what Monsieur Marc Pincherie said after the musical joust back in 1734 between Leclair and Guignon applied to all the musicians in this 2328 joust at the Hollywood Bowl. "There is no clear victory."

"Their performing styles differed profoundly, Leclair's being more precise, more technically delicate, more cerebral, while Guigon's was more colourful, more fanciful."

"From this," said the Chief Justice, "we can say that each musician is a winner and inimitable in his or her own way."

"Well, gentlemen," said Kirk to Spock, McCoy and Scotty, "I told you so."

The crew of the NCC Enterprise planned to slingshot back in time returning each and every virtuoso violinist to his or her proper time period, using "the light-speed breakaway factor" from the sun's gravitational field.    Jean-Marie Leclair and Jean-Pierre Guignon were the first to go back to the Baroque era in King Louis XV's time frame.

Dr. McCoy would run a brain scan so all the contestants would not remember a thing by the time they got back home. Locatelli would be deposited next in the Netherlands.

In these time excursions, H. G. Wells' Time Machine would save Starfleet an immense amount of energy by not requiring the Enterprise, itself, to keep slinging back and forth in time using the gravitational field of the sun. The Enterprise hung hidden on the dark side of the moon for some time, during all this activity, using 1901 as a home base. Fritz Kreisler would be returned to France next, with the hope that he would immigrate to New York in 1938 before the Second World War broke out. Then came Nicola Benedetti and Lenny Solomon. They all would resume their lives as though nothing had ever happened.

The last task left to the crew of the Enterprise was to return H. G. Wells' well-used Time Machine back to him, transporting it intact into the safety of his basement at Spade House. Dr. McCoy did a brain scan of both Mr. and Mrs. Wells, and thanked them profusely for being so kind to Americans with tea and crumpets.

Kirk and his crew would remember the Battle of the Violins fondly. "What a great concert," agreed Scotty and McCoy.

"Indeed," agreed Kirk. "Yes, indeed," commented Spock, raising an eyebrow.

"But." said Kirk again with an air of arrogant foretelling, "I told you so. I knew it would be a tie. They are all great violinists in their own time and in their own way."

---

THE END: i HOPE YOU ENJOYED TIME TRAVELLING WITH CAPTAIN KIRK

**I'D APPRECIATE IT YOU COULD DO A BOOK REVIEW EITHER ON GOODREADS OR AMAZON, IF YOU HAVE THE TIME**

–John Hartig Author

\*\*\*\*\*

# Biography

John Hartig is an up and coming Canadian novelist. He's always been a writer, except when he couldn't speak English. He came to Canada with his parents from Austria in 1954 at the age of 8. The threat of being beaten up by his classmates forced him to learn English...very quickly. Soon he had no accent, and soon he was playing outdoor hockey with the gang, and on weekends reading The Last of the Mohicans.

He started writing poetry in high-school. John acquired a Double-Honours B.A. in English and History from the University of Waterloo, then an M.A. in English from McMaster University. His first job as a writer came at the Chilliwack Progress newspaper in British Columbia. He became an editor at Grande Prairie This Week in Alberta.

John left the writing business for a while because the byline did not pay for gas, rent and food. He became a high-school teacher since he already had a Teacher's degree from the University of British Columbia. In later years, he acquired a degree in Corporate Communications from Sheridan College in the year 2000. Then a

Webmaster Certificate from Mohawk College in the year 2007. Since he had photography experience from the newspaper trade, he became a wedding photographer, and a scenery photographer. It was scenery photography which prompted John to become a more active Web Designer to show his pretty pictures off on the internet.

Now during retirement, John keeps himself busy as an author, writing novels, specifically murder mysteries. There are always new frontiers to conquer.

*****

**You can access my other novels through Amazon or Kindle Books by John Hartig. Here is the direct link:**
https://www.amazon.com/John-Hartig/e/B07PJN8B95?ref_=pe_1724030_132998060

**To order more of John's novels and short stories, just google Amazon Books or Kindle:**
**John Hartig books.**

Website:
www.johnhartig.ca

E-mail:
johnehartig[at]gmail[period]com

Made in the USA
Monee, IL
22 November 2022

17881611R00194